MISSOURI!

The fourteenth compelling story
in the magnificent epic of WAGONS WEST—
thrilling adventures from the pages of history
that come to life as the riverboat's whistle and
the railroad's roar lure colorful men and desirous women
to matchless excitement on the wild frontier.

★★★★★★★★★★★★★★★★★★★★★★★★★★★

WAGONS WEST

MISSOURI!

**THEY TRAVELED THE ROADS, THE
RAILS AND THE RIVERS TO CARRY
FREEDOM'S MESSAGE FROM PRAIRIES
TO MOUNTAINS TO SHINING
WESTERN SEA.**

TOBY HOLT—
Ready to ride toward danger when duty calls, he faces
a cunning new enemy whose evil can only be
stopped by risking his own future.

HANK BLAKE—
Young and fearless, he will fight for the man he
admires, but he may lose the woman he loves.

CINDY HOLT—
High-spirited and headstrong, she burns with
jealousy as much as passion, so the fires she
lights may lead to heartbreak instead of desire.

LUIS DE CORDOVA—
Black gleaming eyes reflect the lust and depravity
of his villain's heart as his schemes threaten a woman's
honor and an honest man's life.

★★★★★★★★★★★★★★★★★★★★★★★★★★★

MILLICENT RANDALL—
Her innocence and frustrated passions could trap her into a shame from which there is no escape.

EDWARD BLACKSTONE—
His wealth and elegance disguise his steely strength until a rare adventure reveals his heroism and his faithful heart.

PAMELA DRAKE RANDALL—
Trapped in a loveless marriage, she flirts with a forbidden attraction and a dangerous infidelity.

THOMASINA HARDING—
Her heart belonged to a riverboat, not a lover, but her beauty made one man want her . . . at any cost.

RUNNING BEAR—
Brave chief of the Nez Perce, he had promised peace, only now an outlaw offered a way to drive the white man from the Indian's land.

Bantam Books by Dana Fuller Ross
Ask your bookseller for the books you have missed

MISSOURI!

DANA FULLER ROSS

 Created by the producers of
White Indian, Children of the Lion,
Saga of the Southwest, and
The Kent Family Chronicles Series.

Executive Producer: Lyle Kenyon Engel

BANTAM BOOKS
TORONTO · NEW YORK · LONDON · SYDNEY · AUCKLAND

MISSOURI!

*A Bantam Book / published by arrangement with
Book Creations, Inc.*

Bantam edition / January 1985

*Produced by Book Creations, Inc.
Chairman of the Board: Lyle Kenyon Engel.*

*All rights reserved.
Copyright © 1984 by Book Creations, Inc.
Cover artwork copyright © 1984 by Bob Larkin.
This book may not be reproduced in whole or in part, by
mimeograph or any other means, without permission.
For information address: Bantam Books, Inc.*

ISBN 0-553-24584-8

Published simultaneously in the United States and Canada

PRINTED IN THE UNITED STATES OF AMERICA

H   0 9 8 7 6 5 4 3 2 1

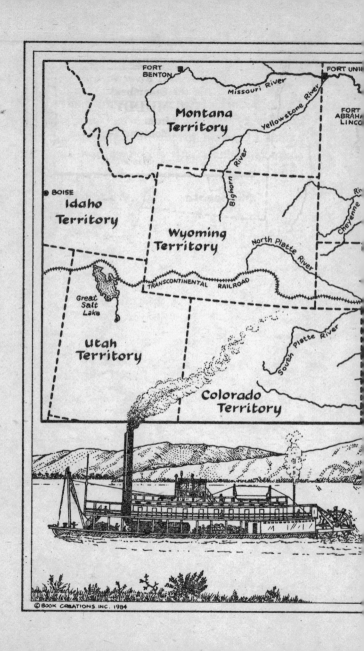

The Missouri River Voyage
of the Steamboat
BIG MUDDY
from
Fort Benton, Montana Territory
to
St. Louis, Missouri

Dakota Territory

BISMARCK

FORT RICE

FORT PIERRE

Red River of the North

Missouri River

Minnesota

Wisconsin

0 50 100 150
MILES

YANKTON

Iowa

Nebraska

Missouri River

OMAHA

Illinois

Platte River

Missouri

ST. JOSEPH

Mississippi

LEXINGTON

Missouri River

ST. LOUIS

Kansas

INDEPENDENCE

JEFFERSON CITY

River

Ohio R.

Kansas River

RON TOELKE '84

★ ★ WAGONS WEST ★ ★

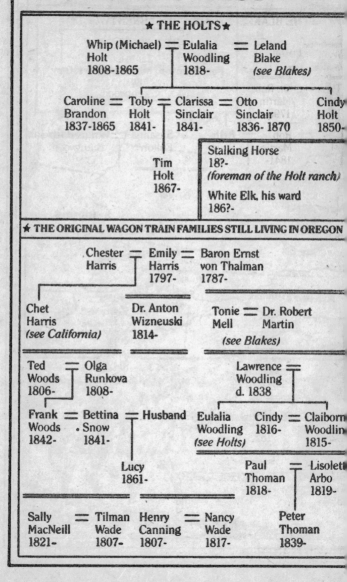

★ THE HOLTS ★

Whip (Michael) Holt 1808-1865 ═ Eulalia Woodling 1818- ═ Leland Blake *(see Blakes)*

Caroline Brandon 1837-1865 ═ Toby Holt 1841- ═ Clarissa Sinclair 1841- ═ Otto Sinclair 1836-1870   Cindy Holt 1850-

Tim Holt 1867-

Stalking Horse 18?- *(foreman of the Holt ranch)*

White Elk, his ward 186?-

★ THE ORIGINAL WAGON TRAIN FAMILIES STILL LIVING IN OREGON

Chester Harris ═ Emily Harris 1797- ═ Baron Ernst von Thalman 1787-

Chet Harris *(see California)*   Dr. Anton Wizneuski 1814-   Tonie Mell ═ Dr. Robert Martin *(see Blakes)*

Ted Woods 1806- ═ Olga Runkova 1808-   Lawrence Woodling d. 1838

Frank Woods 1842- ═ Bettina Snow 1841- ═ Husband   Eulalia Woodling 1816- *(see Holts)*   Cindy 1816- ═ Claiborn Woodling 1815-

Lucy 1861-

Paul Thoman 1818- ═ Lisolett Arbo 1819-

Sally MacNeill 1821- ═ Tilman Wade 1807-   Henry Canning 1807- ═ Nancy Wade 1817-   Peter Thoman 1839-

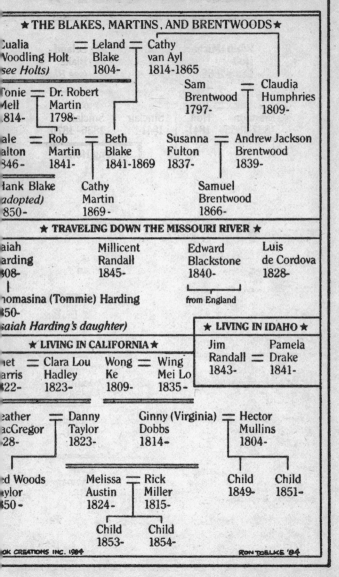

★ ★ FAMILY TREE ★ ★

★ THE BLAKES, MARTINS, AND BRENTWOODS ★

Cualia Woodling Holt *(see Holts)* = Leland Blake 1804- = Cathy van Ayl 1814-1865

Sam Brentwood 1797- — Claudia Humphries 1809-

Tonie Mell 1814- = Dr. Robert Martin 1798-

Hale Dalton 1846- = Rob Martin 1841- = Beth Blake 1841-1869

Susanna Fulton 1837- — Andrew Jackson Brentwood 1839-

Hank Blake *(adopted)* 1850-

Cathy Martin 1869-

Samuel Brentwood 1866-

★ TRAVELING DOWN THE MISSOURI RIVER ★

Isaiah Harding 1808-

Millicent Randall 1845-

Edward Blackstone 1840-

Luis de Cordova 1828-

Thomasina (Tommie) Harding 1850-
(Isaiah Harding's daughter)

from England

★ LIVING IN IDAHO ★

Jim Randall 1843- = Pamela Drake 1841-

★ LIVING IN CALIFORNIA ★

Janet Harris 1822- = Clara Lou Hadley 1823-

Wong Ke 1809- = Wing Mei Lo 1835-

Heather MacGregor 1828- = Danny Taylor 1823-

Ginny (Virginia) Dobbs 1814- = Hector Mullins 1804-

Ed Woods Taylor 1850-

Melissa Austin 1824- = Rick Miller 1815-

Child 1849-

Child 1851-

Child 1853-

Child 1854-

OK CREATIONS INC. 1984

RON TOELKE '84

MISSOURI!

I

The wheels of the three ponderous freight wagons squealed in continuous protest as they jounced along the rutted, hard-packed earth of the famous Oregon Trail in the Idaho Territory. In spite of the difficulties encountered with the road conditions, terrain, and the uncertain March weather, however, the teams of twenty mules per wagon continued to move at a steady pace, and the occupants of the covered wagons clung to their seats, knowing that when they reached the Oregon border, the worst of their troubles would be over. In fact, traveling through Oregon would be easy compared to the hardships encountered in the mountains of Idaho.

The nine men in the little caravan, all of whom wore buckskin jackets and trousers and broad-brimmed hats, were looking forward to spending two nights and a full day in Boise. They had picked up their cargo, which was carried in sealed crates labeled "Iron Bathtubs," in Denver. To be sure, the Central and Union Pacific railroad tracks now crossed the entire continent, from New York to San Francisco, but there was not yet a railroad from Denver to the Pacific Northwest, and it was still necessary to travel by wagon train, as had the first settlers to the region.

On the seat of each wagon was the driver, with a man riding shotgun beside him. At the rear of each wagon sat another man. Only the wagon master, who rode shotgun in the first wagon, knew the actual contents of the crates that the wagon train carried.

When he had accepted and signed for the cargo in Denver, the wagon master had been told in secret that the crates did not carry iron washtubs. Instead, he was charged with the responsibility of transporting precious manufactured goods: The Winchester Rifle Company of Connecticut was sending its latest and most sophisticated product, four hundred new repeating rifles, to Fort Vancouver, the headquarters of the U.S. Army of the West, which was located in the Washington Territory on the Columbia River. Buchanan and Company, the largest transporters of heavy merchandise to be found between Denver and the Pacific Coast, often performed services of this kind for the army.

The members of the company were sufficiently experienced to know better than to drink while they were on duty during the day. They knew they would face immediate discharge if caught by the wagon master. But men who crossed the deserts and mountains of the

West on their way to the Pacific as often as six or eight times a year quickly learned how to deal with their boredom. In theory, they were on their own time, rather than that of Buchanan and Company, whenever they called a halt for the night, and they had discovered that the wagon master left them alone on the condition that they imbibe only at the end of each day's run. So as soon as the drivers and guards made camp around four in the afternoon, they quietly began to pass the bottle before they built their fire and cooked their supper. They were on their own, and as long as they delivered their merchandise safely, no one intervened or chastised them.

No member of the wagon train company realized it, but they were being closely observed from the heights of the mountain chain that ran parallel to the trail. In the shadows of large boulders, two men sat motionless on their mounts, binoculars to their eyes as they studied the encampment. In the background, another dozen men waited patiently, all of them heavily armed. The man who appeared to be the leader of the group was slender and fine-featured, with coal-black eyes and hair. He was wearing hand-tailored boots, expensively made clothes, and across one shoulder was slung a Winchester repeating rifle, similar to the ones that the wagon train carried. At first glance Luis de Cordova often was mistaken for a Mexican or an Indian, but in actuality he was the direct descendant of an old, aristocratic California family that had lived near the Pacific for generations and had occasionally intermarried with Indians.

Continuing to watch the men of the wagon train, de Cordova laughed softly; it was an unpleasant sound.

"Whatever you paid your informant at Buchanan and Company was money well spent, Brennan," he said to the short, husky man beside him. "He knew the itinerary of these guards perfectly. They've stopped for the day a good two and a half to three hours before sundown, and they've started their drinking already."

Tom Brennan joined in the laugh and was pleased that Luis had complimented him. De Cordova was a perfectionist; it was rare for him to praise a subordinate.

"If you were in charge here," de Cordova demanded sharply, "when would you attack?"

Brennan hesitated for a moment and then spoke carefully. "So far," he said, "everything has happened the way it was predicted, so I recommend that we keep to our original schedule. In other words, we stay right where we are, and we give the guards down yonder time to get mellowed and softened by drink. By then it'll be time for their supper, and the minute it grows dark, we swoop down at them out of the mountains. When we move, we hit them fast, and we hit them hard. The whole affair should be ended in less time than it's taking me to talk about it."

"Fair enough," de Cordova said. "That's the way we'll operate. Pass the word along to the men and tell them to be patient until sundown. Then they'll get all the action they want."

De Cordova stayed where he was and continued to observe the activities of the employees of Buchanan and Company. This was typical of him. Whenever he took action against an enemy, he first learned everything he could about his foe. Thus, he reduced risks to a minimum.

Seven of the nine members of the wagon train company drank steadily and over a period of about two hours consumed a great deal of liquor. At about six P.M., several of them lurched to their feet and walked unsteadily to their covered wagons to obtain cooking utensils, while another man built a campfire. Then they began to fry bacon and cook biscuits and beans. Luis was ready to act now, and he carefully took note of the two men who had done little or no drinking. They were the most dangerous members of the party, and he told himself that he would have to take care of them personally, rather than entrust the task to one of his subordinates.

The shadows of night grew longer, and the camp alongside the trail gradually became harder to see. The entire mountain chain to the north was a deep shade of purple.

"Let's go," de Cordova said, and silently led his subordinates single file down the mountain to the trail below.

As he rode, he marveled at his good fortune. The wagon train members had not even observed the basic rules of safety by forming their wagons into a defensive circle for the night. All three of the freight wagons continued to stand side by side, their contents ready for the taking. As they prepared their evening meal, the members of the wagon train company were laughing and talking loudly. The familiar odors of a meal prepared on the trail filled the air as the men helped themselves to the food.

They were just settling down to eat when de

Cordova's band attacked them, seemingly coming at them from nowhere.

Luis de Cordova proved his own claim to leadership, if he required such proof, by firing two pistol shots at the two sober members of the wagon train company. Both of them—one of whom was the wagon master—died instantly. The other guards had no chance to fight for their lives. By the time they put down the tin plates of food and fumbled on the ground beside them for their weapons, they were assaulted by the men riding down on them and firing as they galloped.

Several furious bursts of rifle fire echoed and reechoed across the valley. Then all was quiet, and de Cordova spoke. "Remember, boys," he said, "no personal looting. We haven't time for it." He raised his voice slightly. "Brennan!"

"Yes, sir?" Tom Brennan materialized beside his superior.

"Get your stencils and paint ready. There's work to be done in one hell of a hurry."

"You bet." Brennan dismounted and distributed stencils to several of the men, along with small buckets of paint.

They worked by torchlight. The label "Iron Bathtubs" on the crates was painted over, and in its place appeared a new label: "Farm Implements."

Then, while the paint dried, they awaited the arrival of other confederates. At last they arrived, burly men driving large wagons drawn by teams of four heavy workhorses. The wagons pulled to a halt beside the covered wagons, and the entire group silently went to work, transferring case after case of the latest model

6

Winchester rifles to de Cordova's wagons. They had no need for Buchanan and Company's mules, which were herded into a little ravine that was blocked off by some pine trees the men had hastily cut down. So they left the smaller animals, knowing they would be found within a few days by people sent out to learn the fate of the wagon train.

So efficient were the thieves that their entire task was completed within another half hour. After concealing the crates beneath heavy canvas tarpaulins, a number of men formed a cordon around the wagons, and the new procession started on its way across Oregon, de Cordova riding in the lead.

His problems were not yet at an end, but he had already won an outstanding victory. The rich booty of modern rifles would be worth thousands of dollars to certain carefully selected clients who were as unscrupulous as he was.

On a bluff, graceful weeping willows and clumps of birch trees, their branches still bare, partly concealed the view of the Columbia River below. A half-moon, intermittently covered by thick clouds blown from the direction of Mount Hood, shone on the cemetery, located near the city of Portland. All was quiet and serene in the graveyard, where some of the original members of the first wagon train to cross the continent of North America to Oregon were buried. They had been joined by later settlers, and the cemetery now occupied scores of acres.

The graveyard's metal gates opened soundlessly, having just been oiled for the purpose, and a strange procession made its way toward the graves that were closest to the bluff. Here were Luis de Cordova's three large wagons, each of them moving soundlessly, their axles having been heavily greased. A rifle-bearing man sat beside each wagon's driver, and a third, also armed with a rifle, was perched on top of its tarpaulin.

All three wagons pulled to a halt, and de Cordova, his black eyes gleaming, stepped out of the shadows and gestured. His men immediately began to dig up the nearest graves. They worked swiftly, smoothly, under the supervision of the slender man in the dark suit, and before long, several dirt-smeared coffins were piled up beside the graves.

At last de Cordova signaled to his subordinates, and the digging stopped. The tarpaulins were removed from the wagons, and the services of all three members of each crew were required to unload the heavy crates from the rear of the wagons and to lower them into the empty graves. Then, each grave was filled in again, and the layers of sod were replaced as carefully as they had been removed.

All that remained now was to get rid of the coffins that had been taken from their resting places. They were piled into the carts, which once again were covered with tarpaulins, and the procession departed as silently as it had come. Luis de Cordova led the way on horseback; his lieutenant, Tom Brennan, checked the cemetery to make sure that the disturbance to the graves was as unnoticeable as possible, and then he joined his superior.

The party rode in silence for several miles, heading east along the river, and came to the outskirts of the city of Portland, where many factories and warehouses were now located. De Cordova owned one of these buildings, which he used as a front for his various illegal smuggling enterprises, and it was to this place that the coffins were brought. The hired men went to work at once, unloading the coffins into the warehouse's large, stone incinerator, where they were ignited and went up in flames. Anyone seeing the plumes of smoke rising out of the incinerator chimney would merely have thought the warehouse operators were working late at night, burning trash.

Luis de Cordova hooked his thumbs into the pockets of his waistcoat and sighed. "A very neat, orderly job," he said. "Brennan, give each of the boys a bonus of five dollars and thank them for their work tonight. And while you're about it, be sure you remind them that I'll have the hide of any man who talks out of turn."

"Every member of this team has worked for you for several years, Luis," Tom Brennan replied. "You don't need to worry about them. They're experts at keeping their mouths shut."

"Good," de Cordova replied, removing his hat and wiping his forehead. "I expect to earn a lot of money for all of us on this operation. The rifles are priceless. Indian tribes and bandit gangs will gladly pay fortunes for guns of this caliber. We ought to do a thriving business."

"I sure hope so," his short, chunky subordinate said with a nervous laugh. "Selling firearms to Indians is a federal offense, and there's a death sentence for doing it."

"I've taken every possible precaution to ensure that the authorities don't interfere," de Cordova told him. "That's why we buried the guns in the cemetery rather than taking them to the warehouse. You are in charge of them now, Brennan, and on the off chance that you should be caught, just remember you're getting a very generous cut of the profits. Thus, make certain that my name isn't mentioned and that I'm not implicated in any way."

"Don't you worry, chief," Brennan told him. "If anything should happen, you'll be protected. You'll come out clean as a hound's tooth."

"I sincerely hope so," de Cordova said unpleasantly, "because I have bigger things than selling contraband rifles to Indians and outlaws to worry about. I have much bigger fish to fry."

Clarissa Holt had never been happier. The young matron and her family had just returned to their Oregon ranch from the Idaho Territory, where her husband, Toby, had served with such distinction as military governor. Their small son, Tim, tired after the welcome-home ceremony in Portland, had been put to bed, and another room had been assigned to White Elk, the adopted grandson of Stalking Horse, the foreman of the Holt ranch and lifelong friend and associate of Toby's late father, the renowned Whip Holt.

Too excited to sleep, Clarissa wandered around the house, touching items of furniture and bric-a-brac, staring out the window at the familiar scenes, and grinning at her husband.

Toby, whose exploits in the growth and expansion

of the American West were winning him an enduring reputation, had abandoned all thoughts of getting to bed early and sat now in his favorite living room chair, sipping a glass of good whiskey and stretching out his long legs in front of him.

Clarissa beamed at him. With her red hair piled on top of her head, her green eyes shining, the statuesque woman looked as incredibly lovely as the first time Toby had met her. "We're actually home," she said for at least the one hundredth time, "and best of all we're free to live our own lives again. Ever since we first met, you've had one government assignment after another, first from President Johnson and more recently from President Grant. Now you're finally at liberty to pursue your own private interests, and it's about time!"

Toby thoughtfully sipped his whiskey. As he grew older, his rugged, sun-bronzed features and sinewy build more and more resembled those of his late father. "I don't mind the time and effort that I gave to the government," he said. "My country needed me, and I was glad to be of service to her."

"Oh, I'll always be very proud of the fact that you prevented the Indians in Idaho from going to war against the settlers there," she said, "but I'm still relieved that you're able to look after your own interests."

"Yes," he said, "it's time I buckled down to the horse-raising business again."

Clarissa, standing at the window, suddenly called out, "Look, Toby!"

He was on his feet instantly. "What's the matter?"

"I don't think I've ever seen anything like this

11

before," she said, pointing. "It looks like there's a fire in downtown Portland."

He stared out at the plume of smoke rising high in the distance, and he looked thoughtful. "That's probably an incinerator fire from a warehouse in town, and we're able to see the smoke because it's such a clear, cold night." He shook his head sadly. "I guess civilization and progress affects us even way out here on the ranch."

"I guess I'm not accustomed to living in a civilized area anymore," Clarissa responded. "We spent so much time living on the edge of the wilderness in Idaho, that I forgot how built up Portland is getting."

Toby now laughed and took her hand. "Yes, we've come back to civilization, Clarissa," he said. "But just remember that civilized, built-up areas like Portland are sometimes more wild and lawless than anything we saw in Idaho."

Millicent's, the Boise eating place that the dashing young Englishman, Edward Blackstone, had bought for his cousin, Millicent Randall, was an overnight success. Edward had explained the situation in succinct detail to their mutual cousin, Jim Randall.

"It's urgent that we find something that will keep Millicent occupied," he had said. "You're a married man now, and, naturally, Pam has taken Millicent's place as mistress of your ranch. Since I'm going away shortly on a journey that may keep me away from Idaho for a good many months, Millicent is in danger of being left alone, without anything to do. That's why I've bought her the restaurant, and for her sake, I hope it keeps her occupied and happy."

Somewhat to his surprise, and to that of Jim and Pamela Randall, Millicent took to the management of her restaurant with enthusiasm. She offered good food, well prepared and competently served, in a genteel atmosphere, and there was nothing like it in all the territory, with the result that her place was crowded every evening from the night that it first opened.

With her success, Millicent appeared to lose a measure of her shyness. Still, she continued to wear severely tailored dresses in black, gray, and brown, relieved only by white collar and cuffs. She used no cosmetics whatsoever, tied her long, dark hair in a neat bun at the nape of her neck, and although she greeted her clients warmly, if not jovially, she always maintained a dignified reserve.

She relaxed only in the company of her relatives, as she was doing that night at the little dinner party she was giving at the restaurant in honor of Edward on the eve of his departure from Boise. He marveled at the change in her. She positively sparkled as she joked with her two cousins, and Edward had to admit to himself privately that she actually outshone Pamela, who had come to America with him from England and who wore attractive gowns, ample makeup, and had honey-blond hair that fell below her shoulders.

"Where does your rare adventure begin, Edward?" Millicent demanded with mock severity.

"I daresay that technically it starts the moment I ride out of Boise," he said, "but I won't think of it as starting until I reach Fort Benton."

"Is that where you'll catch the steamer that will take you down the Missouri River?" Pamela interjected.

Edward nodded. "All the way to the Mississippi River at St. Louis, a distance of over two thousand miles." He paused to take a bite of roast beef. "The riverboats are stern-wheelers—that is, they're propelled by paddle wheels that are powered by steam, and they're very large. I've been told that some ships can carry five hundred tons of cargo and have room for at least two hundred passengers."

Millicent sighed. "I find it almost impossible to believe."

"Think of it!" Pamela declared. "Edward will be subjected to all the dangers of the wild, wild West. His ship may be attacked by Indians and by river pirates and by the forces of nature!"

"Don't let your imagination run wild, Pam," Edward said dryly. "You sound as though you envy me my trip."

"Not at all," Pamela replied quickly, placing a hand on Jim's arm and smiling at him. "I'm perfectly content to stay right where I am and to run our ranch as best I'm able."

Jim grinned at her appreciatively.

Edward, who had been her neighbor in England and had known of her many dalliances with men, wondered whether her protestation was sincere, but rather than question her, he turned back to Millicent. "What about you?" he asked. "Would you have liked to come with me?"

Millicent smiled wistfully. "Yes—and no," she said. "I love the idea of seeing so much of America. On the other hand, I'm delighted to have the restaurant to run."

Pamela thought it wiser not to mention that what Millicent needed more than anything was a man. She was certain Millicent would never truly find fulfillment until she had found someone she loved and trusted. But Pamela knew it would be unwise to say anything of the sort to a young woman who had been severely disappointed in love, first when her fiancé was murdered and then when she had lost her heart to the widowed ex-lieutenant governor of Idaho, Rob Martin, only to see him marry his infant daughter's governess, Kale Salton.

They finished their dinner of roast beef with oven-browned potatoes and green vegetables. Then Jim said, "Will you end your journey in St. Louis, Edward?"

Edward shrugged. "If I'm bored," he said, "I might go on to New York by train and attend to some business matters there. If not, I'll be strongly tempted to transfer to another ship and to continue by water down the Mississippi all the way to New Orleans."

Millicent smiled dreamily. "I must admit, Edward," she said, "that I do envy you. But as it is, I'm needed here." She gestured, and the sweep of her hand took in the whole of the busy, bustling restaurant. "I've got to count my blessings. Just look at the beehive that this place has become. I'm very grateful for it."

Toby Holt peered out of the boat that belonged to his stepfather, Major General Leland Blake, as the vessel crossed the turbulent waters of the Columbia River and approached the shores of Washington. "Did my mother happen to indicate in her note to you," he asked his wife, "why she and General Blake are so anxious that we join them for supper tonight?"

"I assumed that you knew, dear," Clarissa replied. "I have no idea what the occasion is."

Toby hoisted his small son, Tim, to one shoulder, preparatory to their docking at the wharves of Fort Vancouver, headquarters for the Army of the West. "No matter," he replied. "We'll find out soon enough."

Clarissa had no intention of letting the subject drop. "Now that you mention it," she said thoughtfully, "there *was* a note of urgency in your mother's letter. She was rather insistent that we accept the invitation and that we not postpone our visit even for a day or two."

The oarsmen expertly propelled the boat up to the wharf, and the sergeant in charge of the detail jumped out of the craft and held it steady while the Holts disembarked.

The general's aide was waiting with a gelding for Toby and a mare for Clarissa, so it appeared that Toby's mother expected the supper invitation to be accepted without question. The couple mounted, and Toby sat his young son in the saddle in front of him. Tim, who was being taught to ride by his father and by Stalking Horse, grasped the reins with an air of familiarity, and they made their way toward the dwellings that faced the parade ground.

The largest of the white-clapboard houses was that of the commander in chief, and the couple was greeted at the door by Eulalia Holt Blake, the dignified, middle-aged widow of Whip Holt, who still retained her thick, dark hair and penetrating dark-blue eyes. Both Eulalia and Lee had lost their spouses in a tragic rockslide in the Washington mountains, and having known each other for more than a quarter of a century since coming out on the original wagon train to Oregon, they turned to each other for love and companionship in their later years. But Eulalia appeared far from elderly as she stood at the door to the house.

As soon as little Tim's feet hit the ground, he ran to his grandmother, embracing her and covering her with wet kisses. Eulalia stood facing her son and daughter-in-law, with her arms around the little boy. "My thanks to both of you for coming here on such short notice," she said. "Lee has been very anxiously awaiting you."

"What's it all about?" Toby asked as he gently moved his son to one side so he could kiss his mother.

"I have no idea, dear," Eulalia replied sweetly. "I've become a good wife to a high-ranking army officer, and I ask no questions. Lee is in his study, Toby, and we'll be in the living room any time you're able to join us." Carrying her grandson, she ushered Clarissa toward the living room.

Toby went immediately to the study that occupied one wing of the house and tapped on the door.

"Come in, please," General Blake called.

Toby entered the room, and his stepfather rose from his desk to shake hands with him.

Major General Leland Blake, gray-haired and looking fit and trim, was impressive in his blue uniform with the twin stars of rank twinkling on each shoulder. He carefully closed the study door, went to a small bar

17

in one corner of the room, and mixed mild drinks of whiskey and water, one of which he handed to his stepson. Then he resumed his seat.

"Do you still have your clearance, Toby, to receive secret U.S. government information?" he demanded bluntly.

"I guess I do," the younger man replied, concealing his surprise, "unless, of course, it was automatically rescinded when I resigned as military governor of the Idaho Territory."

General Blake shook his head. "No, it's never automatically rescinded. You'd have been notified in a special communication if you'd been taken off the government list."

Toby smiled as he shook his head. "I've received no communication," he said.

"Good," Lee Blake said crisply. "That saves us a great deal of extra bother. It goes without saying that this entire conversation is confidential and never took place."

"I understand, sir," Toby replied gravely, and tensed slightly as he leaned forward in his chair.

"I'm reasonably sure," the older man said, "that you've never seen and probably haven't even heard of the new model repeating rifle."

"No, sir," Toby replied. "What's that?"

"A marvelous new weapon that's much more powerful than any of its predecessors. It's been developed at the Winchester Rifle Company in Connecticut."

Toby nodded thoughtfully.

"If you're interested, and I assume you are," his stepfather said, "I'll be glad to discuss the mechanism with you on some other occasion. It isn't relevant right now. What is relevant is that General Sherman, as the army chief of staff, has ordered a large number from Winchester for army use, and President Grant has approved. This is all being done in great secrecy, and none of it has been publicized. I was scheduled to receive a fair share of the weapons direct from the manufacturer in recent weeks."

"Just a moment," Toby interrupted. "I want to make sure I have this straight. The rifles were being delivered to you by the manufacturer rather than through the army ordnance bureau?"

"That's correct," General Blake said. "Rather than slow up the distribution of the guns by having them go through army channels from New England, it was decided by the War Department that that responsibility would remain with the manufacturer. A cargo containing a number of crates of the guns—I'm still waiting to learn from Washington precisely how many—was sent by rail as far as Denver, and the crates were transferred to covered freight wagons. The wagon train was ambushed along the Oregon Trail in Idaho, and the guards and wagon drivers, nine men in all, were brutally shot to death. Their bodies were left as carrion for wild animals, and the wagon train's mules were found corralled in a ravine that had been closed off with some pine trees. The mules were half starved and badly in need of water, too, when they were found. Not a word of this has appeared in print, of course. We've kept the entire incident confidential."

"Have you found the rifles?" Toby asked.

The general shook his head. "No, there's been no

trace of them. They seem to have vanished from the face of the earth."

"And you don't know who committed the robbery?"

"I'm afraid not," Lee Blake told him. "The garrison at Boise has opened an investigation. They were joined by some experts on the staff stationed at the Presidio in San Francisco, and according to their reports, they've managed to track the crated weapons as far as Portland, at which point the trail disappears. There's simply too much traffic in the area to distinguish one wagon train from another."

He handed a file folder across the desk. "This contains every report that's been written on the subject, and you'll find whatever clues have been discovered to date—and there are damned few of them—on paper here."

Toby took the folder and leafed through the meager contents. "There isn't much here, I've got to say that."

"I'll concede to you," the older man said, "that we're stabbing in the dark. Which makes this unfair of me, but, nevertheless, I'm asking if you'll take charge of an investigation into the entire affair."

"What do you want me to do?"

"Find the rifles and turn them over to me."

Toby was lost in thought for some moments. "You have a number of professional investigators on your staff," he said at last. "Why choose me instead of them to conduct the search?"

"Oh, they'll conduct their own hunt," Lee said, "and they'll be under orders to report any findings directly to you. I've chosen you for a very good reason, however. Whoever took the guns hopes to make a profit from them. That brings up the question of who has use for such weapons. Well, various bands of criminals—bank robbers and the like—would find it very convenient indeed to gain possession of these powerful, new-model repeating rifles. I should think, however, that heading the list of potential buyers would be various Indian tribes that are either at war with the United States or are contemplating starting such a war. Well, I know of no man in the entire nation who has your knowledge of Indian tribes, their current state of affairs, and their long-range plans."

"I am forced to admit," Toby said, "that at least half a dozen tribes come to mind at once as potential buyers of the rifles. There's no question that the thieves could command an exceptional price for them from various Indians."

"I've hesitated before asking you if you'll take the responsibility of conducting this investigation, Toby. I realize you've already made many personal sacrifices in order to serve your country. Your recent assignment in Idaho was just the latest in a long string of important tasks that you've undertaken on behalf of the government. Your mother has told me that you've been anxious to return to your own affairs at the ranch, and I certainly can't blame you for that. If you don't look out for your own interests, no one will."

"If I'm needed," Toby said quietly, "I'll accept this assignment."

"I was hoping that would be your attitude," Lee said, "and personally, as well as on behalf of the United States, I'm deeply grateful to you for it. For whatever

21

consolation this may be to you, I don't believe that the chore will take up too much of your time. In the first place, I strongly suspect the thieves will let the furor over the robbery die down before they make any move whatsoever, and when they do, I'm hoping it won't be too difficult or time-consuming for you to set up a network in which to trap them."

"I'd like to let a little time elapse," Toby said, "and just sit back and wait for developments, if it's all right with you. That will give me time to continue to look after my own affairs."

"Deal with the problem in any way you see fit, provided you keep your activities confidential," a relieved Lee Blake told him. "You have no idea what a burden is taken from my shoulders just to know that you're going to be working on the case!"

Cadets who had completed two years at the United States Military Academy at West Point were granted their only vacation during their four years of study, an extended furlough of a few months. So the atmosphere that evening was highly charged in the dormitory of the second-year cadets, and laughter echoed up and down the corridors as the students prepared for their eagerly awaited visits home. In the room occupied by the class leaders, Henry Blake and David King, an air of calm efficiency prevailed as the two young men busied themselves, packing their civilian clothes for their homeward journey.

"I'll arrive home late tonight, Hank," Dave said. "That's where I hold an advantage over you. It will take you about ten days before you reach the Pacific Coast."

"Not quite ten days, Dave," Hank replied. "I'll arrive in San Francisco by train one week from this morning, and then it's just two days by coastal steamer to Fort Vancouver. Until the transcontinental railroad was established, it took many weeks to reach the Pacific Northwest. So long, in fact, that it was impossible for cadets from that part of the country to go home on furlough."

"I guess you're fortunate at that," Dave replied. "Are you taking any uniforms with you?"

"You bet I am!" Hank replied. "What with my father commanding the Army of the West, there's no telling when I may be required to appear in uniform, and the Lord have mercy on me if I'm unprepared."

"When we were plebes," Dave said, "I envied you, being the son of a general, but seeing what you have to go through, I'm not so sure."

"I'll admit that more is expected of me than of other cadets," Hank said. "The officers on the staff at the academy demand more, and so does my family, but I don't really mind all that much. Their expectations spur me on to trying a lot harder."

"And getting results," Dave added. "General Blake has to be mighty proud of you with your present record—first in the class academically, first in military affairs, and first in athletics. You can't rank any higher than that."

Hank looked up from the open suitcase on his bed. "I'll tell you something, Dave, strictly between us," he said. "My father told me months ago that General Sherman is keeping an eye on me, so I don't have any choice in the matter. I've got to produce."

Dave King whistled softly under his breath. *"The General Sherman?"* he wanted to know. "General W.T. Sherman, the commander in chief of the whole blamed army? Wow! I'll say you've got to produce!"

"All I know," Hank said, "is that if I rank first in the class when we're commissioned, General Sherman will have a special assignment for me."

"What kind of an assignment?"

Hank shrugged.

"Suppose you aren't first in the class," Dave persisted. "What then?"

"We didn't discuss that, either," Hank told him. "A fellow in our line of work who's the son of a general is at a distinct disadvantage when discussing military matters with his father, believe me," Hank said. "You listen, you say, 'Yes, sir,' and you do what you are told. You ask no questions. It's assumed that I'll graduate first in the class. The possibility that I might rank any lower when I graduate has never occurred to my father, nor to me."

"I've got to hand it to you," Dave said earnestly. "You sure do hold up under pressure."

Hank grinned at him. "If I do," he said, "it's because I have no choice in the matter."

Dave shook his head. "It's no wonder that Alice is crazy about you."

Hank was startled. Alice Snyder was the older sister of Dave's girlfriend, Joyce. At Dave's request Hank had acted as her escort over a weekend the previous fall. "What do you mean she's crazy about me?" Hank now asked.

"You aren't supposed to know this," Dave said

reluctantly, "but Joyce has written me any number of times, saying that Alice has spoken of nothing but Hank Blake this and Hank Blake that ever since they were up here for that weekend last fall. As a matter of fact, Alice was hoping that you wouldn't be able to go all the way out to Fort Vancouver during this furlough and that I'd bring you home to Baltimore with me."

"Sorry I can't oblige you," Hank said lightly, "and don't go feeling sorry for Alice. I told her the last time I saw her that I have a private understanding with Cindy." Cindy was Eulalia Holt's daughter and the stepdaughter of General Blake. She and Hank had met when the general and his wife had taken Hank in. Later, the Blakes had adopted Hank, and during this time Hank's romance with Cindy had grown.

Dave understood all of this, and he nodded.

"I wish to goodness that Alice would believe me," Hank continued. "I don't need her complicating my life."

"My impression of her," Dave said, "is that she's a girl who knows what she wants and doesn't give up easily."

"She'd better latch on to somebody else," Hank said, "because I'm counting the days and the hours until Cindy and I are reunited!"

The quarter troop of the U.S. Cavalry, twenty-five strong, was strung out in single file on the palisade road that stretched along the Columbia River on the Washington side. The men rode at a steady gallop, brandishing their old-fashioned rifles in a mock display of warlike anger. Preceding the group was the detachment leader,

Second Lieutenant Eric Hoskins, who waved his sword in a futile effort to induce his men to ride still more rapidly.

In advance of the entire unit, crouching close to the neck and back of a small horse, was a figure that, at first glance, might have been mistaken for a boy. On closer examination, however, twenty-year-old Cindy Holt could be nothing but an exceptionally attractive young lady. Her riding outfit, an open-necked white shirt, riding breeches, and boots, showed off her high bosom, tiny waist, and long, lean legs. The kerchief tied around her head held in place her sandy-blond hair, and the freckles that were dusted across her pert nose gave her a mischievous look as she smiled in pleasure at winning the race from the seasoned cavalrymen. Passing close to a huge oak tree that marked the finish line, Cindy reined in her mare, then halted and awaited the approach of the column.

When Lieutenant Hoskins pulled to a halt beside her, Cindy laughed and patted her mare. "It was just too easy to beat you, Eric," she said, breathing a trifle rapidly. "I really should cancel our bet."

He shook his head. "Certainly not! A wager is a wager!"

The quarter troop approached one by one, and they, too, drew to a halt after they had passed the big oak tree.

"Well, boys," Lieutenant Hoskins said, standing in his stirrups, "I don't know what we have to say for ourselves. We're supposedly the champions of Fort Vancouver, the very best in the West, but we've been beaten today by a girl. We can always claim that she was riding a lot lighter than we were, but I'm not sure that would be too fair."

A grizzled sergeant raised his right hand to his hat in a salute to Cindy. "We ain't makin' no excuses to nobody," he said, acting as spokesman for the group. "The unit lost the race fair and square, but we didn't just lose to a girl; we lost it to a very special girl. She ain't just the stepdaughter of the commanding general, but her father was Whip Holt, and don't we ever know it. Miss Holt, in case nobody never told you this before, you sure do ride like the wind!"

Cindy inclined her head prettily. "Thank you very much, Sergeant," she murmured.

"Take the detachment back to Fort Vancouver, Sergeant," Lieutenant Hoskins said. "I'll join you there shortly."

"Yes, sir," the sergeant replied, and after saluting, he led the quarter troop toward the fort at a rapid clip.

Eric Hoskins remained behind with Cindy. "I owe you the best dinner that's available in the area," he said. "I reckon we'll ride into Portland for it."

"I feel guilty accepting a prize from you, Eric," Cindy said. "Winning it was just too easy."

"Look at it this way," he said. "It gives me a wonderful excuse to take you to dinner. What I can't for the life of me understand is how you won the race so easily."

"It's really very simple," she said. "I learned to ride about the same time I could walk, and I've spent most of my life on horseback. My father—and Stalking Horse, our foreman—taught my brother and me just about every trick of horsemanship there is to learn. The last couple of years of my father's life he kept saying that I was moving into his class as a rider. I wasn't, of course, but it was awfully nice to hear."

"As far as I'm concerned," he told her, "you're in a class by yourself." He hesitated only briefly. "When do you want to go out for dinner?"

Cindy was glad he was giving her a choice and not forcing her to reveal that Hank would be home in a week and that she would be occupied, consequently, for some time thereafter. She had told Eric some months earlier—at gunpoint, when he had made an unwanted advance to her—that she had an understanding with a West Point cadet. Lieutenant Hoskins had graduated from the military academy himself the previous June, so he understood that such a betrothal was necessarily informal, but he had had the good sense not to bring up the subject again and to treat her with the greatest respect from that time forward. Now that she was home from college, she continued to see him because she enjoyed his company and because her parents insisted that she maintain at least the semblance of an active social life during Hank's long absence.

"Either tonight or tomorrow night will be just fine," she said.

"Tonight it will be, then."

They rode to a side gate at Fort Vancouver, and the sentinels on duty there saluted Lieutenant Hoskins. According to regulations, Cindy was required to identify herself, but no sentinel ever found it necessary to ask her for identification. She was universally recognized, and the guards grinned at her as they waved her through the gate.

"I'll see you at six," Eric told her, raising his hand to the visor of his cap. Then he cantered off to rejoin his unit.

Cindy rode on to the commanding general's imposing mansion. Her victory in the race meant nothing to her, and she dismissed it from her mind. She had expected to win, and so she had; it was as simple as that. She took a measure of satisfaction in the fact that her mother had been similarly independent and strong-willed when she was a young woman. Her mother certainly would not have lectured her to the effect that she should never beat a suitor in any form of competition. The fact that it was impossible to convince her mother that she didn't regard Eric Hoskins as a suitor in any way was another matter entirely.

In fact, just the realization that Hank would be home in a week was enough to cause Cindy's heart to pound and bring a rush of color to her face. It was almost too good to be true! she thought. After spending two years at the military academy, Hank was actually coming home, and they would be reunited under the same roof. Her parents, Cindy reflected, had made no foolish rules to the effect that she had to continue to see other people during the nearly three months that Hank would be home, and she felt certain they would deal sensibly with the matter. Actually, the period that stretched out ahead was going to be a perfect interlude in her life, a blissful time that would be surpassed only when she and Hank were married after he received his commission in two years.

MISSOURI!

*   *   *

Luis de Cordova sat in the small parlor of his suite at the Portland House, Oregon's finest hotel, and examined the travel documents that his underling, Tom Brennan, had obtained for him. He was scheduled to go with a commercial party from Portland to Boise, and a horse would be provided for him, as would his meals and his sleeping accommodations. After a layover of two nights in Boise, he would be accompanied by a professional guide, who also would supply him with a horse and living essentials and would escort him to Fort Benton on the upper reaches of the Missouri River in the Montana Territory. There, in accordance with his specific instructions, his local representative had been ordered to obtain passage on the first stern-wheeler of the Harding fleet to leave Fort Benton for St. Louis when the shipping line opened its spring run.

"What about my reservation for a suite on one of the Harding Line ships to St. Louis?" he demanded testily. "After all, I'm not making the journey for my health!"

Worry clouded Brennan's pudgy face as he sifted through a sheaf of papers, and then his expression cleared when he came to a telegram at the bottom of the pile. "Ah, here it is," he said. "Gibson in Fort Benton has reserved you a space on board the *Big Muddy*, the flagship of the Harding Line."

De Cordova nodded thoughtfully. "Good," he said. "And will Isaiah Harding be on board personally?"

Brennan again consulted the telegram. "He'll be there, Luis," he said reassuringly. "In fact, Gibson

30

stresses in the telegram that Captain Harding will act as his own ship's master on this particular voyage."

"I sincerely hope so," Luis de Cordova said, "because that will simplify my task enormously. I want to take over all four of the Harding Line ships, and I intend to have them by the time the *Big Muddy* reaches St. Louis."

"I'll bet on that!" Brennan said loyally.

"After all, my time is worth something to me," Luis said self-righteously. "I'm not going to waste two months meandering down the Missouri River on board a creaking stern-wheeler unless I have something concrete to show for it. Seeing that every river steamer, properly managed, stands to earn thousands of dollars on each voyage she makes, this little jaunt can be well worth my time. Meanwhile, you know what you are to do."

Brennan nodded. "I sure do, boss. While you're heading down the Missouri, ah, seeking new business opportunities, I'll be busy contacting gang leaders and young war chiefs who would just drool over these guns we got hidden away."

Luis de Cordova grinned in satisfaction. It appeared that all the pieces were falling into place for him to control a business empire extending all the way from Portland, Oregon, to St. Louis, Missouri.

Only a few months after she had married Jim Randall, Pamela Drake Randall was distressed to find herself bored with her new life. It served her right, she supposed, for marrying a man whom she didn't love.

As she well knew, she could find no fault with Jim.

He was honest, forthright, and courageous, qualities that he demonstrated constantly, and he was tender and thoughtful in his lovemaking. He was dark, handsome, and distinguished-looking—always the gentleman—and he was generous as well as wealthy, so she lacked for nothing in her daily life. And having lived for years in Baltimore, he was sufficiently sophisticated and worldly to meet her on her own level.

The more she thought about it, the more she realized that Jim was in no way to blame for her boredom. The weather, she finally decided, was solely responsible. Winter lingered in the vicinity of Boise, and the ground was still covered with thick layers of snow, making outdoor activities virtually impossible. She dared not ride into Boise, and so she was restricted to the ranch. When she did venture outdoors, she habitually wore snowshoes in order to prevent herself from floundering in deep drifts.

Jim's extensive library, to which he was constantly adding books sent from Baltimore and from Chicago, proved to be a godsend, but after a time, she read so much that the words began to blur on the pages, and she had to find other ways to keep herself busy. Ah-Sing, the Chinese cook she had inherited from Millicent, was so efficient that she stayed away from his kitchen, and eventually she began to interest herself in improvement projects on the ranch, activities that kept the hired hands occupied during the winter months. The men built an addition of two rooms to the main house, and then, at her instigation, they started to enlarge and improve the quarters in their bunkhouse. She eagerly took charge of this activity.

One morning after Jim had eaten a hearty breakfast—Pamela confining herself to a single slice of unbuttered toast and a cup of black coffee—he went off to the library to struggle with his meticulously kept ledgers. She went to the so-called "snow room," where she had to prepare for the short walk across the open yard to the bunkhouse. First, she wound a long, woolen scarf around her head and neck, and then, after putting on high boots and buckling on a pair of cumbersome snowshoes, she donned a sheepskin-lined coat and a pair of lined leather gloves. Only then did she venture out into the open.

Several inches of fresh snow had fallen during the night, increasing the difficulty of walking across the yard, and a biting wind blew down from the mountains, numbing the young Englishwoman and forcing her to lower her head as she hurried to the bunkhouse.

Red-faced and gasping for breath, she reached the bunkhouse, where a cacophony of sawing and hammering greeted her. The hands were busily engaged in building new sleeping quarters for themselves, and they greeted her with smiles and waves but did not interrupt their work.

Removing the scarf from her head, Pamela shook out her blond hair, then began to divest herself of her outer garments as the ranch foreman, Randy Savage, approached her.

He was tall, sandy-haired, and broad-shouldered, with a natural, easygoing charm that had won him great popularity among the unmarried young women of Boise. Grinning broadly, he said, "If I were you, ma'am, I'd wear my greatcoat in here. We're open to the elements,

33

you know, and it gets mighty chilly without a fourth wall to protect us."

"I suspect you're right, Randy," she replied, and shrugged back into her sheepskin-lined coat. "My! This new dormitory room is so big!"

"One thing is sure," he said. "There's going to be more than enough room, even after we put up partitions, to assure each man of his privacy."

"And you're going to have your own room?" she inquired.

"Yes, ma'am! I never heard of a foreman with a private room all to himself, but I never saw quarters like this for hands on a ranch in my life!"

"It made complete sense to my husband," she said. "He works the boys hard and expects them to produce for him, so he feels he should exert himself for them in return. Also, if they have comfortable quarters, good food, and are treated right, they'll work that much harder for him."

"That makes sense, ma'am," he replied. "You want to see the recreation room? We closed the fourth wall off after you left us yesterday."

"By all means." She followed him out of the new dormitory into a smaller chamber. Because it was enclosed, it was warmer, and Pamela promptly opened her coat.

"The heating stove will go over yonder," Randy told her. "The billiard table you've ordered for us will go here. Over there we're going to partition off another room for reading and letter writing. When word goes around about the way we live here," he declared, "just about every hired hand in the West will be beating down the doors to get a job on the Randall ranch."

Pamela laughed.

Randy placed one hand on the unfinished wall behind her and leaned against it, his eyes searching. "How come you're being so all-fired nice to me and the boys?" he demanded.

Pamela found his direct gaze disconcerting. "I'm treating you the way I'd expect to be treated if our positions were reversed. That's all," she said lightly.

Randy's attitude remained solemn. "Well, ma'am," he replied, "any time you want anything from me, all you have to do is holler."

Pamela conveniently forgot that she was dealing with her husband's employee and close associate. Ever since she'd been an adolescent, she'd made it a practice to flirt with attractive males, and she saw no reason to change her habits of a lifetime now. Parting her moist, full lips, she gazed up at him seductively. Randy, whose face was only inches from hers, became flustered.

She continued to regard him steadily, enjoying the sense of power she exerted over him.

Gradually Randy's expression and attitude changed. Until that moment, he had been dealing with her strictly as the wife of his employer, a woman who was kind enough to look out for his interests and those of his subordinates. Now, suddenly, he was aware of her as an exceptionally attractive female, as someone who was signaling her possible availability to him.

Pamela knew she was playing with fire, and a warning bell clanged in the back of her mind, but she paid no attention to it. Instead, she moved closer to him.

One of the ranch hands suddenly called out from the adjoining room, "Hey, Randy, I need a hand," and the spell was momentarily broken. Pamela knew, however, that this was not the end but instead marked the beginning. The road ahead was uncharted, and adventure beckoned. Time promised to pass far more rapidly, as well as pleasantly.

II

In spite of the heavy snows that blocked the trails on the heights, Edward Blackstone made splendid time as he rode through the lower passes that took him from Boise to Fort Benton. Toby Holt had given him a recent surveyor's map before leaving Idaho, and by following it, Edward avoided major difficulties. Occasionally, thick snow forced him to make detours, also shown on his detailed map, and by closely following the advice that Toby had given him, Edward always managed to return to the main trail.

Attired for late winter travel in a fur hat, a coat with a broad fur collar, and fur-lined boots, Edward made a dashing figure, with his handsome face, pencil-thin mustache, and clear, bright eyes. He rode a spirited gelding, leading an equally active workhorse behind him. The latter animal was heavily laden with the equipment that Edward required for travel alone through those lonely, rugged parts. There was his canvas tent, neatly folded and packed away, as well as cooking utensils, tins of food, and a host of personal items, including a spare rifle in addition to the English repeating rifle that he carried in a sling behind him in the saddle.

He gloried in the magnificent vistas that he encountered as he rode through the mountains, and most of all he relished the all-encompassing solitude of the mountain vastness. His one regret was that he had not lived several decades earlier, when such fabulous mountain men like Kit Carson and Whip Holt were making their reputations in these remote regions. As it was, he felt privileged to have made the acquaintance of young Toby Holt.

Edward traveled for days on end without seeing another human being, but he knew, nevertheless, that he was not alone in this seemingly unpopulated region. This belief was dramatically confirmed one afternoon when he was riding through a section of evergreen forest where patches of snow were interspersed with larger areas of forest rubble. Suddenly there was a sharp cry, the sound of someone in severe distress.

Peering ahead through the trees, he saw eight or ten Indian braves, who he knew would be members of the Shoshone nation, since according to his map he was riding through their territory. In their midst, lying on the ground and writhing in pain, was a boy of prepuberty age whose leg was caught in the steel teeth of a bear trap. The child's agony was excruciating, but the years of training he had endured stood him in good stead, and he did not cry out again. Instead he clamped his teeth shut and rocked back and forth in pain, sweat pouring down his face and into his eyes.

One warrior, wearing a feathered bonnet that marked him as having greater rank than any of his comrades, moved through the underbrush toward the child to try to help him.

Edward took in the situation at a glance and then called out, "Stop! Don't move!" As he jumped to the ground, the chieftain and the other braves all stared at him.

After dismounting, Edward picked up a long, dead evergreen branch from the ground and, poking it into the rubble ahead of him, began to advance toward the stricken Indian child.

Most of the braves had not understood the white man's command, but they nevertheless halted their advance and watched him curiously.

Suddenly, a loud, crunching sound echoed through the forest, and the jaws of a second bear trap snapped shut with such force that the pine branch Edward carried was broken in half. Edward had known that whenever one bear trap had been set, there was usually another, to prevent a captured animal from dragging the first trap away. This was what the hunter had done in this case. Having satisfied himself that both traps were sprung, Edward advanced quickly to the stricken boy.

The Shoshone chieftain was close behind him, careful to follow in his footsteps and not stray onto land where there might be other traps.

Together they caught hold of the jaws of steel that

held the child prisoner and, using all of their strength, pried the trap open. The little boy was freed, but his discomfort was far from ended. Blood smeared his bare leg, and Edward saw that the cruel steel teeth had ripped a long gash in the boy's flesh.

Edward hurried to his packhorse and took down a saddlebag, which he opened hastily, removing a small flask of brandywine and a sewing kit containing a length of strong yarn and a stout needle used for mending tears in greatcoats.

"Hold the boy firmly," he said to the chieftain. "This is going to hurt like the very devil."

The Shoshone nodded, apparently understanding English. Taking the child onto his lap, he addressed him at some length in his own tongue.

Edward, who had acquired first-aid experience when serving as an officer in the Royal Cavalry in India, first threaded the needle, wiped the wound clean with a small quantity of brandywine, then swiftly sewed up the gash in the child's leg.

The boy buried his face in his father's buckskins during the operation, but he made no sound.

Edward tied off the yarn, cut it, and, relieved that he had completed the operation successfully, took a small swallow of brandywine.

"You friend of Shoshone," the chief said, struggling to make himself understood in English. "You come camp, eat supper with us."

It would have been rude to decline, and Edward consoled himself with the thought that the Shoshone had gestured toward the east, so he knew that he would continue in the general direction of Fort Benton, his destination. He insisted that the injured boy ride in his stead and lifted the child up into his flat English saddle.

Then he accompanied the braves on a trek of several miles through the wilderness. Shortly before dark, they came to a small plateau beside a mountain stream that was running free and clear, even though winter was not yet over. To the surprise of the visitor, the camp was being tended by an Indian girl in her late teens, and judging from her relationship with the chief and his son, she was the leader's daughter.

The girl took immediate charge of her brother, washing off his injured leg with water from the stream and then smearing the wound with a salve of some kind made from the pulp of a plant. The ointment was crude, but from the boy's expression it was apparent that it was immediately effective. Before long, he fell sound asleep, rolled up in a blanket near the fire.

The girl proved to be a model of efficiency in other ways, too. She had roasted large amounts of venison meat, obviously shot earlier during the Shoshone's stay at the camp, and with it had prepared varieties of dried vegetables, which apparently the Indians had brought with them from their main village. She had even found time to fish in the stream and to broil her catch over the fire. Her father held a long talk with her and evidently told her in detail of Edward's deed. Consequently, she could not do enough for the visitor and insisted on treating him as an honored guest, serving him a whole, broiled trout followed by a choice cut of venison and a generous portion of the boiled vegetables.

The language barrier made it impossible for Edward to converse easily with the Indian girl, just as he could not speak with the braves. Night came while they were eating their evening meal, seated near various fires in the encampment area. The girl lighted a pipe, which she presented to Edward. He tried it and found the tobacco strong and bitter to his taste but smoked it rather than offend the girl and his hosts. He noted that he and the young woman were now alone at their fire and that the braves were grinning at him in a strange way. Whenever he caught the eye of a warrior, the man grinned even more broadly and then turned away.

At last, the mystery was explained. Using careful sign language, the girl offered herself to the young Englishman. Stunned, Edward stared at her. Her figure, revealed beneath her buckskins, was rounded but slender. She wore her coal-black hair in a single braid down her back, her features were clean-cut, and her eyes were huge and softly feminine. She appeared to be about eighteen or nineteen years of age, and she was in earnest as she made it clear to him that she was willing to go to bed with him.

He guessed that he was being so favored because of his quick-thinking kindnesses to her little brother. It was possible, he had to concede to himself, that the young woman found him attractive, but the fact remained that she was compelled to offer herself to him because of tribal customs.

Edward decided instantly that he could not accept her invitation. He very much doubted that she had indulged in affairs with many men, and he refused to be one of the first. She was thanking him in the only way that she and her people knew, but as far as Edward was concerned, the efforts he had exerted on her brother's behalf would be spoiled if he took this kind of a reward.

However, he knew he had to exercise great care to ensure that she did not lose face. Somehow he had to convince her that his rejection was in no way based on a refusal to admire her charms.

Using sign language and the few words of Shoshone he had learned while living in Idaho, he slowly and painfully concocted a story for her benefit. He was married, he told her, and he loved his wife. He would be dishonoring her if he engaged now in a relationship with someone else. He was very sorry, but the rules of his people demanded fidelity; as an honorable warrior, he was required to obey the law of his people.

He was greatly relieved when the girl accepted his explanation and went off unhurt.

Edward slept soundly, alone, in the midst of the Shoshone. The following morning, the warriors clustered around him and watched curiously as he took out his shaving brush, soap, razor, and mirror and began to shave his face, then wash in the icy waters of the mountain stream before donning his clothes again. Breakfast was a repetition of the previous night's supper, and then the time came for him to be on his way.

Before Edward departed, he presented his spare rifle to the little boy, whose leg was now on the mend. He told the child—through his father—that by learning to use this rifle, he could grow up to become a mighty hunter and a main source of food supplies for his people. The Shoshone cheered him as he rode off, and Edward was convinced that the Indians and the settlers could truly learn to live in peace and friendship if they would only try.

At least a score of sturdy stern-wheelers sat in long rows at the Missouri River docks in the booming frontier town of Fort Benton, Montana. To an extent, the ships were very similar. All of them had snub-nosed prows that could slide up on sandbanks when necessary. All of them had glass-enclosed wheelhouses high in their superstructures, surrounded by narrow, cleated walkways. Twin smokestacks rose like rabbit's ears on either side of most of the wheelhouses to carry away the smoke from wood-fired boilers, which provided the steam for the stern-wheelers.

Most of the river steamers looked top-heavy and squat. They had at least two, and sometimes three, decks above the waterline and were about half as wide as they were long, which was unusual because they ranged in length from forty to eighty feet. There were seats for as many as a dozen oarsmen forward of the enclosed storage space, and it was common to see a small brass cannon in a swivel mounting on the bow.

Most ships also boasted a mast that took a sail and was attached to a long rope called a cordelle. With cargo piled high on their main aft decks and covered with canvas, the larger riverboats were towed in shallows or hauled through heavy brush along the banks of the river when they could not be rowed or sailed. Miraculously, even the largest and most cumbersome of the river vessels could navigate in a scant thirty inches of water.

Of all the ships tied up at the waterfront docks, the

Big Muddy stood out because she was bigger and sleeker than her sister vessels. She was eighty-five feet long and only twenty feet wide, boasting three decks, including excellent private cabin accommodations for more than thirty first-class passengers. She also carried in excess of five hundred tons of cargo and was superior in construction.

Seated in a leather-padded swivel chair in the wheelhouse high above the docks was one of the most renowned of the river captains, Isaiah Harding, who had been navigating on the Missouri for more than forty years. He had carried the furs trapped by Jim Bridger, Kit Carson, and Whip Holt to the markets in St. Louis, and it was said of him that he was familiar with every twist and turn in the Missouri, that he knew the location of every shifting sandbar and underwater obstacle.

No one knew his age, but his snow-white hair and his wrinkled, leathery skin were evidence that he was far from young. However, he was broad-shouldered, carrying himself with the air of one long accustomed to command. His eyes were pale, exceptionally bright, and penetrating; he had the ruddy complexion of one who has spent virtually his entire life outdoors.

He sat back in his chair now, frowning as he tried to read through several closely written legal documents. They appeared to make no sense to him because he repeatedly turned back to the first page, started over, frowned, and shook his head.

He was so immersed in the documents that he failed to hear someone entering the wheelhouse. At first glance, the newcomer appeared to be a slender male youth but on closer examination was revealed to be a girl in man's attire, an open-throated shirt and work pants several sizes too large for her. She wore boots, and her sandy-blond hair was tied up beneath a faded bandanna that concealed it from view. Her eyes were huge and luminous, identical to Captain Harding's, which was not surprising, since she was his daughter Thomasina, known by all as Tommie.

Captain Harding sighed, then blinked as he looked up from the documents he had been studying. "Hello, Tommie," he said, giving her a weary smile. "How's the world been treating you all day?"

"Not too bad, Papa," she replied, throwing herself into a chair adjacent to the big steering wheel. "The work crew has cleaned the aft hold, and we're ready to start loading cargo," she went on. "Beginning tomorrow morning, we're going to start painting the first-class suites and cabins."

Ordinarily her industry would have pleased him, but he merely nodded and said absently, "Good."

Instantly alert, she looked at him, her eyes searching. "What's wrong, Papa?" she asked quietly.

"Nothing," Captain Harding protested, then changed his mind. "All right, dammit," he went on, "there's a great deal wrong. I've had another letter from that confounded Luis de Cordova. He claims that I'm deeply in debt to him, that I still owe him interest on that loan he made to me a couple of years ago. He's demanding payment, and he says if I don't have the cash—and he knows blamed well that I won't have any cash at all until after we make this voyage to St. Louis—then I've got to pay him by turning over one or more of my ships to him."

Tommie reached for the communication he was holding and read it slowly, then reread it. "This makes no sense to me," she said at last, frowning. "I think that what Luis de Cordova is saying to us is that the interest on his original loan to you has multiplied and multiplied until it has reached an astronomical sum that can be met only by his taking possession of some of the ships of the Harding Line fleet, including the flagship, the *Big Muddy*."

"How my debt to him could just keep doubling every month is beyond me," her father growled, "but one thing is sure: I've put my soul into the building of the *Big Muddy*, and it's going to pay off, and pay off handsomely, for me and for you. She'll earn at least ten thousand dollars by the time we take her to St. Louis and back here to Fort Benton. You'll notice that in that letter de Cordova threatens to have the law on us and says he'll take the *Big Muddy* from us by force. Well, I'm damned if he will! I've got to sit down with him and talk some sense into the man's head."

"You'll be wasting your time," she said emphatically. "I didn't like de Cordova when I met him in the past, and I never will. I can't prove that he's dishonest, but I really don't trust him as far as I can throw him. I think he's cheating us when he tosses these figures of his around in the air, and I don't mind telling you, when he intimated to me that he wanted to marry me, my flesh crawled!"

"All I ask of you," Isaiah said, a pleading note in his voice, "is that you say and do nothing to offend the man. His agent asked me to hold a suite for him on board the *Big Muddy*, and that's what I'm going to do.

All we have to do now is to stall off paying him until we make the voyage, and at the end of it, we'll have enough money to pay him a portion of what he demands."

"I don't like to tell you how to run your business, Papa," Tommie said, "but if I were you, I'd turn all of this over to a smart lawyer and let him handle it for you."

Captain Harding bridled. "For forty years," he said, "I've made my living on the Missouri River. I haven't needed any help from any lawyers, and I'm blamed if I'm going to start relying on them now. No matter what happens, I'll handle my affairs myself, and not get some mealymouthed lawyer involved in my business!"

Tommie knew it was useless to argue with her father once he had made up his mind. He was intending to see his problems with Luis de Cordova through to a finish on his own, regardless of the consequences.

Luis de Cordova took himself to Millicent's, which he had been told was the best restaurant in Boise, shortly after he had arrived in town on his way to Fort Benton, Montana. He had hated living in a wagon on the trail all those days, and consequently, he enjoyed the luxurious atmosphere of the first restaurant in which he had dined since leaving Portland. The white table linen and crisp napkins, the genteel chinaware and graceful flatware, and the thin, delicate glasses all appealed to him. His predinner drink was delicious. In short, Luis de Cordova was enjoying himself thoroughly.

Absently twirling his whiskey glass, he watched the proprietress, Millicent Randall, as she conducted people to their tables, made sure they were comfortable, and took their dinner orders. He had long considered himself an expert in judging feminine beauty, and he was amazed by Millicent's appearance. Granted that her dress of midnight blue with white collar and cuffs was modest, that she wore no cosmetics, and that her hair was pulled into a bun at the nape of her neck. But he judged her figure, beneath the loose-fitting dress, to be excellent, and he noted that her features were regular and chiseled. She had beautiful, large eyes, her hair was thick and shiny, and when it was let down, he was sure it would be very long. He imagined that properly dressed and with the appropriate use of cosmetics, she could be spectacularly beautiful.

As he sipped his drink, he became vaguely conscious that the blowsy, overdressed blond woman at the table adjoining his was studying him. He knew at a glance that she was a bordello keeper, but he had no interest in her girls that night, and so he paid no attention to her.

Suzanne, however, continued to watch him closely. His clothes were expensive, and his gold cuff links and the diamond-inlaid gold ring he wore on one hand had obviously cost a small fortune. A bold idea was forming in the back of her mind. She had tried repeatedly to buy the restaurant from Millicent Randall so that she could move her brothel to a bigger building in a better part of town, but to date, her efforts had been rebuffed. Indeed, she often came here for supper, before her own place got busy, in the hopes she could persuade Millicent to sell. Perhaps now if she tried a new tact and pressed hard, she might be able to gain her goal.

Sipping her own glass of wine, she spoke softly but distinctly. "I gather," she said, "that you find Millicent attractive."

Luis de Cordova's expression did not change, and he did not look at Suzanne. "By Millicent," he said, "I gather you refer to the hostess?"

He was nibbling at the bait! "Yes," Suzanne said, matching his blunt tone. "Millicent Randall is the proprietress of this place."

He nodded distantly. "I see."

She was afraid he intended to break the tenuous thread of conversation, so she persisted. "I've noticed you eyeing her," she said boldly. "It's been rather obvious to me that you admire her."

Luis got right to the point. "Don't tell me," he said, laughing, "that you're in a position to make her available."

"I might be in a position," she replied cautiously, "to strike up a deal with the right person for the right price."

His shrewd glance measured her, and he saw she was not joking. He slowly finished his drink, then signaled his waiter to bring him another and to serve Suzanne again as well. Suzanne saw the gesture and knew that he was now biting at the hook.

"In my opinion," he said evenly, "the young woman you referred to as Millicent Randall has dazzling potential. I'll grant you that she's totally inexperienced and needs awakening. With the proper guidance, however, she could become explosive."

"I'll defer to your judgment, sir," Suzanne said smoothly.

He shrugged and waited for her to continue.

"I haven't always earned my living in the West," Suzanne said. "In fact, for many years I operated in New York, America's largest city. There I had an opportunity to befriend a man who lived with me and my girls for a time. He had traveled widely in Europe and presented me with a rare gift in return for my, ah, hospitality. He gave me some unusual dried mushrooms that he had obtained from Gypsies in their native Hungary. The mushrooms, when powdered and mixed with a tincture of alcohol, had remarkable properties. I have a vial of the liquid available at this very moment."

Luis laughed mockingly. "Just what are the properties of this liquid?" he scoffed.

Suzanne remained serious. "One drop of the fluid placed in a woman's drink will change her whole future for a long, long time," she said. "I guarantee it. That single drop will make her easy to arouse and hypersensitive to lovemaking. No matter how restrained she has been all her days, that one drop will transform her into an alley cat who cannot get enough of masculine lovemaking. In fact, repeated use of the potion completely alters the individual's personality, and the effects are long-lasting."

"What you say," Luis replied, "sounds too good to be true."

"But it is true," Suzanne insisted. "See for yourself. Feed one drop to Millicent—it's colorless and odorless so you can do it without her knowledge—and watch the miraculous transformation that takes place in her personality."

Luis de Cordova returned to his observation of the

brown-haired young woman, who was busily moving about the restaurant. "Suppose you and I reach an understanding. It should be self-evident to you that no agreement between us will be binding unless it is proved conclusively and without a shadow of doubt that the claims you make for this potion of yours are accurate. If your claims prove to be accurate, what price would you demand of me?"

Suzanne's retort was prompt. "When you are satisfied that my claims are accurate," she said, "I will ask you to buy this establishment for me. Millicent refuses to sell to me personally, but once you have her in your thrall, she will do whatever you ask of her. And having this building for my own will be most helpful to me in establishing my business for the rest of my days."

Luis's instinct as a gambler had been touched. What was more, if this potion worked as the bordello keeper said it did, he would not only have his own way with Millicent but would also find other uses for her. "Very well," he said eagerly, "you will provide me with a container of your magic Gypsy potion. I will try it out this very night, and if it lives up to your claims for it, I will buy this establishment for you. If the potion is valueless, however, all bets are off."

"That's very generous of you," Suzanne told him, and congratulated herself on having maneuvered him into making a wager that was even more beneficial to her than she had dared to hope.

They ordered supper, and while their meal was being prepared, Suzanne excused herself and hurried off to her nearby bordello. When she returned, she had an expression of smug satisfaction on her face. "Now, sir," she announced, "you shall see for yourself that I always keep my word." She handed him a small, smoke-colored bottle.

Taking it, he removed a glass stopper and put a drop of the contents onto the palm of his hand. As she had indicated to him, the fluid was colorless, and when he held it up to his nose, he found that it had no odor. Carefully drying his hand on his napkin, he slipped the bottle into his pocket and began to eat his dinner. They conversed occasionally as they ate, and Luis's attitude made it clear that he expected no results from the use of the potion. Suzanne, however, seemed confident that it would be effective, and her mind was already racing as she planned the alterations she intended to make in the interior of the restaurant.

When they finished their meal, Luis asked their waiter to include her check with his, and then he stood up to shake Suzanne's hand as he bid her farewell. "I'll meet you here tomorrow noon," he said, "and we'll settle our debt—if there's anything to be settled at that time."

"I look forward," Suzanne said with finality, "to the conclusion of our business arrangements at noon tomorrow. I'm sure you'll find that the potion is effective. It has never yet failed me."

Luis waited quietly for a time after Suzanne had left the restaurant. Then, as Millicent walked past his table, a sheaf of menus in one hand, he beckoned to her.

"I hope you enjoyed your supper, sir," she said mechanically, her smile artificially bright.

"It was delicious," he told her gravely. "The best

meal that I've eaten in many weeks, but I've grown tired just watching you pacing around the floor of this place all evening. You haven't sat down once. Perhaps you will honor me by joining me for a nightcap."

Color rose in Millicent's cheeks as she thanked him but refused the offer, saying she did not drink.

Luis persisted. "Have a cup of coffee with me, then," he said. "You really need a few minutes of rest."

Millicent thought it would be not only bad manners but also bad business if she rejected his appeal. He appeared to be a respectable gentleman, so she graciously consented to sit. After he ordered two cups of coffee from the waiter, they introduced themselves, with Millicent shyly stammering as she told him her name. She thought it strange that this handsome, dashing stranger should show an interest in her.

Luis feigned surprise when she revealed her identity. "I never dreamed," he said, "that the owner of Millicent's restaurant would be such a wonderfully attractive young lady!"

She turned beet red and could not reply.

Luis de Cordova had no trouble keeping up a steady monologue. He was accustomed to dealing with women, and he found it easy to flatter her.

They were interrupted from time to time as various waiters came to their table to obtain Millicent's initials on the bills they were about to present to customers. On each of these occasions, she was distracted for several moments, and thus it proved to be a relatively simple matter for Luis to remove the stopper from the end of the small bottle and shake the glass rod attached to it over the woman's coffee cup. To his satisfaction, the two or three drops of liquid that clung to the stopper dropped into her coffee.

When the waiter who had come to the table moved off and Luis had Millicent's attention again, he offered her cream and sugar. She took a small quantity of the latter and stirred it into her coffee.

In spite of his innate skepticism, he found himself watching her face anxiously as she drank her coffee.

All at once her voice trailed off in the middle of a sentence, and her eyes became glassy. She stared into space for several moments, obviously disoriented. The color was high in her cheeks. Then gradually she returned to normal and resumed her conversation, apparently not realizing that she had behaved oddly or that anything had been amiss.

Luis, however, realized that something had happened after she had consumed the potion-laden coffee. He had no idea whether it would be effective in the manner that Suzanne had outlined, and he had to make sure before he went any further and made a fool out of himself.

While continuing to chat about inconsequential matters, he maneuvered beneath the table in such a way that one of his legs pressed against Millicent's leg. Instead of breaking off contact, as he expected her to do, she surprised him by continuing to allow their legs to touch. For the first time, he began to believe that Suzanne's potion had been effective, and he swiftly planned his moves accordingly.

"We're holding down the last table in the place," he told her. "Must you stay on here much longer?"

Millicent was surprised to discover that, as he had

indicated, every other table in the restaurant had been vacated. "Oh, dear," she murmured with an embarrassed laugh, realizing that her dining room and kitchen help were prepared to depart for the night. "I've lost all track of time. Maybe I've been working too hard or something, but I'm feeling a little giddy." She couldn't help letting out a little giggle. "Actually, I feel just fine . . . wonderful, really. But I guess we'll have to go, too."

"I hope you'll allow me to escort you to your home," he said as he rose to his feet.

"Thank you," Millicent replied, "but that won't be at all necessary. I live close by the restaurant. I've taken possession of a suite that was used for some time by my cousin, Edward Blackstone, at the Boise Inn."

"You're not taking me out of my way at all," he assured her. "I'm staying at the Boise Inn myself."

She laughed at the seeming coincidence and agreed to accept him as an escort.

Luis waited for her while she locked up the restaurant, and then he helped her into her fur coat. Donning his own greatcoat, he took her arm as they went out into the late-night street.

A light rain had fallen earlier in the evening and then had frozen, forming a slippery crust on the snow-laden streets. Luis put an arm around Millicent, ostensibly to steady her and prevent her from falling. Again, she made no attempt to pull away from him; instead, she leaned against him. By this time he was convinced that the potion was at least strong enough to rid her of a number of obvious inhibitions.

When they came to the inn, Luis released her and

kept his distance from her as they made their way together through the lobby. Millicent began to bid him good night in the lobby, but he insisted on seeing her to her door. When they arrived at her suite, he asked if he could come in for a cordial and, giving her no chance to respond, quickly stepped inside.

Although somewhat flustered, Millicent did her best to be a good hostess and poured him a small glass of brandy, which until now she had kept for medicinal purposes.

By this time Luis had divested himself of his great-coat and had lighted the fire that the chambermaid had prepared in the hearth of the sitting room. As Millicent handed him his snifter of brandy, he caught hold of her hand and led her to the couch facing the fire, where he sat down close beside her.

"Oh, this feels so nice and warm," she said, the drug having taken full effect. "I could stay here all night."

Sliding an arm around her shoulders, he sat back on the sofa, ostensibly intending to watch the fire with her. To his gratification she made no attempt to get away from him but sat very still. As nearly as he could judge, she was totally relaxed.

He knew now precisely what he was doing. First, he removed the pins and combs from the bun at the nape of her neck and let her thick, dark hair tumble freely across her shoulders and down her back. Then he began to gently caress her arm.

Sighing contentedly, Millicent inched closer to him and put her head on his shoulder. Increasingly convinced that she would offer no resistance to his lovemaking, he put his hand over her breast and began to stroke it. Still meeting no protest, he began to toy with the nipple. The depth and ferocity of Millicent's reaction astonished him. Breathing hard and squirming in unconcealed delight, she threw herself at him, throwing her arms about his neck, pulling him close, her lips parting for his kiss. She pressed herself against him, and one hand at the back of his head exerted great pressure on him to kiss her that much harder.

If she acted like a woman possessed by demons, it was because that was exactly how she felt. Never before had she cast aside all her inhibitions; never before had she eagerly sought a sexual union with any man. The feelings she had kept bottled within her all her life were released, and her abandon was complete.

She craved total fulfillment and was oblivious to the way in which she achieved it. Neither then nor later did she recall precisely whether Luis had undressed her or whether she had assisted him. Similarly, she could not remember how he had divested himself of his own clothes, although she seemed to recall that she had eagerly helped him.

He took her on the sofa, and although she was a neophyte, her ardor was even greater than his, and her movements matched his. Straining and thrusting, her hands moving up and down his bare back, she dug her nails into his flesh and screamed in delight as his thrusts became more powerful, more deeply penetrating.

At last she found glorious release, and in that moment she had an experience that was unique to anything she had ever known. She distinctly heard the crashing chords of a Beethoven symphony ringing in her ears, and she gloried in the sound, reveling in the sensation as never before.

Luis could scarcely believe his good fortune. He had found a woman who was ultrasensitive to his slightest touch and who completely lost herself in their mutual sexual experience. Surely he could put what he had found to good use and could earn himself a handsome profit.

Millicent and Luis made love again the following morning, and again she could swear that she heard the soaring notes of a symphony as she reached a climax. Her lack of experience left her bewildered, and convinced that she was not dreaming, she concluded that she must be in love with Luis de Cordova. She could find no other reason for reacting to him as she did.

As they ate breakfast together in the dining room of the inn, Millicent completely unconcerned about the wondering looks on the faces of the other guests, Luis was aware of the young woman's rapt gaze fixed on him. He knew the moment had come to strike, to put his scheme into operation.

"I am planning on hiring a guide and horses and getting together supplies for a trip to Fort Benton in Montana," he said. "From there I'm intending to travel down the Missouri River by stern-wheeler all the way to St. Louis." He noted with satisfaction that she appeared crestfallen, so he added very gently, "Will you come with me?"

Millicent reacted as though he had offered her the sun, moon, and stars. Believing that she loved him, she jumped to the inevitable conclusion that he also was in love with her. The journey to Fort Benton and subsequently on by steamer to St. Louis could be a honeymoon, she told herself, and she was convinced that although he had not mentioned marriage as such, he fully intended to make her his wife. Because her whole background was so staid and proper, the thought did not occur to her that he might be proposing that they live together without bothering with a marriage ceremony.

"Oh, Luis, do you mean it? Do you really mean it?" she asked in something of a daze.

He merely nodded.

For a moment she looked troubled. "But there's my cousin Jim and the restaurant and . . ." She remembered, too, that her other cousin, Edward Blackstone, was also traveling down the Missouri by riverboat. What if she ran into him; what would he say? Then she put all these thoughts from her mind. "Of course I'll come with you!" she blurted out, and looked at him adoringly.

Luis smiled at her, stroked her arm, and then became crisp. "There are many things to be done before we leave," he said. "I can't delay my departure because I've got to reach Fort Benton in time to sail on board the *Big Muddy*, the best of the river steamers. In fact, I've already reserved a suite on her for the voyage. Obviously," he went on, "you'll want to dispose of your restaurant."

"Yes, yes, of course," she said. "I'll want to repay my cousin for his expenses in buying it for me."

Luis was completely businesslike now. "How much do you figure you owe him?"

"I'm sure that five thousand dollars would cover everything," she said.

"I'll get twice that amount for you," he said forcefully. "I know just where to go for it. Sign a power of attorney, granting me the right to deal on your behalf, and I'll have the cash in hand before we go today."

She believed that he could accomplish anything. "That will be wonderful," she breathed.

Being long familiar with the necessary form, he promptly wrote out a power of attorney for her. As soon as Millicent signed it, he was on his way.

First Luis busied himself telling the guide who would lead them to Fort Benton to rent horses for himself, Millicent, and their equipment, and then concentrated on purchasing the various supplies that they would need on the trail.

Promptly at noon, he went to Millicent's restaurant and was waiting for Suzanne when she appeared a few moments later. Not bothering to discuss with her the efficacy of her Gypsy potion, he contented himself with showing her the power of attorney that Millicent had signed. "Pay me ten thousand in hard cash here and now," he said, "and this place is yours."

Suzanne made no attempt to conceal her disappointment. "Ten thousand?" she said. "That seems mighty high. Can't you shave that figure some?"

"Take it or leave it, the price is firm." He was brutally frank. "I agreed to sell you the place, but I mentioned nothing about price. If you want it badly enough, you'll pay what I ask."

Realizing she had been outsmarted, Suzanne gave in. Luis accompanied her to the Boise territorial bank, where he signed a document turning the property over to Suzanne, and she, in return, gave him ten thousand dollars in cash, which he promptly deposited in a new account in Millicent Randall's name. He wisely took not one penny for himself.

Then he returned briefly to the inn. Millicent was deeply impressed when he gave her the bankbook and tore up the power of attorney document in her presence. He arranged to meet her in two hours and told her to be ready to leave Boise at that time.

The young woman barely had time to ride out to the Randalls' ranch in order to bid them farewell.

She arrived just in time to sit down to a hasty meal with them, and while they ate, she told them her fantastic news—that she had fallen in love with a man named Luis de Cordova, who had sold her restaurant for her, and that she was accompanying him on a long journey that would terminate in St. Louis.

These developments stunned her cousin and his wife, particularly as they were so uncharacteristic of the usually conservative Millicent.

When they questioned her, however, and tried to persuade her to take her time before making such major changes in her life, she brushed aside their protests. Her mind was made up, she told them, and nothing would dissuade her from carrying out the instructions that Luis had given her. She turned her various bankbooks over to them, making it clear that she did not anticipate needing money for any purpose and that she would repay Edward for the restaurant in due time. She also arranged that Jim and Pamela would keep her mare, Lady, for her until she returned to Boise for it.

Then, before they could protest further, she bid them farewell and hurried back into town to keep her rendezvous with her lover.

Jim and Pamela remained seated at their dining room table. Jim, who had lost one eye while serving with the Union Army during the Civil War, sat absent-mindedly smoothing his eye patch. It was a gesture he used only when he was badly upset. "I'll be damned," he said.

"I don't mind saying I'll be damned, too," Pamela replied humorlessly. "This is the most extraordinary thing I've ever heard."

"I can't believe it's happening to Millicent," he said, shaking his head.

"Neither can I," she replied. "You must have noticed Millicent's face whenever she mentioned this chap de Cordova. She beamed and blushed like a schoolgirl in her first romance."

"I'm afraid," Jim said, "that you've hit the nail right on the head, Pam. That's exactly what Millicent is: a schoolgirl floundering in the throes of her first real romance. It's pitiful in a grown woman, but her music has meant so much to her that she's never really had a chance to learn about personal relationships until now. Yes, she was engaged once, but that was all so proper and formal—hardly like what's going on now. I'm afraid she's going to pay the penalty for her lapse."

"I must say one thing for this de Cordova person, whoever he is," Pamela declared. "At least he's not after Millicent's money. I was impressed by the fact that he turned over every penny of the sale of the restaurant to her. I know that because she gave us the bankbooks."

"You may or may not be right," Jim told her. "I've never set eyes on de Cordova, and I know nothing about him, but it's certainly possible that he gave up a short-term profit on the restaurant in return for a much larger profit later. If he knows that Millicent has money back East in savings and bonds worth many times ten thousand dollars, perhaps he's just playing a shrewd game."

"You may be right," she said thoughtfully. "Indeed, if he's as sophisticated and worldly as Millicent seems to think, what else could his interest in her be?"

"Quite true," he said. "We know she's generous, talented, and has a lovely spirit, but those qualities might not be so evident to a stranger, particularly some-one who's known her for less than twenty-four hours. I attribute her extraordinary statement that she loves him to her complete lack of experience in the world, but I can imagine no valid reason why he would think himself in love with her in so short a time unless he's after her money."

Pamela stirred, drumming her fingers on the table. "What can we do about all this?"

"Absolutely nothing," her husband told her flatly. "No matter what we may think of Luis de Cordova and his motives, and no matter what we may feel about Millicent's action in all this, we have no say in the matter. She's of age and so is he, so our hands are tied, I'm afraid."

They fell silent, staring bleakly at each other.

"There *is* one thing we can do," Pamela said tentatively. "We can send a telegram to Edward in Fort Benton acquainting him with the facts and telling him to keep watch for Millicent."

Jim thumped the table in sudden excitement. "You're right! Why didn't I think of that? I'll get off a telegram to Edward immediately, and perhaps he can come up with an understanding of the true situation when he sees Millicent. He might even be able to influence her where you and I have failed."

"You're too hard on us, darling," Pamela said. "We didn't fail. We had no chance to succeed because Millicent wouldn't listen to us. She acted like someone who was bewitched!"

III

Cadet Henry Blake, wearing civilian clothes for the first time in two years, sat in the plush upholstered seat of the transcontinental railroad train and stared out the window as the luxurious car jounced across the flat Iowa landscape heading for Nebraska. The knowledge that every hour of travel brought him that much closer to Fort Vancouver so excited him that it became impossible for him to read, and he stared instead at the rich farmland, at the newly tilled cornfields that stretched out all the way to the horizon.

For some reason, he thought of his own boyhood on a Montana ranch in the years before his own father had met an untimely death, and the clock seemed to turn back.

He was lucky beyond belief, he told himself. Instead of growing up as a professional gunslinger, after having avenged his father's death, he'd been befriended by Toby and Clarissa Holt. Then he had been adopted by General and Mrs. Blake, and this association ultimately had led to his appointment to West Point. Best of all, he had lived under the same roof with Mrs. Blake's daughter, Cindy Holt, for whom he had conceived an adolescent love that was maturing rapidly into an adult relationship. The knowledge that he and Cindy would soon be reunited filled him with delight, and he positively glowed. As he sat in a euphoric state, the train conductor made his way slowly down the center aisle, pausing when he reached a spot where he could observe Hank.

He looked at the young man carefully and then studied the leather case in which Hank carried his recently issued Winchester repeating rifle. Then the conductor came and sat down beside him. "You got a minute for a chat, young feller?"

"You bet," Hank told him.

"After we reach Council Bluffs in another hour," the man said, "we'll leave Iowa and come to the new railroad bridge that connects us with Nebraska. We'll stop in Omaha for fuel, water, and supplies. Then, as we cross the eastern Nebraska plains, we're likely to run into trouble."

"What kind of trouble?" Hank asked.

"There are bands of brigands—no-good robbers—that are infesting the Plains these days. They've halted a good many trains and have taken every last penny that the passengers carried."

Hank shook his head. "That's awful," he declared.

"It sure is," the conductor agreed. "Our head office has thought of asking the U.S. Army for help, but the troops are needed farther west to keep Indians under control, so we're trying to see if we can't make out on our own. We're asking passengers who know how to use firearms if they'll volunteer their services to help protect the train when we reach the Plains west of Omaha."

Hank smiled. "I reckon I can handle a rifle," he admitted.

"That's what I figured, seeing you're carrying one with your luggage. What do you say, young feller? Are you willing to give us a hand?"

"You bet I am!" Hank told him.

"Good," the conductor said. "I'll meet you at the engine at the end of our Omaha stop."

Hank looked after him as the man went on, searching for other volunteers among the passengers. All at once, the journey promised to become livelier.

After the train had crossed the new railroad bridge between the Iowa and Nebraska shores of the Missouri, it pulled into the new station at Omaha, where it was scheduled to remain for half an hour while various supplies were taken on board. Hank promptly went into the station, where he looked around, bought himself a newspaper, and then returned to the train. Filling the pockets of his suit coat with bullets, he picked up the case containing his rifle and went forward to the engine. Directly behind the engine stood the coal car, and there a half-dozen men were grouped around the train's fireman, who was in charge of defenses. Hank promptly joined the group, noting at a glance that the others were, without exception, many years his senior.

"When a train is attacked," the fireman said, "the robbers usually fire a shot or two as a warning and force the train to stop. While it's halted, they go from car to car and help themselves to the money and valuables that belong to passengers, and then they vamoose. They're out of sight before we can do a blamed thing about it. We're hopin' that you gents can discourage 'em and maybe even scare 'em enough to drive 'em off. Look around the locomotive and the coal car, if you will, and pick out your locations." He waved them on board.

One location above all others appealed immediately to Hank. At the front of the engine was the cowcatcher, a platform of iron that projected about three feet ahead of the body of the engine itself. It was intended, quite literally, to pick up cows, buffalo, and other large animals that might otherwise be standing on the tracks when the train approached and, after being struck, might cause a derailment unless moved out of harm's way.

"I figure the cowcatcher up yonder is as good a station as any—better than most," he said.

The entire group stared at him openmouthed. "Don't you think it's a mite too exposed?" the fireman demanded.

Hank shrugged. "Most robbers are terrible shots," he said. "Besides, it's best to beat them at their own game if we're going to get into a pitched battle with them."

One of the older passengers, a man who sported a bushy, walruslike mustache, clapped a hand patronizingly on Hank's shoulder. "I hear tell them newfangled Winchesters are tricky guns," he said. "Do you s'pose you can handle one of 'em?"

"I reckon so," Hank replied laconically. "Leastwise, I can try." He removed his rifle from the case, which he placed carefully in the engineer's cabin, and then climbed up onto the cowcatcher, making himself more or less comfortable by squatting down at a point beneath one of the engine's kerosene lights.

Eventually the train pulled out of the Omaha station, and leaving the produce and manufacturing town behind, it headed due west across broad, fertile fields. Hank busied himself making certain his weapon was in good condition and then carefully loaded it. For the first time since he had entered the military academy two years earlier, he would be firing a weapon in something other than target practice.

He knew that two of his fellow volunteers were riding in the cabin of the engine, while the fireman and the other four were located on both sides of the coal car, which was directly behind the engine, but he could see no one from the vantage point of the cowcatcher, nor could his colleagues see him. The engineer tooted his whistle once, briefly, in an attempt to make the youth feel less isolated. Hank waved his rifle over his head, then shoved it out to the left of the train as a way of letting his colleagues know that he was aware of their presence and appreciated it. For a half hour or more, Hank rode on the cowcatcher, swaying and being jolted and occasionally being forced to grasp the metal handhold welded to the engine behind him in order to keep from being thrown off the train. Under the circumstances, it was virtually impossible for him to relax his vigilance.

The engineer slowed the train to a crawl as he negotiated a very sharp curve, and Hank noted idly that it was difficult to see more than a few feet ahead because the dried cornstalks in the field beside him were so high. They had not been cut down since the beginning of the winter, and they formed a perfect obstacle to sight.

All at once, he grew tense as the train stopped rounding the curve and he saw a dozen masked men directly ahead on either side of the track, all of them mounted on horses and all brandishing rifles. The engineer, who had been awaiting just this development, applied his brakes, and air hissed as the train slowed to a speed of no more than five miles per hour.

This is it! Hank thought as he raised his rifle to his shoulder, quickly took aim, and then squeezed the trigger.

The nearest robber, who was approximately forty yards away, promptly crumpled to the ground.

Hank had called attention to himself, and the other robbers instantly concentrated their fire on him, their bullets making loud, clanging sounds as they bounced off the thick iron of the engine. As Hank had indicated, the robbers were anything but expert marksmen. Without exception, the shots of the first volley directed at him went wild.

The train continued to crawl forward, and Hank was grateful to the engineer, realizing that any motion made him a more difficult target to hit. Again, he raised his rifle to his shoulder, and this time he selected a

71

broad-shouldered, heavyset man, whom he also felled with one shot.

He was beginning to enjoy the experience, and he chuckled aloud when his third and fourth shots resulted in the killing of two more men. Suddenly the remaining bandits decided to withdraw. Their shots were leaving the enemy on the cowcatcher untouched, and in the meantime, his rifle was taking a continued, deadly toll.

No one gave an order, no one shouted a command, but all at once the remaining robbers grabbed the reins of the riderless horses, spurred their own mounts, and began to beat a retreat across the fields.

Hank Blake showed no mercy. He brought down one robber with a shot in the left side of his back, and he shot another at the base of his head. The others who managed to escape got away only because he had no time in which to take aim at them and fire.

At last the train drew to a halt, and the engineer and fireman ran forward, as did the half-dozen volunteers. They found Hank squatting on the cowcatcher, still studying the landscape around him.

"I never seen such shootin' in all my born days," the fireman shouted, and ecstatically pounded Hank on the back.

"I feel like a consarned fool," the passenger with the walrus mustache shouted. "Just imagine my askin' the boy if he knew how to fire one of them newfangled rifles." He laughed heartily at his own folly and then looked curiously at the youth whose marksmanship had single-handedly won the day. "What are you, boy, a star performer in some wild-west show?"

"No, sir," the embarrassed Hank replied quietly.

"I'm a cadet at the U.S. Military Academy, and I'm on my way home to enjoy a furlough."

The entire group crowded forward, staring at Hank.

"If you gents will give me a helpin' hand," the man with the walrus mustache said, "we'll go through the train and take up a collection for the boy. I say let's give him somethin' solid in the way of gratitude for gettin' rid of those scum today."

"Thank you, sir," Hank said, politely but firmly, shaking his head, "but I can't accept money or any other gift in return for doing my duty."

"Hellfire, boy," one of the other passengers said, "it wasn't your duty to get rid of a whole band of cut-throats all by yourself."

"Shucks, mister," Hank said, grinning, "I had me a right good time. I don't get the chance to practice my marksmanship on live targets every day of the week!"

Running Bear, the husky young Nez Percé warrior who had led a rebellion of his own nation and the Shoshone against the United States, was well satisfied when he returned to the main town of the Nez Percé in the mountains of central Idaho from a three-day hunting trip. Not only had he and the friends who had gone with him enjoyed the best of good fortune in their early spring hunting, bringing down several deer and an elk, but—even more important—Running Bear had made peace with himself.

Now he slept soundly every night, enjoyed his food, and relished the knowledge that he was young, alive, and in the best of health. Certainly he had made the right decision when he had agreed to the demands of Governor Toby Holt of Idaho that he abandon his rebellion against the United States.

For a time he had been reluctant to accede to Governor Holt's wishes, but he had been given no choice when he had been roundly beaten after challenging the governor to a deadly form of hand-to-hand combat.

Now, with the altercations behind him, he finally realized that he had done the wise and sensible thing. The young braves of the Nez Percé and the Shoshone were no longer in danger of losing their lives to army sharpshooters. The older men, the women, and the children were at peace, too, free to live their lives as they saw fit, and to live in peace with their neighbors, the American settlers.

Yes, life was far happier this way. In fact, Running Bear had found a young woman in whom he was interested, and he could look forward to a life as a husband and father free of complications. It was a good feeling.

His contentment was short-lived, however. A scant forty-eight hours after his return to the main town of the Nez Percé, he received a communication in the mail, which was brought to the nation's reservation once each week by the U.S. Postal Service. To his surprise there was a letter for him that bore a smudged, illegible postmark.

Running Bear could read, for he had been educated in a white man's mission school. As he tore open the envelope, he wondered whom he knew well enough to write him a letter.

What struck him instantly as odd was that the

letter was printed by hand instead of being written in longhand, and it bore no signature. The message was equally curious:

> Greetings to Running Bear, who has proved that he is a true patriot who has the best interests of the Nez Percé and of their brothers, the Shoshone, at heart.
>
> You now have an opportunity to bring even closer the day when you shall be independent and free for all time. A delicate matter like this cannot be explained in great detail in a letter. You will excuse our caution, but we can afford to take no risks, any more than you can afford to take them yourself.
>
> There is no need for you to reply to this letter. Instead, we suggest that you come to the western base of Jersey Mountain due north of the great forks of the Salmon River.
>
> We look forward with great pleasure to doing business with you, and we know that the Nez Percé and the Shoshone will benefit greatly from our association.

Running Bear read the communication several times, but it made no sense to him, and finally, in his frustration, he took it to the leaders and the elders of the Nez Percé community, where he read it aloud, translating as he went along.

The mature braves made no comment, but they knew each other sufficiently well that they only needed to exchange glances in order to know what each other thought. Finally, the Nez Percé chief spoke to Running Bear.

"This is a strange communication," he said. "It may be legitimate, and it may be a trick of some sort being played on us by white men who are unscrupulous. We authorize Running Bear to go to the base of Jersey Mountain near the great forks of the Salmon River and there to meet with the writer of the letter and to learn his business."

Running Bear nodded.

"However," the chief went on, "do not commit yourself to any agreement or to any course of action, either for yourself or on behalf of our nation. Tell those who meet with you that you must refer their offer or their suggestions or whatever they may have in mind to the High Council of the Nez Percé and that the council alone will determine the action to be taken."

"Running Bear understands and will obey," the young warrior said.

The following morning at dawn, Running Bear left the town of the Nez Percé and rode westward across the mountains on the first leg of his journey to the rendezvous. Perhaps he was wasting his time, he thought, but it was always possible, on the other hand, that the Nez Percé might benefit. He was certain only of one thing: By the time his journey came to an end, the strange message would be deciphered, and he would know where he and his people stood in this odd matter.

The opening of a spur that reached north to Boise from the Central Pacific transcontinental railroad line would end the isolation of the Idaho Territory from the rest of the United States. As the time drew closer for the opening of the auxiliary line, the significance of the event was not lost on the ranchers and farmers of Idaho, who could look forward to ordering what they needed for the coming season and have it quickly sent to them, instead of sending for it on a long haul by freight wagon across the mountains.

Jim Randall made a careful estimate of his ranch needs, then rode into Boise to place an order with a San Francisco transfer company. The coming of spring had melted the snow, and the one road to town was transformed into a river of mud, so Pamela Randall refrained from accompanying her husband and instead remained at the ranch to attend to a number of chores there. She spent the better part of an hour doing some mending, a chore that she hated, and then she adjourned to her private sitting room, where she wrote checks to pay some bills and tried to make certain that her account was accurate.

While she wrestled with a column of figures, a dark, tall shape loomed in the open doorway. "Excuse me, ma'am," Randy Savage said, "but if you're busy, I can always come back later."

Startled by the unexpected interruption, Pamela looked up quickly and then brushed from her face a lock of wheat-blond hair that had fallen forward.

"Oh, it's you, Randy," she said, and hoped that her pleasure at seeing him wasn't too obvious.

"Yes, ma'am." The foreman turned his broad-brimmed hat in his hand. "The cook said I'd find you here, but if you're too busy to see me, I can come back later."

"No, don't leave," she replied, showing more haste than dignity. "My arithmetic can always wait. Please, come in."

As Randy entered the little room, he saw that one of the two visitors' chairs was filled with books and papers and that the other was covered with a new dress that was having a panel sewn onto it. There was no place for him to sit.

"Oh, dear." Pamela tried to conceal her flustered feelings. "I think we'd better adjourn to the parlor." When they got there, she told him, "Help yourself to a drink, Randy, and then make yourself comfortable."

"If it's all the same to you, ma'am," he replied, sounding strained, "maybe I'd better light a fire in the hearth. It's a mite chilly in here."

"It's freezing, now that you mention it," she responded, and rubbed her arms vigorously. Then she sat on a divan facing the fireplace and watched him as he placed kindling and logs in it and started a fire.

He knew what he was doing, and soon a crackling fire leaped high. Going to a collection of liquor bottles and glasses standing on a small table in the corner, Randy availed himself of her invitation and poured himself a drink that was typical of what the Westerner who worked with his hands consumed. He poured three fingers of whiskey into a glass, then downed the contents neat, in a single gulp.

"That was good," he muttered politely, "and I thank you." Then he became businesslike. "I've brought you the plans, ma'am, for the last of the improvements in the bunkhouse." He approached the divan and stood before her.

"Please sit down, Randy," she said, patting the cushion beside her in invitation.

He lowered himself to the divan but, embarrassed by their proximity, perched on the edge of his seat.

Loving his naive approach, Pamela waited expectantly. She smiled up at him, her face drawing close to his.

Red-faced and uncomfortable, he reached into his hip pocket and drew out a crumpled wad of paper, which he carefully opened and smoothed. "Here," he said, speaking a trifle too rapidly, "is the floor plan for the bunkhouse. This here," he said, pointing, "is the way we've decided to divide it up, putting my private quarters right here."

She was aware of his hesitation. "Does the plan meet with your approval, Randy?"

He squirmed in his seat. "Now that you mention it, ma'am, the room we built for reading and writing is kind of a joke. No one uses it. If it was my bunkhouse that I was building, I'd eliminate that room and I'd add onto the billiards and card room."

"It is your bunkhouse, Randy," she told him earnestly. "The whole thing belongs exclusively to you and to the boys. I'll have nothing to say about it, and neither will Jim, but I urge you to leave the reading and writing room the way it is. You well may be surprised to see many of the hands eventually using it."

"If you say so, ma'am." He shrugged indifferently, refusing to be drawn into a dispute with her.

"I'm perfectly willing to be proved wrong," Pamela said, "but I believe that when an opportunity is created for someone, that person always responds and takes advantage of it. Don't you think so?"

Randy glanced at her and saw her blond hair framing her face in waves. Her kohl-rimmed eyes looked enormous as they regarded him solemnly and steadily, and her moist, parted lips were an invitation that beckoned to him.

"I reckon you're right, ma'am," he said huskily. "When a fellow don't take advantage of an offer, the offer, like as not, dries up and blows away in the next wind that blows down from the mountains. When you get an offer that looks good to you, you go after it with all you got, and you hold onto it so tight that you shake the daylights out of it!"

"You're a man after my own heart," she told him smugly, and reaching out, patted him on one knee.

Randy reacted as though she had burned him with a red-hot poker. Jerking his leg away from her, he reached down and rubbed his knee as though it had been blistered.

Somehow Pamela managed to restrain the merriment that welled up within her, and she refrained from laughing aloud or even smiling at his exhibition of gaucherie. But it proved impossible for her to hide the laughter that welled up in her eyes.

Randy saw her expression and knew that she was enjoying herself at his expense. His complexion turned a deep, dull red, and his long jaw jutted forward. "Begging your pardon, ma'am," he said, restraining himself with difficulty. "I don't mean any disrespect, but you've got your own way of doing things over in

England, and they aren't even remotely like the way we do things here in America. We're different people!"

Pamela sucked in her breath. "I do beg your pardon, Randy," she said contritely. "I didn't mean to laugh at you, and I certainly wasn't mocking you. As for being different, I'm afraid I can't agree with you. Men and women everywhere are alike. They have the same yearnings, the same joys, and the same sorrows."

"I reckon you're right," he muttered.

She placed a slender hand on his arm and looked up at him, her eyes large and round and infinitely appealing. "Am I forgiven, then?"

By now he was thoroughly confused and couldn't even remember what had caused their dispute in the first place. "Hell, yes, ma'am," he muttered. "I'm not carrying a grudge against you, and I'm not mad at you, no how!"

"I'm so glad," she replied softly, her face still raised to his.

Randy became even more bewildered. All he knew was that they had quarreled and had made up, that he felt a sense of infinite relief, and that he wanted her badly, more than he had ever wanted any woman. They continued to gaze at each other without speech, and as they did, their self-control and sense of propriety slipped away from them.

Pamela knew she was playing with fire, that she was a married woman whose husband loved and trusted her, and that she was willingly on the verge of betraying him.

Randy, too, faced a terrible dilemma. He was conscious of the fact that this lovely, delectable young woman who challenged him was married to his employer and, consequently, should be beyond his reach. On the other hand, the only women with whom he had associated in several years had been the prostitutes who worked at Suzanne's brothel in Boise, and the mere knowledge that this lovely young lady who stood so far above him, socially and financially, was at least toying with the idea of engaging in an affair with him, drove him to distraction.

Casting aside all caution, all fear of the possible complications and consequences, Randy reached for her.

Pamela thrust from her mind the thought that she had sworn to forsake all others when she had married Jim. The realization that she had never really loved Jim Randall was the only excuse she needed now to push her fidelity to one side. Her lips, glistening and inviting, parted slightly as she continued to raise her head to his.

Randy's sense of self-discipline abandoned him, and he put his hands on the woman's soft shoulders, then drew her to him. Pamela moved toward him willingly. Their lips met, and time stopped.

An inner voice, demanding and insistent, told Randy he was getting into waters deeper than he could negotiate. He knew they were treacherous waters, that he could not swim in them, and that he would surely drown. All at once, he straightened, raised his head, and withdrew from her.

Stunned by the abrupt termination of their intimacy, Pamela blinked, then stared at him. The expression in his eyes spoke volumes, and for the first time she regarded her own situation. She knew she was being unbelievably cheap, common beyond measure, and she knew that her self-respect and her lifelong belief in right and wrong had to be obeyed now. She dropped her hands from his neck, moved away from him on the divan, and picking up a tiny, lace-edged handkerchief, she pressed it to her lips.

"I beg your pardon, ma'am," Randy said stiffly, "I had no call to treat you like that!"

Pamela wanted to shout that he was mistaken, that she alone was to blame. By then it was too late, however; he had already risen to his feet, bowed, and stalked out of the parlor.

Tired but exhilarated after his trip across the mountains, Edward Blackstone arrived in Fort Benton, Montana, and checked into the comfortable Senator Benton Inn. Not bothering to rest, he went out to examine his surroundings and found that the town itself, located a few miles below some impassable falls high on the Missouri River, was a typical frontier community that was enjoying a boom period.

Huge warehouses lined the riverfront and were used for storing the furs, lumber, and other cargo to be transported down the Missouri to St. Louis and to towns on the way. Some of the large buildings were filled with food supplies, clothing, and other items that had been carried to Fort Benton on board the river steamers, on which the community depended for its life.

On the river itself, scores of stern-wheeler steamers stood side by side, tied to the docks. They comprised the heart and soul of Fort Benton.

The dock area teemed with activity because the

ships' captains were busy hiring their crews for the more than four-thousand-mile journey to St. Louis and back. Most of the men were roustabouts, who would pull the shallow draft vessels over sandbars and other obstacles encountered in the river. Firewood to provide fuel for the engines of the steamers was arranged in neat, mountainous piles near the riverfront, and the ships' masters dickered with wood sellers as they bought enough cordage to feed their engines' demands for the initial stage of their voyage downriver.

Passengers intending to travel eastward, ranging from those who engaged entire first-class suites to those who barely scraped together the funds to rent sleeping space on an open deck, had come to Fort Benton by the hundreds. They overflowed the town's shops as they purchased firearms, foods, and other delicacies to augment their ship's fare. Even clothing merchants did a lively trade, and Fort Benton's many bordellos and equally numerous saloons remained open twenty-four hours a day, doing steady, heavy business.

The busy spring season had arrived with a vengeance. The town truly had come to life and would remain active until the next winter, when the river would freeze.

Before venturing out into the busy streets of Fort Benton, Edward dressed in a way that he hoped was inconspicuous and strapped on the pair of six-shooter pistols that were regarded as essential in the American West. His hopes of blending into the crowd were in vain, however: His tailor-made English clothes fitted him to perfection and obviously were extremely expensive, as were his superbly crafted boots and his broad-brimmed hat.

Taking his time, Edward wandered down to the river, ignoring the stares and sometimes deliberately provocative comments of passersby. He was surprised to see so many vessels tied up at the docks, and he paused to examine each of them in turn.

The ship that most impressed him was a long, sleek vessel that bore the river's nickname, the *Big Muddy*. As he stood on the dock studying the ship with approval, a half-dozen crew members were working busily nearby, hauling heavy crates of cargo to the ship and then storing them in holds that stretched from forward to aft. The leader of the gang, a slender young man wearing heavy boots, was so busy that he backed into Edward without looking, hitting him with such force that the young Englishman was propelled forward several paces and teetered precariously on the edge of the dock directly above the swirling waters of the Missouri several feet below him. He swayed perilously at the edge of the dock for a moment or two, finally regained his balance, and took a single step toward safety.

"Why don't you watch where in the devil you walk?" he demanded angrily.

"Why don't you keep the hell out of the way?" the foreman responded in a soprano voice that revealed her to be a woman.

Edward stared at the young woman in astonishment. Most of her hair was hidden by an old bandanna, which was tied above the center of her forehead, revealing only a small patch of sandy-blond hair. She was dressed in a man's work shirt and trousers, both several sizes too large for her, and on her feet were a man's heavy boots.

Recovering his mental equilibrium was as difficult as regaining his physical balance had been a few moments earlier. "I was minding my own business when you crashed into me," he said, realizing that his words lacked force. Had he been dealing with a man, he could have pushed the argument until it resulted in a fistfight, but under the circumstances, there was little he could do or say.

"You have no business loitering where you don't belong!" Tommie remained deeply annoyed.

Totally frustrated, Edward terminated the conversation by stalking down the dock toward the gangplank that led to the ship. He had caught a glimpse of a white-haired man wearing a gold-encrusted captain's cap in the glass-enclosed wheelhouse, high on board the vessel, and he was determined to obtain passage. It availed him nothing to continue arguing with the clumsy, bad-tempered woman.

He went on board, noting with approval that the ship was spotless, and climbed the narrow steps that led to the wheelhouse. He introduced himself to the master.

Isaiah Harding had no idea what had brought the Englishman to his ship but, nevertheless, greeted him cordially, as he did virtually everyone.

Edward explained his desire to rent a single, first-class cabin for the entire voyage. Isaiah consulted a booking chart, and the deal was quickly made, with the appreciable sum of three hundred and fifty dollars in cash changing hands.

✳ When Edward learned he had booked passage on a ship of the Harding Line, he told the captain how he had, on Toby Holt's recommendation, written ahead from Boise to make reservations on a Harding ship. "I daresay the letter never arrived," the Englishman said, "since there was no message waiting for me at my hotel, confirming my reservation."

"The mail is extremely slow, Mr. Blackstone," Isaiah Harding said. "I would say you got here before your letter did." Then the captain leaned back in his padded leather chair and inspected the newcomer curiously. "You're a long way from home, Mr. Blackstone," he observed.

"That I am, sir," Edward replied cheerfully.

"Ranch owners and sometimes trappers who are well-off frequently engage first-class accommodations from me," Captain Harding said, "but this is the first time that a foreigner has ever booked passage for a voyage of this length down the river. If you don't mind my asking, Mr. Blackstone, is this a business trip you're making?"

"Not exactly," Edward said. "I've spent the better part of a year in Idaho, and I've had a strong desire to see the whole of the American West close at hand. The closest I can come to it, as far as I can figure, is to take the *Big Muddy* and stay on board until she reaches the end of her run."

"You must like this part of the world," the captain said.

Edward nodded emphatically. "There's no doubt of that, sir," he replied. "There's enough space here for people to breathe, and speaking of people, they're not like those you meet anywhere else."

Captain Harding grinned amiably. "I reckon you're right," he said. "Most folks you meet are honest and decent and straightforward. You know them for what they are the minute you meet them." His smile faded as he thought of Luis de Cordova. "As for the other kind, they make it pretty plain that they're no good from the first time you set eyes on them. Folks out this way don't cover themselves up with much of a veneer of civilization. You know as soon as you meet them whether they're decent and law-abiding or whether they're just plain no good."

As Edward made his way back to his hotel a short time later, Captain Harding's words continued to ring in his ears. The American West was unique, and he was fortunate to be able to know the region and share in it as its destiny unfolded.

When he reached the Senator Benton Inn, he found a long telegram awaiting him from Jim and Pamela Randall. The news that Millicent had sold the restaurant in order to travel to Fort Benton with a man whom she had just met and with whom she imagined herself in love was shocking, and the knowledge that they might appear there at any day startled him. Realizing there were only a small handful of first-class hostelries in Fort Benton, he reflected grimly that if he kept a sharp watch for Millicent and her lover between now and the time he sailed, he would be sure to find her. Then he would get to the bottom of the mystery.

The vast expanses of Idaho were still mostly virgin wilderness. The forests of pine and birch, oak and maple, stretched as high as the timberline, and above it stood the peaks on which the snows never melted. Smaller ranges were covered with forests all the way to their tops.

Travel through such country was difficult, and as Running Bear made his way toward the great fork of the river that lay directly south of Jersey Mountain, he reflected that the people who had set such a rendezvous had certainly chosen a place far from civilization and as inaccessible as possible. The young Nez Percé went on doggedly, eating sparingly from his supply of parched corn, finally halting only after he reached the area in which the meeting with the stranger who had written him the mysterious letter was to take place. He found no one there, and making a modest camp for himself, he settled down to wait.

As noon approached the following day, with no one showing up, Running Bear began to hope that the author of the letter would not keep the engagement. He was sorely disappointed a short time later when Tom Brennan, Luis de Cordova's first assistant, appeared out of the wilderness, riding horseback. The pair stared at each other in a mutually hostile silence for a time and then grudgingly identified themselves. Only then did they relax somewhat.

"I hope you don't mind if I eat something before we have our talk," Brennan said as he dismounted. "I can't think good on an empty stomach, and I haven't touched a bite of hot food since I started out to this place."

An eloquent shrug indicated Running Bear's indifference to the other's activity.

Brennan built himself a far larger cooking fire than

he needed, a mistake commonly made by neophytes in the wilderness, and then, taking two potatoes from his saddlebag he threw them onto the coals. Eventually he fished a frying pan out of the bag and then cooked some beans and bacon, which he proceeded to share with the Nez Percé, together with the potatoes.

Running Bear was anything but hungry but never refused the offer of food and ate everything that was given to him. When they were finished eating, Brennan took a long swallow of whiskey from a bottle and then handed his new Winchester repeating rifle to the Indian. "Take a good look at this," he said, "and tell me what you think of it."

Taking his time, Running Bear carefully examined the weapon. It was obvious that he was impressed. "This appears to be a fine gun," he said at last. "Running Bear has never seen another like it."

"I have access to many that are just like it," Brennan said carelessly, "and they fire more than once without reloading."

"Is it effective?" Running Bear asked.

It was the white man's turn to feign indifference. "It's loaded," he said. "Try it for yourself."

Running Bear selected a target at random, a small branch of an oak about forty yards away. He fired two shots in rapid succession at it, scoring a hit with the second that caused the branch to break partway through and to dangle in the air. "This is a marvelous gun," he said sincerely.

"As you can see," Brennan said, "you can fire many times without reloading. Try it again."

This time the two shots succeeded in breaking off

the branch and sending it plummeting to the ground below. "Never has Running Bear seen such a weapon," the Nez Percé said in wonder.

"Keep it with our compliments," Brennan told him, and rummaging in his saddlebag, he produced a whole box of cartridges, which he proceeded to hand to the young Indian. "Show this to your followers and let them try it, too. It's a remarkable gun, and it's going to change the very nature of warfare. With enough rifles like this in your possession, the Nez Percé easily can win the freedom you crave from the United States."

Running Bear peered hard at him but made no comment. Apparently the white man believed that the young warriors of the Nez Percé and the Shoshone were still in rebellion against the United States government and that Running Bear was their leader.

"Imagine," Brennan persisted, "what you could do with twenty-five of these guns, with fifty, or even one hundred."

Running Bear's imagination was strained to the breaking point, and he shook his head.

"My employer is in a position to make these remarkable new rifles available to the warriors of the Nez Percé and the Shoshone," Brennan went on. "The usual price for them is one thousand dollars per rifle."

The fee was so enormous that Running Bear laughed aloud.

"However," Brennan went on, "since you'd be buying them in bulk, and more importantly, since my employer sympathizes with the cause for which the Nez Percé and the Shoshone are fighting, he's willing to let you have the weapons at a measly two hundred and fifty dollars per rifle."

Remembering the instructions he had received from the Nez Percé council, Running Bear knew it would be necessary for him to temporize. "Two hundred and fifty dollars," he said, "may be a very small amount of money to you, but to the people of my nation it is a fortune and—multiplied by a minimum of one hundred, in order to obtain enough of the rifles to make them effective in combat—would be a far larger sum than we could pay."

"I reckon I didn't make myself clear," Brennan said hastily. "We realize only too well that the Nez Percé don't have thousands of U.S. dollars at their disposal, so my employer is perfectly willing to wait for his money. If you'd like, we'll turn the rifles over to you at once—as many of them as you wish—and during the time you are winning your tribe's freedom, you can repay us with the gold and silver you take from the white man as you drive him out. If you don't get cash, we'll be glad to settle for real estate, livestock, furs— whatever you take in booty as you set yourselves free."

The payment that the gun merchant would demand would be worth many times the cost of the weapons, Running Bear knew, and he was stunned by the audacity of the offer. He was tempted to terminate the negotiations instantly but again recognized the need to keep them alive for a time, in the hope that he could learn more about the men making the offer.

"Running Bear will report your offer to his nation's council," he said, "and then he will have an answer to give to you."

Brennan demonstrated the customary impatience that white men showed with the dilatory tactics of Indians. "How soon will you have an answer for me?" he said. "This offer won't be kept open indefinitely."

Running Bear remained calm. "A new moon will appear in the sky overhead tonight," he said. "When the next new moon comes, Running Bear will have the word of the Nez Percé for you."

"You will be in a position then to confirm a deal in a month?" Brennan demanded eagerly.

"That is so," Running Bear said, "provided that the council of my nation gives its approval." He knew, however, that under no circumstances would the leaders of the Nez Percé nation approve such a shady deal, which would be disadvantageous to the tribe under the best of circumstances and would demonstrate grave disloyalty to the United States. In fact, the young brave decided, perhaps the best thing he could do, even before meeting again with his elders, would be to see his friend Toby Holt in Oregon and get his opinion of the matter.

"Where shall we meet to settle this matter?" Brennan asked.

"Running Bear will meet with you here, at this same place in the wilderness, when the next new moon appears in the sky overhead."

IV

Luis de Cordova owned warehouses and buildings in many cities and towns in the West, so it was only natural that he should own a small warehouse and dwelling in Fort Benton, Montana, a thriving trading center. His house there was nominally owned by Ben Gibson, the head of his freighting concern, operating along the Missouri River.

Living with Gibson was a brown-haired woman known only as Clara, who was the star inmate of one of the local bordellos. Strictly speaking, she was not in de Cordova's employ, but she frequently performed errands for him and was exceedingly well paid for the work she did.

"You need a rest," Luis said to Millicent Randall as soon as they arrived at the house, which he would use during their stay over in Fort Benton. "The long trip from Boise no doubt has tired you. Clara," he added to the young woman who was hovering in the hallway, "see to it that she has plenty of hot water for her bath, will you, and then bed her down in my room. After she goes off to sleep, I want a word with you."

"You bet, Luis." The trollop promptly disappeared.

Luis kissed Millicent, the expression of sheer adoration in her eyes assuring him that his hold over her was as strong as ever. Then she turned and obediently followed Clara toward the rear of the house.

Luis smiled in self-satisfaction and followed Gibson into the parlor, where the latter poured them shots of gin to be washed down with steins of beer.

"Who's the honey lamb?" Gibson demanded.

Luis's smile remained unwavering. "She's a very special young lady, Ben," he said. "I've already invested a lot of money in her, I'm about to blow a couple of thousand more on her, but for every penny I spend, I'm going to be getting many more dollars back in return, never you fear."

Gibson sipped his gin, then took a long swallow of beer. "Are you going to put her to work in the same joint where Clara hangs out?"

Luis shook his head emphatically. "Under no circumstances," he said flatly, "will she work in a brothel. She's far too valuable for that, and she's going to earn me ten times as much as she could make in a bordello."

Gibson whistled soundlessly. "Doing what?"

Luis chuckled. "Never you mind," he said. "Now then, what have you got ready on Harding's company?"

"The system we've been using has been enormously

successful," Gibson said, "so I see no reason to change it. I've already had various documents drawn up for delivery to Harding, and you'll present one of them to him as soon as you're safely on the water, en route to St. Louis. It's a demand for payment of over fifty thousand dollars; I've arrived at the sum by charging him the usual exorbitant rates of interest. No matter how much he may earn on the voyage, there's no way he could accumulate the sum of fifty thousand, so we'll have our attorneys waiting when the boat reaches St. Louis. You can take possession of it there."

"Good," Luis said, sniffing his gin but not drinking it.

"That move," Gibson went on, "should break his back. His fleet will then be reduced to only three major ships, and they'll be unable to provide sufficient revenues to pay the balance of his debt. We can then pick up the remaining ships from him for pennies. He'll be lucky to get out of this with his skin in one piece."

"It sounds pretty good to me," Luis said. "Do you have the documents?"

"Yes, sir, they're right here." Gibson went to a desk and took several papers out of a drawer, which he handed to his employer.

Luis studied the documents one by one, smiling and nodding his approval as he perused each of them. As he was going over the documents with Gibson, Clara came into the room. "How would you like to pick up a couple hundred dollars in return for an hour's easy work?" Luis asked her.

"That's for me," she told him.

"Good." His voice became crisp. "Go to your bordello right now and get a cosmetics kit for Millicent. I want everything for her, lip rouge, the stuff you use on eyes, cheek rouge—everything. Then I want you to go to several of the tall, slender girls—yourself included— and pick up an entire wardrobe for her, the kind of things you girls wear when you call attention to yourselves. When you're on parade, so to speak, through the town."

"I get you," she replied.

"These outfits needn't be new," he directed, "but I insist that every one of them has to stand out. Make good and sure that they're daring, and bring me a complete wardrobe. How much do you suppose you'll need to buy them from the girls?"

Clara pondered quickly. "I'd say a thousand ought to be enough," she told him.

Luis de Cordova reached into a pocket and began to peel bills from a wad of money. "Don't stint," he said. "Here's two thousand, and whatever you don't spend you can keep."

She was almost overcome by his unexpected generosity. "This is great, Luis!"

"Nothing is too good for Millicent," he said. "When you come back here, wake her up and dress her in one of the outfits. Then teach her how to use the cosmetics, and you don't have to use too light a hand."

She left immediately, and Luis settled back to work with Ben Gibson. They were still conferring, with documents relating to the Harding ships spread out before them, when Clara returned. She knew what had to be done, and Luis waved her toward the upstairs portion of the house. She disappeared up the stairs, hauling two carpetbags filled with clothes. Three quarters of an hour passed before Clara reappeared in the doorway. "Here she is!" she said triumphantly.

Millicent Randall stood framed in the archway entrance to the living room, her expression registering both fear and self-loathing. The change in her appearance was little short of astonishing.

Her luxurious, dark brown hair surrounded her face and fell well below her shoulders in loose waves. Her eyes, her most arresting feature, were emphasized by a heavy rim of kohl, and there was a shiny lavender salve painted on her eyelids. Her high cheekbones were emphasized with rouge, and her lips were a provocative scarlet color. Also helping to make her appearance striking was a black velvet beauty patch affixed to one cheek.

Her attire did wonders in bringing out the assets of her figure. Her feet were encased in slippers with such high heels that she teetered precariously when she walked, causing her gently rounded hips to sway seductively. Her ankle-length skirt was slit high on both sides, revealing her shapely calves and a portion of her slender thighs. Her tiny waist and flat stomach were emphasized by a broad belt. The silk blouse she wore appeared to be a size too small for her. The open-throated neckline showed off her deep cleavage, and her nipples were clearly outlined through the fabric, indicating that she wore nothing underneath.

"Millicent," Luis said heartily, "you look great, just great! Doesn't she, Ben?"

Gibson swallowed hard as he stared at the woman. "You bet she does," he murmured.

Millicent refused to be comforted, her expression revealing her misery. Luis crooked a forefinger and beckoned. Millicent responded reluctantly, timidly, approaching him very slowly. It was obvious the realization had not occurred to her that she epitomized feminine sexuality.

Luis reached up and pulled her roughly onto his lap, so roughly that she almost fell, but he caught her in both arms. Then, unmindful of the presence of his two associates, he began to caress and kiss her.

For no more than an instant, Millicent resisted him. Then there was an amazing change in her attitude. She clung to him, squirming ecstatically as her passion mounted, and she seemed to melt in his arms. Gibson and Clara gaped at the unusual scene.

Luis, not wanting her to become overly aroused, rose and stood her on her feet. "You and I," he told her, "are going out on the town now."

An expression of doubt appeared in Millicent's eyes for a moment, but Luis's touch, as he put an arm around her, totally melted her and made her amenable to his slightest wish. She had no mind of her own. She was willing and even anxious to do whatever he wanted.

"Make sure she has plenty of cosmetics in her reticule," he said to Clara.

The woman nodded. "She not only has them there, but she knows how to use them now."

"Good." Luis picked up the bag by its long strap and draped it over one of Millicent's shoulders. "Come along."

Without further ado, and not bothering to offer any explanation, Luis de Cordova led Millicent outside and then tucked her hand through his looped arm.

There was a chill in the air, now that the sun had lost its intensity late in the day, and Millicent was inadequately clad, having neither a coat nor a cloak to protect her. Consequently, her nipples hardened, and Luis noted with great satisfaction that they showed even more boldly through the fabric of her blouse. That was all to the good, he told himself, and made her appear all the more desirable.

As they left the quiet residential street on which Luis's house was located, they drew nearer to the center of town, and the dirt road became increasingly clogged with pedestrians. Millicent, her gait mincing in her high-heeled shoes, felt a wave of deep discomfort and gripped Luis's arm more tightly as she realized that she'd become the center of attention. They passed man after man, and these total strangers stared at her, taking in every detail of her appearance.

The lust in their eyes was plain to see, and it was easy enough to read their minds from the way they clenched their jaws and moistened their dry lips. A sense of shame suffused Millicent, and she gripped Luis's arm all the harder.

The crowds became still thicker, and little by little she became more accustomed to the stares of the men. Gradually, a strange transformation came over her. The realization dawned on her that for the first time in her life that she, Millicent Randall, was attractive and desirable to men. To *all* men.

Her embarrassment began to dissipate, and she started to enjoy the unique experience. Men of every class, ranging from gentlemen in black suits and high hats to grubby roustabouts in work clothes, demonstrated, clearly and emphatically, that they wanted her.

Her confidence began to grow, and eventually she was somewhat startled to discover that she was enjoying the stir that she caused. Gaining self-esteem, she became less taut and began to experiment. She rolled her hips from side to side with increasing abandon as she walked, and in time, she was boldly returning the stares of the men.

Luis de Cordova became aware of the change in her attitude and rejoiced silently. She was making his task far easier and was fitting in perfectly with the plans that he had made for her.

At last the couple came to their destination, a huge establishment that was a combination restaurant-saloon-gambling hall. By this time Millicent was positively strutting. Every pair of eyes in the place was riveted on her as the couple made their way to a table.

Luis ordered predinner drinks of sack and then said to her, "You'd better go to the powder room and freshen your makeup."

She went off obediently.

Their drinks arrived at the table during her absence, and Luis took his time as he removed the small bottle of Hungarian Gypsy potion from his pocket, shook a few drops of the substance into her drink with the stopper, and then put the container away again. He well remembered Suzanne's injunction that the potion, whatever it contained, had a longer effect on the human system if used repeatedly, that it would eventually effect a long-lasting personality change.

But that was not Luis de Cordova's concern. He

was eager to see Millicent play the role that he had in mind for her, and he was totally unconcerned about any lasting effects that the potion might have on her. He intended to use her as the central figure in a scheme that would earn him nearly as much as he was making from his other enterprises, and as long as she fulfilled that function, he was in no way worried about what might become of her after she had served his purposes.

Every man in the establishment gaped at Millicent as she returned to their table. Her smile was radiant as she sat down.

"Here's to your success," Luis told her, and lifted his glass in a toast to her.

"If I've changed," she replied, "and even I can see plainly that I have, it's all due to you." She lifted her own glass to him. "I'm eternally grateful to you, Luis."

He would remind her of that statement if it should prove necessary, but for the present, he was content to keep silent.

She raised her glass to her lips, drank, and then placed it on the table. Her reaction was precisely what it had been on each of the previous occasions when she had swallowed a dose of the potion. Her eyes became momentarily glazed, she stiffened, clenching her fists, and she experienced difficulty in breathing. Then she shuddered slightly and shook herself, as though awakening from a deep sleep.

Her smile was ravishing as she looked at Luis, and he knew that she was ready for the next act in the drama that he was preparing for her.

They took their time eating a leisurely dinner, with Luis deliberately giving the other patrons ample opportunity to watch and study his companion. From time to time he caressed her thigh beneath the table, and she responded at once, looking at him adoringly and leaning toward him in order to touch him. The patrons who watched her actions concluded that she was an exceptionally passionate young woman, as well as an extraordinary beauty.

When the couple finally finished their meal, they rose, and Millicent took Luis's arm as they wandered through the establishment, going past the bar into the quarters where extensive gambling was taking place. Many men in Fort Benton had become rich overnight in shipping, fur trading, and the like, and they seemed eager for the opportunity to squander their money. There were tables for roulette, dice were being thrown, and several poker games were in progress.

When they paused occasionally to watch one game or another, Luis slid an arm around Millicent and stroked her shoulder. She unfailingly responded to him, as the men who comprised her growing audience were quick to note.

Finally Luis was ready to spring his trap. "Gentlemen," he said to a group of two dozen or more men who were clustered nearby, "you appear to have great admiration for my lady, and I can't say that I blame you. You show excellent taste."

Millicent's cheeks burned at his unexpected public compliment.

"It's no secret to me—nor is it to her—that each and every one of you is imagining himself making love to her. How would you like to spend an entire night with her? It's within your reach, and I'll make each of you a sporting offer."

The crowd stirred, and Millicent became rigid in his grasp.

Luis pulled her closer, and as he gently caressed her, he whispered in her ear, "Don't worry, my dear, I won't let you down, now or ever."

Simultaneously soothed and aroused by his touch, Millicent relaxed somewhat.

"I'll play each and every one of you a game of high-low," he said. "We'll draw cards. If you draw the higher card, you can spend a night with the lady. If I draw a higher card, you owe me five hundred dollars. That's fair, isn't it? You're betting a measly five hundred against the possibility of spending an entire night with this delectable lady." He placed an arm firmly about Millicent's waist and drew her closer as his gaze swept back and forth across the crowd, challenging them to meet his terms.

Millicent regained her equilibrium. Not only had Luis reassured her in words that no harm would come to her, but his arm encircling her waist offered her further assurance. She had no idea what he had in mind but knew that she had nothing to fear, and she reacted accordingly, enjoying her role as the center of attention. She planted her feet apart, squared her shoulders, and stood with her chin and breasts outthrust. Her gaze traveled slowly around the semicircle of faces, and she found herself inadvertently flirting with one man or another. These gestures were instinctive rather than deliberate, and she soon found that she was enjoying herself thoroughly. In every instance, the man reddened, blinked, or straightened, and she knew that she was exerting a power over them that she never before realized she possessed.

Luis chuckled encouragingly and stroked the nape of her neck, a gesture that caused her to breathe more rapidly and to part her lips suggestively.

This was too much for her audience, and at last one of the men stepped forward. Pulling out a large stack of bills from his pocket, he counted out five hundred dollars. Then he and Luis de Cordova seated themselves at a vacant table.

Luis reached into an inner pocket and drew out what appeared to be a new pack of playing cards. He broke the seal on the package, removed the cards, and shuffled them a number of times, swiftly and expertly. Then he offered the deck to Millicent to cut.

Still standing, she clumsily did as she was bidden, never before having handled playing cards.

Luis gestured, and his opponent drew first. It was very quiet in the room as he turned up the seven of diamonds.

A hush of tense expectancy settled over the crowd, and Luis drew a card, and then there was a long, drawn-out sigh as he turned up the eight of hearts. He was the winner.

Millicent's brilliant smile of relief goaded several other spectators and impelled them also to take part in high-low games. But Luis appeared to lead a charmed life. When an opponent drew a ten of clubs, he pulled the jack of clubs. When an opponent turned up a queen of diamonds, he had the king of spades. He appeared incapable of losing, and each time he faced an opponent, he grew richer by five hundred dollars.

As Millicent's confidence in his talents grew, her manner became increasingly bold. She continued to flirt with the men, smiling encouragement at them, and eventually she lost count of the amount of money that Luis was winning.

Watching him as he manipulated the deck of cards with practiced ease, she wondered if his victories could be entirely accidental. He had assured her that she had nothing to lose in these supposed games of chance, and his prediction was absolutely accurate. How could he know for certain that he was going to win every hand against all opponents?

She began to wonder if he was cheating. Luis saw her quizzical look and instantly sensed her changed mood. "That's all for tonight, gentlemen," he called, and placed the deck of cards into his pocket. "Sorry to disappoint you, but the lady is still mine."

Smiling blandly at the disappointed men, he put an arm around Millicent's shoulders, then rapidly left the hall with her, not pausing until they had walked several blocks away from the gambling establishment.

She found it difficult to believe that he had used her as bait while he cheated at cards in order to win many thousands of dollars. She tried to frame a question in a way that he would not find insulting, but her mind refused to function.

The real truth of the matter was that she didn't want to know whether or not he had been cheating. The knowledge that she had been a party to his crime would devastate her.

His pockets bulging with the cash he had won, Luis kept one hand on the hilt of his six-shooter as he walked home with Millicent. His other arm curled around her, and he could sense her withdrawal. Her display of

106

coolness did not worry him in the least, however; he knew precisely how to handle her. "Your behavior tonight with those yokels was absolutely perfect," he told her, his hand roaming freely as he patted and stroked her. "You had them eating out of the palm of your hand."

Her brain ceased to function, and the only thing she knew was that she wanted him.

Luis decided that after they reached his house, he would "reward" her by making love to her. That would soften her and guarantee that she would act in the same way the next time he decided to avail himself of her very special services.

Luis's contentment was complete as they continued to walk toward his house. Of all his money-making ventures, Millicent Randall was proving to be by far the most enjoyable. She was expensive, to be sure, but she was well worth the money and time that he was forced to lavish on her. She had earned him a small fortune in a few short hours that night, and his journey on the Missouri still loomed ahead. By the time the voyage drew to an end, he anticipated he would be many times richer than he had ever dreamed possible.

An hour before the *Big Muddy* was scheduled to sail, the passengers began to line the decks. There were several ladies on board, all of them apparently traveling in first class, while the male passengers represented every economic spectrum. The well-to-do had private suites or individual cabins, while the poor were forced to share the open deck space below with the roustabouts.

On sailing day, however, all passengers were equal.

Though no one dared to express it aloud, everyone shared the hope that the vessel would reach her destination safely in approximately two months. Superstitions about travel on the Missouri dictated that hopes and fears remain unmentioned.

So many things could go wrong. There were unseen obstacles in the river, such as sandbars and tree roots, which could smash through the hull of a ship. And there was the ever-present danger that the boiler might explode. Hostile Indians might be encountered, and it was always possible that gangs of robbers and other outlaws would attack the unwary. Every year several stern-wheelers cracked up in midjourney and, for one reason or another, had to be abandoned. It was not uncommon for passengers to go ashore, make their way to the nearest U.S. Army post, and wait there for troops traveling eastward to act as their escorts.

Edward Blackstone had secured a place on deck amidships for himself and watched the presailing activities in fascination. He saw the last crates of cargo being hauled on board under Tommie Harding's supervision, and he watched as large packages of smoked meat were placed on the deck for distribution to various army posts along the way. Firewood was piled on deck to meet the insatiable demands of the ship's boiler, and someone standing near Edward commented to the effect that most of this wood would be held in reserve against the day when the *Big Muddy* passed through regions where trees were sparse. For the present, there would be woods on both sides of the river, and firewood would not be a problem to obtain.

Promptly at noon, the lines that held the *Big*

Muddy tied to the dock were removed, and as the vessel began to inch out into the rapidly flowing waters of the Missouri River, Tommie Harding leaped effortlessly on board and immediately made her way up the stairs to her father's wheelhouse.

A long, low ship's whistle sounded, soon to become familiar to everyone on board. The master and his crew were bidding farewell to Fort Benton, which they did not anticipate seeing again until midsummer.

In spite of Edward's sense of excitement over the beginning of the voyage, he felt restless and disturbed. He had been unsuccessful in his attempt to locate his cousin Millicent; she had not been registered at any of the hotels or inns in Fort Benton. He searched the deck for her but could not see her among the passengers. He caught sight of the rear of a spectacularly dressed brunette, but he immediately dismissed her from his mind. She was deeply engaged in conversation with a slender, dark-haired man and seemed oblivious to the fact that the ship was now in motion.

The woman's lightweight silk dress clung to her in the breeze, clearly outlining her body. When her thick brown hair was ruffled by the breeze, Edward caught a quick glimpse of her heavily made-up face. Paying no further attention to the woman, he continued to search for Millicent, but in vain.

Two elderly gentlemen and an old lady were standing directly to Edward's left at the rail, and he vaguely noted their presence. They obviously were old hands at river travel and were so engrossed in their conversation that they were oblivious to others on board.

Edward's attention now was drawn to a shabbily

dressed man of middle years who was standing between
him and the elderly trio on the deck. The man was
insignificant-looking, but what made him stand out was
a small monkey perched on his right shoulder. The
little animal had a typical monkey's face, looking like an
old man one moment and like a wise baby the next. His
attire was striking. He wore a doublet and breeches of
brilliant green, a pair of tiny boots, and a cap that
sported a long, curling feather. It was obvious that his
costume imitated the illustrations of Robin Hood found
in an extremely popular children's book of the era.

While Edward watched, the little man, unaware
that he was under surveillance, nodded his head almost
imperceptibly to the monkey.

The animal lowered himself to the man's middle,
where he wrapped his tail around his owner's arm in
order to obtain balance. Then, showing the greatest of
delicacy, the monkey picked the hip pocket of one of
the elderly gentlemen, removing a wallet so smoothly
and deftly that the victim had no idea he was being
robbed. The little man promptly took the wallet and
dropped it into his own pocket, while the monkey
hopped up onto his shoulder and resumed his perch
there. The entire incident had taken place within
seconds.

Normally no one would have been aware of the
theft, but Edward Blackstone had witnessed the entire
incident. Acting without thinking, Edward tapped the
man on the shoulder, and they moved together toward
the bulkhead, out of hearing of the other passengers.
"Your small friend is exceedingly clever," Edward began.

The man managed a sickly laugh. "Yeah," he replied in an American accent that was unfamiliar to Edward, "Robin here is a real card, he is. Always jokin' and doin' things to make folks laugh."

Edward remained unsmiling. "I'm afraid I don't share your sense of humor—or his," he said severely, "and I suspect that the gentleman who was robbed of his wallet will feel even more strongly about the matter. I hate to interfere in a matter that is none of my business, strictly speaking, but I've witnessed an illegal act and must respond accordingly. I'm afraid that if you don't return the gentleman's property to him intact, I shall be obliged to report this incident in full to the captain, and you'll have to take the consequences."

"Give me a break, mister," the shabby-looking man said, tears appearing in his eyes. "You don't know what a tough time I've had. I came out here from Brooklyn, New York, lookin' for gold, and all I've found is misery. Six months ago I won Robin here in a stud poker game, and that's the last good thing that's ever happened to me. I had just enough money to pay for my passage, and now I'm dead broke, and I ain't got a penny to my name. I haven't eaten a decent meal in longer than I can remember, and neither has Robin. Don't turn me in! Please!"

In spite of Edward's high standards, he couldn't help feeling sorry for the man. Reaching into an inner coat pocket, he withdrew a billfold and took a crisp five-dollar note from it. "Here," he said brusquely, "this should get you a couple of good meals on ship. When you run out, come to me for more."

"God bless you, sir!" the little man babbled. "Robin, shake hands with the gentleman and thank him properly for the fine supper you're going to eat tonight!"

The monkey solemnly extended his right hand.

Feeling slightly foolish, Edward shook hands with him. "Now," he said sternly, "be good enough to return the wallet."

"You bet, sir! Right now, sir." The man moved to a place on the deck close behind the gentleman he had robbed, then silently handed the wallet to the monkey, who climbed nimbly down to his waist and then, displaying infinite deftness, replaced the wallet. Edward turned away, pleased that he had done a very good deed.

All through the rest of the first afternoon on board the *Big Muddy*, Edward Blackstone was intrigued by Tommie Harding's activities. He watched her as she supervised the setting of the sail, unlimbered the brass cannon on the foredeck, and had several iron balls used as ammunition brought forward for it. She threw a plumb line over the prow regularly, to test the depth of the river's water, and frequently she reported on the results of her various activities to Captain Harding, on the bridge.

Edward realized that in spite of her man's attire, she was a very feminine young woman, and as he watched her, he admired her grace and her skills.

His cabin proved to be small but snug, more than adequate for his needs. In it were a small table, two chairs, and a bunk long enough to accommodate his frame. His quarters also boasted a closet more than large enough to hold the clothes he had brought with him for his voyage.

The *Big Muddy* made excellent time that afternoon,

and when evening approached and shadows lengthened across the towering, snow-covered peaks of Montana in the background, Captain Harding dropped anchor for the night in a small cove. He was establishing a routine that he hoped to follow until the end of the voyage. The bed of the Missouri River underwent drastic changes from season to season, and hidden obstacles could sink or permanently cripple a ship if it sailed onto them. Thus travel after dark was far too dangerous, and captains always tied up for overnight stays. They were subjecting themselves to the increased likelihood of attacks by Indians, bandits, and others who sought to interrupt a ship's journey, but it was far better to set a schedule for men who would keep watch through the night than it was to try to sail down the river after dark.

In his cabin Edward donned a dark silk cravat and a coat of black velvet before proceeding to dinner in the ship's great cabin, or saloon. He found it curious that he was thinking of Tommie Harding and was eager to see her again. He wondered if she would show up in her usual man's garb for dinner.

The great cabin was located on the main deck below the first-class quarters, and as Edward made his way to the staircase that would take him to the saloon, he came face to face with the exceptionally handsome young woman he had seen earlier that day on deck. She was wearing a daring black dress studded with bugle beads, and she was heavily made up.

He glanced at her, started to step aside so that she and her companion could precede him down the stairs, and then suddenly halted. "Millicent?" he asked uncertainly.

Millicent was better prepared for the confrontation

than was Edward. With one hand resting lightly on the arm of the scowling Luis de Cordova, she said lightly, "Why, hello, Edward. Mr. de Cordova, may I present Mr. Blackstone? Mr. de Cordova is my fiancé, Edward."

The two exchanged brief nods, each making it plain that he had little use for the other.

Edward recovered his equilibrium sufficiently to ask politely, "Do I assume correctly that you're making the journey to St. Louis, Millicent?"

"Indeed," she replied, adding with a slight emphasis, "Luis and I are making the voyage together."

Edward held his ground. "If you don't mind, I'd like a word with you at your convenience regarding your travel arrangements."

Luis neither knew nor cared about the Englishman's identity. He had jumped to the conclusion that, strange as it seemed, the handsome, self-contained young Englishman had once been a suitor of the shy Millicent, which could account for his shock at seeing her in her present dress and makeup. Regardless of his identity, it was time to intervene.

"Allow me to remind you, Mr. Blackstone," he said harshly, "that Millicent is of age. As a woman who is free, white, and has passed her twenty-first birthday, she is in charge of her own destiny, and it is her privilege to make whatever travel arrangements she wishes, without outside interference. From anyone," he added emphatically.

Millicent moved closer to him, her eyes enormous as she gazed up at him. Then, as she turned to face Edward, a defiant look appeared on her face. "My fiancé," she said, "has put the matter far more succinctly than I am capable of doing, but he has spoken the truth. I am free to do as I wish, and what I wish is to travel with Luis!"

The shocked Edward wondered if she was intoxicated or under the spell of a drug of some sort. She appeared to be in complete command of her faculties, however, and he had to content himself with the obvious, that she was deeply infatuated with the man and very much under his spell.

Edward became even more distressed when Luis added, "What we're both telling you, Mr. Blackstone, is to mind your own business. I trust you'll heed the advice."

Too shocked to reply politely, Edward stood aside and let them pass before following them at a distance to the ship's saloon.

The great cabin was furnished elegantly. Candles flickered in wall brackets and in two crystal chandeliers, and the long table, which was set for twenty-four persons, was covered with a sparkling white cloth. The dishes were made of real silver.

Places were assigned to the first-class passengers for the entire voyage, and Edward was relieved to discover that his seat was at the opposite end of the table from those of Millicent and her companion. He knew it would be virtually impossible to remain civil if he were forced to have much contact with the man whom his cousin had identified as her fiancé. He was able to put Millicent out of his mind temporarily when he discovered, to his delight, that he was seated to the right of Tommie Harding, who had the place at the head of the table.

The change in her was startling. Tommie had removed her bandanna, and her sandy-blond hair formed a halo around her face as it descended to her shoulders. Her intense eyes, which looked blue one moment and green the next, sparkled in the candlelight. Her mouth, which she had rouged very lightly, was soft and appealing, and her forehead, nose, and chin had a distinctly patrician look. She wore a simple, beige-colored gown that did far more justice to her lithe figure than did the man's attire in which she customarily appeared. She greeted Edward politely but coolly, no doubt remembering their earlier run-in.

Wine had already been poured in the goblets located at each place, and before the assembled company sat, Tommie Harding rose and offered a toast. "God save the President of the United States and preserve this company, keeping it from harm."

Everyone drank, and Edward politely held Tommie's chair for her when she sat. She thanked him without looking at him.

"Ladies and gentlemen," Tommie said, "Captain Harding craves your indulgence and expresses the hope that he can join you for supper tomorrow evening. As this is the first night of our voyage, he wants to make certain that the ship's guards and other personnel attend to their appointed duties."

As soon as Edward tasted the fish and vegetable chowder, which was ladled out of a huge tureen, he knew for sure the voyage would be as grand as he had hoped. The food was delicious. Obviously the *Big Muddy*'s principal cook knew his business.

To the Englishman's surprise and pleasure, Tommie Harding proved to be a pleasant and an exceptionally well-informed dinner companion. Speaking to all the passengers seated at her end of the table, she told them in detail about the history, past and present, of the Montana Territory, especially the region through which they were currently passing, the Missouri River basin.

"You'll find," she said, "that for some days to come the conditions of the journey will be as pleasant as any you will find on the entire trip. The falls that are located north and west of Fort Benton give the Missouri a considerable impetus in this area, and the water here is usually fairly deep—sixteen to eighteen feet—which means that we can sail without fear of hitting sandbars, fallen trees, and other obstacles. The water is clean here and is quite safe for drinking and washing."

"Do we maintain good relations with the Indian tribes that we find on this stretch of the river?" an elderly lady asked.

"Indeed, yes," a smiling Tommie told her. "We anticipate no troubles with Indians until we reach the country dominated by the Sioux, who remain a very belligerent nation anxious to oust the United States from what it regards as its territory."

Tommie vanished quietly at the conclusion of the meal. Edward, however, remained at the table for a time, drinking coffee with the other passengers. Occasionally he caught glimpses of Millicent and Luis de Cordova at the opposite end of the table, and that sight filled him with such misgivings that he finally decided to go to Captain Harding with his suspicions. Finishing his coffee, he left the saloon and climbed to the wheelhouse, where he found Isaiah Harding eating a meal from a tray that Tommie had just brought him. She was seated nearby.

"Come in, Mr. Blackstone," the captain called.

Edward was apologetic. "I don't want to disturb you when you're eating, Captain Harding," he said. "I'll come back later."

"Nonsense!" Harding replied heartily. "Come in, sit down, and let's hear what's on your mind."

Tommie's gaze seemed to be fixed on a point somewhere above Edward's head, and she appeared to be taking no notice of him.

"I'm very much disturbed about a cousin of mine who is currently traveling on board the *Big Muddy*," Edward said as he sat down opposite the captain. "Not only is her appearance completely altered, but she's traveling with a man, which in her case is totally unthinkable."

Tommie's interest had been captured. "Is the brunette with the flamboyant style of dress and the rather—ah—exuberant makeup your cousin?"

"She is," Edward replied grimly.

"The lady in question," she said to her father, "is traveling with Luis de Cordova."

Captain Harding sighed but made no comment as he continued to eat his dinner.

"You wouldn't know it from her appearance," Edward said, "but Millicent Randall is a lady. She is wealthy in her own right, born and bred in Baltimore, and happens to be an accomplished flutist and a well-regarded composer of music for the flute. A mutual relative sent me a telegram at Fort Benton before we sailed warning me that she was being accompanied by some man, but I didn't see her until after we'd set sail, and I must say she and de Cordova gave me an exceedingly rude reception. That isn't at all like Millicent!"

"When Luis de Cordova becomes involved with someone," Captain Harding said, "you can be sure that no good will come of the association."

"What can you tell me about him?" Edward asked.

"Not much," Isaiah Harding replied. "He's a man of considerable means and has his finger in many pies. He's hooked me, and I still don't know quite how he's done it."

"What happened?"

"A couple of years ago I needed ten thousand dollars in cash to put together enough money to buy a riverboat, a much smaller vessel than the *Big Muddy*. I borrowed the money from de Cordova. Since that time, I've repaid the ten thousand, plus a considerable sum in interest, but he keeps insisting that I owe him a very large amount of money, well over fifty thousand dollars, and he demands to be paid, or he's threatening to take possession of the *Big Muddy*."

Edward frowned. "The only way a debt of ten thousand dollars could be compounded into a sum more than five times that much would be for de Cordova to have been charging you usurer's rates of interest, compounded monthly."

"You see, Papa?" Tommie demanded. "That's exactly what I told you, but you wouldn't believe me!"

"I've spent my entire life on this river," Captain Harding said slowly, "and I've met all types through the decades. I find it very difficult to believe that any man could be that dishonest."

119

"If your cousin is really a lady," Tommie said with a sudden show of emotion, "she'll soon get wise to de Cordova and will have nothing more to do with him, believe me. He's an absolutely loathsome man. He's actually hinted—more than once—that he'd like to marry me. I'd rather die first! I don't dare tell him what I really think of him, however, because he'll take out his anger financially on Papa."

Edward looked at the captain. "May I ask what you're doing to end this man's threat to you?"

Father and daughter exchanged a look, and Captain Harding said, "There's nothing mysterious about it, really. Between the cargo we're carrying and the passengers, I anticipate making a profit of ten to fifteen thousand dollars on this trip."

Edward whistled appreciatively.

"That's not an unusual sum," Captain Harding hastened to assure him. "Any of the larger riverboats can earn that kind of a profit on a single voyage, provided that underwater obstacles are avoided and the vessel completes her journey. The way I figure it, with that amount of cash in my pocket, I can reason with de Cordova and pay him a sufficient amount to get him off my back."

"I'm afraid he's not going to be satisfied until you pay him every penny he's demanding," Tommie said. "I refuse to trust him, no matter what!"

Captain Harding smiled wanly at Edward. "I may represent the laws of the United States on this voyage," he said, "but I'm afraid there's nothing I can do for your cousin without her specific consent. If de Cordova were forcing her to travel with him against her will, for instance, I could intervene and put a stop to it, but this way. . . ." His voice trailed away.

Edward clenched his fists in frustration. "Thank you for your interest and for filling me in on de Cordova's background," he said. "I can see there's no way you can intervene, and I'm afraid I'm handcuffed, too. Both de Cordova and Millicent have told me in so many words to mind my own business, so all I can do—at least for the present—is to sit tight, wait—and hope for the best."

The voyage was resumed shortly after daybreak, in accordance with Captain Harding's long-established custom. Edward arose early, and after eating a light breakfast in the saloon, he went on deck to watch the passing scene. In the background the silent, snow-covered peaks of Montana rose majestically, blending with the horizon. The *Big Muddy*'s engine throbbed, turning the paddle wheel that was located in the stern of the ship, and twin plumes of black smoke rose from her high stacks and curled lazily toward the limitless blue sky overhead.

Captain Harding, manipulating the steering wheel in the wheelhouse, was following a course roughly in the center of the river, which was about sixty to eighty feet wide at that point. The current was swift, and the waters were muddy due to the silt that was being washed into the stream from the drainage that came down from the mountains. It was impossible to see more than a few inches below the surface, and as Edward had learned at supper the previous evening, it was useless for the ship's master to use charts as navigational aids.

All at once, the serenity of the voyage ended when the *Big Muddy* ground to a sudden, jarring halt.

Tommie Harding, in her customary man's workday attire, appeared on the run out of nowhere and cupped her hands. "Grasshopper!" she shouted. "Grasshopper!"

Crew members, including deckhands, cabin attendants, and roustabouts, all swarmed up to the opposite sides of the catwalk that straddled the top deck on either side of the wheelhouse. The men grasped two exceptionally long spars, or poles, which they lowered to the bottom of the river at forty-five-degree angles.

These long, strong timbers were driven down and back like crutches by cables attached to a capstan, which was powered by a little steam engine. This forced the *Big Muddy* to slide a few yards ahead before halting again, and then it was necessary to move the spars again in a forward position. This was done first with the pole on the left, then the pole on the right, and each time, the vessel moved forward a short distance on the sandbar that had mired her. Eventually the *Big Muddy* floated free in deeper water beyond the obstruction, and Tommie breathed more easily. As Edward would learn, in the event that the ship had not been freed, the roustabouts—or roosters—would climb into the water and, sometimes wading up to their necks, haul the ship free. A portion of the cargo, as much as fifty percent if necessary, would be unloaded until the vessel floated again, and then the cargo would be reloaded in the holds.

Such activities were known to slow the ship's schedule by a half-day, but on this occasion they enjoyed good fortune and were on their way again after a delay of no more than a half hour.

What fascinated Edward was Captain Harding's uncanny ability to navigate completely by feel. He was so familiar with the Missouri after a lifetime of travel on the river, so sensitive to its currents and the way his ship reacted to them, that he could sense every change in the channel that had occurred during the winter months when the river traffic had been suspended.

At noon, Tommie, still in work clothes, again assumed the place at the head of the table, and again she was cool toward Edward and conversed mostly with the other diners.

As Edward and the other passengers were leaving the dining room after their meal, a sudden scream sounded from the first-class passenger deck above. Edward was the first through the door and bounded up the stairs two at a time.

The shabby little man from Brooklyn was lying on the deck, bleeding profusely from several deep cuts. His monkey, jabbering in terror and clutching a man's wallet in one paw, was clinging precariously to a light fixture on the wall and trying to stay out of the way of a burly passenger, who was slashing at him with a knife.

Edward took in the scene at a glance and knew instantly what had happened. The little man obviously had not heeded Edward's advice and had directed the monkey to steal from another passenger. The outraged victim had not only slashed the animal's owner severely but also was trying to attack the monkey.

"Just a moment!" Edward called urgently. "Don't hurt the animal. Whatever's happened is hardly his fault."

The burly passenger paid no attention and continued to slash the air wildly, trying to reach the tiny, terrified monkey.

Edward felt compelled to intervene. Keeping away from the man's knife, the young Englishman delivered a lightninglike series of jabs to the man's face and torso. A solid blow with his right fist sent the man reeling. He crashed to the deck, his knife slipping from his grasp. A well-aimed kick sent the knife down the width of the deck and overboard into the river. Then Edward dropped to one knee beside the gravely wounded Brooklyn man.

"I should—have listened—to you," the man said, barely able to speak. "I'm—sorry. Please, sir—look after Robin for me. He has—no one else." He closed his eyes and died quietly.

Edward looked up and saw a sea of faces around him, including Tommie, several crew members, and a number of passengers. Conscious, too, of the still-quaking monkey clinging to the light fixture, he rose easily to his feet.

"Robin," he said sternly, "give me the wallet." The little monkey unleashed a stream of unintelligible gibberish.

"Now!" Edward said, and extended a hand.

The monkey obediently dropped the wallet into his hand. Edward flung it to the deck beside the burly passenger, who was now sitting up, appearing ashamed of his murderous outburst.

The little monkey decided it was safe to leap down and find sanctuary on Edward's shoulder.

Edward reached up and stroked the little animal soothingly. "That's a good boy, Robin," he said. "Everything is going to be all right."

One of the passengers held out a bit of candied fruit left over from dinner. Edward took the sweet and handed it to the monkey. Robin Hood stopped shaking and concentrated on eating. At that moment a firm friendship was born, and Robin transformed his past loyalties into unwavering affection for the Englishman.

Crew members removed the Brooklynite's body from the deck, and the ship's carpenter built a coffin for him out of scrap lumber. Frontier justice, swift, bold, and uncompromising, had been observed. That evening, when the day's run was completed, the victim's coffin was taken ashore, and Captain Harding read the Twenty-third Psalm as the little man was lowered into his grave. Only Edward Blackstone, with Robin Hood perched on his shoulder, came ashore and attended the last rites for the unfortunate man who dared to flout the law of the West.

V

The *Big Muddy* settled into a routine as smooth-flowing as the waters of the Missouri River itself. All the days seemed alike as the ship gradually worked her way eastward. All of her overnight stops in Montana were made in the wilderness, the territory being only sparsely settled except in the gold-mining districts. Then the mountains fell away to hills, and the river basin became flatter as the vessel dipped into the Dakota Territory. Due to the belligerence of the Sioux nation, who refused to make their peace with the United States, the atmosphere changed from that of a nation at peace to one that was prepared for instant warfare. A number of major army posts were located on the Missouri in Dakota, and these communities depended on the *Big Muddy* and other steamers to provide them with guns, ammunition, and food staples. Halts were scheduled at Fort Union, Fort Buford, Fort Berthold, and Fort Stevenson. The removal of cargo from the *Big Muddy* was undertaken at each army post by military personnel, and Captain Harding and his daughter went ashore to dine with the colonels who commanded the forts.

Although no one on board realized what he was doing, Luis de Cordova did not go ashore at any of the army posts. He was out of touch with the subordinates handling various matters for him, and he had no idea of the status of the stolen Winchester repeating rifles. It was possible that the guns had been discovered and that one or more of his subordinates had talked out of turn. But as long as he was inconspicuous and the army didn't know where to find him, he was safe, even if the secret had been uncovered.

At last, the ship came to the town of Bismarck, in Dakota, the first major community that had been encountered on the voyage. A stay of two days and a night was scheduled there; business was also to be conducted at Fort Abraham Lincoln, a major army post, directly across the river. Arms, ammunition, and foodstuffs were to be delivered to Fort Lincoln, and goods were not only to be dropped off but also taken aboard in Bismarck.

At the urgent suggestion of Captain Harding, male passengers who went ashore in Bismarck wore sidearms, and women did not go into town without escorts. Bismarck was a rough frontier community with more than its share of rogues, and the bordellos and saloons of the community were important industries.

Not wanting to make himself too conspicuous, Edward Blackstone decided to leave Robin Hood on board the *Big Muddy* when he came ashore, and following the captain's advice, he strapped on two six-shooters. Various passengers banded together for mutual protection, and Edward joined one such group, which included a middle-aged schoolteacher traveling east to her former home for the first time since she had settled in western Montana.

Meanwhile, at Luis de Cordova's instigation, Millicent Randall wore one of her more revealing costumes and heavily made up her face.

Luis took her to Bismarck's largest and most opulent gambling hall, where they dined in style, and then, following the custom he had established previously, he challenged the habitués of the place to games of high-low, wagering a night with Millicent against five hundred dollars a draw.

The night held no surprises for Millicent. She knew exactly what to expect, and she was helpless to prevent Luis from using her as he saw fit, even though she was degraded and cheapened in the process. He patted and caressed her enough so that she could not help but do whatever he demanded, and then she willingly acted as a shill for him while he cheated man after man at cards—and she was now certain that he was cheating. For a time Millicent tried to keep her sanity by counting the number of victims Luis snared into losing large bets to him, but there were so many that she eventually abandoned her efforts.

Luis's diabolical game suited to perfection the mood of the gamblers of Bismarck, and it was the small hours of the morning before the clamors of the last contestants were stilled. By this time Luis had made so much money that he was forced to hire two off-duty constables to act as escorts to take Millicent and him back to the ship.

Millicent was afraid that she and Luis might be attacked and killed by men who realized belatedly that they had been cheated, for the men here seemed of a tougher caliber than those in Fort Benton. She did not breathe easily until they reached the *Big Muddy* and went aboard the ship shortly before dawn broke. She closed and locked the door of their suite behind them, and the following day she was very happy to remain in isolation on board the vessel. It did her peace of mind no good that Luis, having made a financial killing, was content to stay on board until the *Big Muddy* sailed that afternoon and make love to her all day. Even though she was unable to stop herself from responding to him, she discovered that his lovemaking, for the first time, left her with a sense of self-loathing and disgust. She realized that he had the power to render her physically helpless, but her mind was reasserting itself, and she knew that she had no respect for him and none for herself, either.

Edward Blackstone, who had not bothered to go ashore since the previous evening, encountered the captain on the stairs a short time before they sailed.

"Let me tell you something for your private information, Mr. Blackstone," Captain Harding said. "We're going to put in to a small cove on a lake that empties into the Missouri River tonight, and we'll be spending the night there. The water is deep and very clean, and I understand that it's excellent for swimming. It'll be a mite chilly, being spring and all, but you still might want to have yourself a little swim before we set sail again tomorrow."

Edward thanked the captain. The prospect of a swim the following morning was delightful.

Rising early the next day, before any of the other passengers were about, Edward went promptly to the stern, where the great paddle wheel was now idle. Removing his clothes, he dived into the waters of the cove.

The experience was exhilarating. The water was indeed clean, and though it was cold, it was superbly refreshing. As he struck out lazily for the shore, Edward realized he was not alone in the water. Directly ahead, riding at anchor, was a small boat that was obviously the property of the captain, for it bore the name of the *Big Muddy* on her prow. He saw someone swimming to it, and he caught sight of a blond head of hair.

"Oh, dear," said Tommie Harding as she noticed Edward and began treading water near the boat. Then she added indignantly, "I always swim here. Every time we come down the river and stop in this cove, I go swimming."

"I sincerely beg your pardon," Edward said. "I had no wish to intrude on your privacy, but obviously I didn't know that you swam here, or I wouldn't have come into the water myself."

For the sake of keeping peace between father and daughter, he refrained from mentioning that the captain had suggested a swim in the cove.

Tommie was still treading water, taking care to keep her body totally submerged. "I trust you're going to be a gentleman, Mr. Blackstone," she said rather primly.

Edward had to laugh. "What's sauce for the goose is sauce for the gander, you know," he said. "You may be vulnerable, but so am I."

Tommie joined in his laugh. "That's very comforting to know," she said.

"What do you suggest?" he asked, treading water, too. For some reason, he couldn't stop chuckling.

Tommie had recovered her equilibrium and spoke in her usual crisp manner. "Remove yourself from proximity to my boat," she said. "Swim some distance from it. Then be gentlemanly enough to avert your gaze and not to peek while I climb out of the water and put on my clothes, which are in the boat."

"I give you my word that I won't peek at you."

"I'll row back to the *Big Muddy* as fast as I'm able, and you can then finish your swim at your leisure and return to the ship whenever you wish."

"It strikes me you're being unfair to yourself, Miss Harding," he said. "You're cutting your own swimming time short."

"If you please, Mr. Blackstone," she said urgently, "do as I ask! I can't tread water indefinitely!"

Edward turned away without saying another word and began to move off through the water. Still facing away from the boat after he had gone about twenty feet, he halted but kept his face averted. A series of splashing and scraping sounds told Edward that Tommie was pulling herself into the boat.

He recognized that he faced a dilemma. He had agreed with the young woman's plan and had given his word on it. He supposed that, as a gentleman, he was honor bound not to look at her. On the other hand, his sense of curiosity threatened to overcome him. When she dressed in man's clothes, she emphatically wasn't worth a second look, but the dresses she wore to dinner in the evening hinted that she had a figure well worthy of inspection. He had to find out. There were times in a man's life—and this was one of them—when a man's quest for information took precedence over his standing as a gentleman.

Partly turning in the water, Edward surreptitiously looked at Tommie and was stunned. In the soft light of early morning, she was so beautiful that, for a moment, he thought he might be seeing an illusion.

She had a perfect figure. Her shoulders were broad but feminine, and she had a long, swanlike neck. Her breasts were high and firm. Her waist was incredibly tiny, her stomach was flat, and her legs were long and beautifully shaped. Edward was so affected by the sight of her figure that he submerged, swallowed a quantity of water, and rose to the surface again, sputtering.

"All right, Mr. Blackstone," Tommie called from the boat, "you may look now."

He saw that she had donned her man's shirt and pants.

"Thank you so much," she said primly, and began to row steadily toward the *Big Muddy*.

Edward stayed in the waters of the cove until Tommie had boarded and the lifeboat was hauled up on deck. Only then was it safe for him to return to the ship. He knew that life from then on would be different than it had been until that day. He could not help but be permanently affected by the glimpse he had had of Tommie Harding's glorious figure.

Cadet Henry Blake arrived safely at Fort Vancouver, and his parents were delighted to see him. Cindy Holt was ecstatic, and Hank reciprocated her feelings. They were inseparable from the moment of his arrival, and their romance appeared to pick up where it had left off when they had last seen each other at West Point some months earlier.

At the first opportunity, Clarissa Holt invited the Blakes to the Holt ranch for supper, and for the occasion she also extended an invitation to Rob and Kale Martin, Rob having been very friendly with Hank when he'd been a forlorn orphan in Montana. He and Toby, along with Clarissa and Rob's late wife, Beth, had been jointly responsible for the boy's rehabilitation.

Toby, who had not seen Hank in more than two years, was struck at once by the young man's maturation. His features had solidified; his green eyes were penetrating, and his jaw jutted forward prominently. His expression was that of a man, not a boy, and it was clear at a glance that he was someone with whom to contend in a dispute.

Cindy blossomed in Hank's presence, and she and Hank made no secret of their mutual affection. They sat side by side on a sofa in the parlor of the Holt ranch house before supper, holding hands. At the least, their shoulders touched, and when convention forced them to move apart, they seemed to find countless excuses to reach out and touch each other. They were obviously so much in love that their elders were reminded of their own premarital days and felt waves of nostalgia for that earlier period.

Conversation was general at the supper table, and both Lee Blake and Toby Holt refrained from mentioning any of the problems that currently troubled them. Rob Martin amused the gathering with a story of his recent activities.

"I was all set to open an office for the sale of lumber from the property that Toby and I own in Washington," the red-haired man said, "when I got an offer that I couldn't resist. Apparently I've acquired something of a reputation as a surveyor for railroad lines—"

"And with good reason!" Kale interrupted loyally. "There's no one in the country who knows more about the subject than you do!" She beamed at him, and it was clear her former life as a courtesan was completely behind her, that she was happy living in Portland as Rob's wife and the stepmother of his little girl from his first marriage.

Rob took her hand. "Be that as it may, honey, I've been hired by the Southern Pacific Railroad Company to lay out the line that will extend from Portland across the mountains to the east and will form a trunk line with the major northern transcontinental route. In addition, I'm going to determine the location of the connector line between San Francisco and Portland."

"I envy you the fun you'll have surveying, Rob," Toby said sincerely.

"Join me," Rob said, grinning. "The company will be very pleased to have you, I know."

"I can't do it," Toby said regretfully. "The operation of the ranch takes my complete time." He did not mention that he was also obligated to his stepfather to search for the missing army rifles, a hunt that had so far proved fruitless.

Everyone was interested in the life that Hank was leading at West Point, and the young man, with typical modesty, answered the questions quietly, never referring to the brilliant record he was creating for himself at the military academy.

Eulalia beamed during Hank's recital, but General Blake, who had to be careful in meting out praise, was more restrained and tried to conceal his pride. However, the broad smile on his face gave him away.

As dessert and coffee were about to be served, a tap sounded at the front door. Toby excused himself and answered the summons, then stared in openmouthed disbelief. On the threshold stood one of the ranch hands, accompanied by none other than Running Bear, the young Nez Percé whom Toby had last encountered as the leader of the Indian rebels in Idaho.

Running Bear was uncomfortable. Though he had attended missionary schools, this was the first time in his life he had visited the home of a white man, and he was conscious of his buckskin clothing and of the other differences that separated him from those who represented a more advanced civilization.

Nevertheless, he struggled valiantly to overcome these feelings. He had traveled on horseback a long distance across the mountains to the east in order to see

Toby Holt, and he was determined not to be deterred from his goal.

The Nez Percé raised his left arm, palm extended, in greeting. Trying to hide his surprise at seeing Running Bear, Toby responded with the same gesture. Next they exchanged almost interminably long, formal greetings. Only after the amenities had been observed did Toby invite the Indian to enter the house, instructing the ranch hand to look after Running Bear's horse and to see that there was a place for him to sleep that night in the bunkhouse.

Running Bear hesitated for a moment and then stepped inside, but he balked and refused to enter the dining room when Toby tried to take him into the family supper party.

Thoroughly familiar with the sensitivities of Indians, Toby did not insist. Instead he led Running Bear into the sitting room, then went to fetch Rob and to bring to the unexpected guest a slab of juicy peach pie, which Clarissa had baked that afternoon.

Running Bear went through the long rigamarole of exchanging greetings with Rob and finally settled down to eat the piece of peach pie. It was important that he accept the refreshments offered by his host, and ignoring the presence of a fork on his plate, he picked up the slab of pie with his fingers and began to eat.

The peach pie was the first he had ever eaten, and he demolished it swiftly, licking the plate and then popping his fingers into his mouth one after the other in order to clean them and again taste the delicious dessert.

Trying without success to make himself comfortable in his white man's chair, Running Bear belched politely and at last was ready to reveal his reasons for having come all the way to Portland. Toby and Rob settled back in their seats and listened.

Running Bear told them about the note that he had received and his meeting with an unidentified man, in the wilderness of northern Idaho, who had offered him as many Winchester repeater rifles as he wanted for a very large fee per rifle.

Giving him no chance to finish his story, Toby hurried back into the dining room and fetched General Blake, whom he also wanted to listen to what appeared to be the first break in the mystery of the stolen Winchester rifles. Running Bear was awed by the presence of the man he regarded as the great war chief of the whites, but he warmed to his theme as he repeated his tale at Toby's request.

Making no comment, the general allowed him to finish his story. Then he asked, "What arrangements did you make with this man when you parted company with him?"

"It was arranged," the young Nez Percé replied, "that we would meet again deep in the wilderness of Idaho in one moon's time. I am to give him my reply then and tell him whether the Nez Percé wish to possess these new rifles and to arrange payment for them."

General Blake did not even glance in Toby's direction as he asked his next question. "You and your people are willing to cooperate with the United States in this matter?"

Running Bear nodded emphatically. "I have sworn an oath, and so have my elders," he said, "that we are the brothers of Americans, and we will stand together with our blood brothers against our common foes for all time."

The general smiled and nodded, showing pleasure at the response. "Are the Nez Percé willing," he asked, "to help us capture those who stole valuable rifles from our army?"

Running Bear could not conceal his surprise. "The new rifles are stolen?" he asked in wonder.

"They are," Toby assured him. "That is why you were offered these weapons. In case you don't realize it, it is against the law of the United States to sell firearms to any Indian nation."

"I have long been familiar with that law," the young Nez Percé said, and pondered for a moment. "It is my wish, and the wish of the elders of my nation, to do the bidding of the United States in this matter. We will obey the word that we are given by the great war chief."

"You won't regret this decision," the general said. "Keep your rendezvous with the representative of the thieves. Pay him for a limited number of rifles—perhaps ten—in order to whet his appetite for more sales. Show him that you have even more money and arrange to buy additional rifles—all he has available. Set another time and place in the wilderness for these weapons to be delivered. Instead of meeting with you, however, he will come face to face with my representatives."

Running Bear shook his head sadly. "I regret," he said, "it will not be possible for the Nez Percé to heed the words of the great war chief."

The general first looked astonished, and then his expression changed to disgust.

Toby intervened swiftly and addressed the young Indian in his own tongue. "Do I understand correctly," he said, "that what is causing the trouble is a matter of finances?" He spoke in the language of the Indian deliberately, in order that Running Bear not be embarrassed by being forced to admit publicly to poverty.

Grateful for his delicacy, Running Bear answered in the same language. "That is so," he said. "It would be needful for us to trap many animals and sell their furs for us to gain the sum of one thousand dollars—which would buy only four rifles. I am not certain there are enough beaver and fox in the entire territory of Idaho to provide the sum of thousands of dollars, which is what ten rifles would cost us."

Toby hastily explained the situation to his stepfather.

General Blake looked relieved. "I'm willing to take the risk," he said. "It's well worth thousands of dollars to stop the operations of these munitions thieves and to catch them red-handed. Toby," he continued, "go to my finance officer at headquarters first thing tomorrow morning, and he'll give you ten thousand in cash." He looked at the young Indian and smiled. "You shall have the money that will serve as bait for those who would sell you rifles. Tell their representative that you acquired the money by killing and stealing from the white man. That will convince him that you mean business."

He shook hands with Running Bear, then returned to the family gathering in the dining room.

Toby grinned at the Indian, feeling ebullient for

the first time since he had accepted the assignment from his stepfather. "You and I have much to arrange, Running Bear," he said. "We have a trap to set and some thieves to catch. For the first time, I have real hope that this problem will be solved."

Stalking Horse, the Cherokee foreman of Toby Holt's ranch and the lifelong friend of Toby's father, Whip Holt, had left Oregon for Idaho several days earlier, accompanied by White Elk, the orphaned Indian boy whom he had first befriended and then adopted as his grandson. They rode on horseback, taking two additional horses to carry their supplies of cooking utensils, blankets, and extra ammunition. Julia, the little burro that White Elk had made his pet, also accompanied them.

As always, they hunted for their own food, and Stalking Horse was gratified to see how White Elk put to use all the knowledge that had been taught him, bringing down game with a gun or bow and arrow, cleaning it, cooking it over a campfire, and saving the skins for future use.

Their trip took two weeks, and when they arrived in the vicinity of Boise, Stalking Horse went straight to the ranch of Pamela and Jim Randall.

The previous year, the orphaned White Elk had been found by army troops on patrol in Idaho. They had turned the boy over to Toby Holt, who was then military governor, and he had made an arrangement with Pamela and Stalking Horse, who had been visiting his employer in Idaho. Under the terms of the agreement, Stalking Horse was to look after the child in

Oregon for part of the year, then release him into Pamela's custody for the remaining months of each year, in order that the boy be taught the ways of the civilization that she represented. In this manner, it was hoped that White Elk would grow to manhood and become a bridge between the Indians and the white men.

The arrival of little White Elk filled Pamela with a sense of relief as well as pleasure. She had found herself drifting ever closer to an affair with Randy Savage, and even though she had never loved Jim, she was opposed to being unfaithful to him. Bored by her day-to-day existence at the ranch after a lifetime of high living in cosmopolitan London, Pamela had been unable to resist the drift toward an affair. Now, however, the situation was drastically changed, and she knew that her days would be occupied by White Elk.

Stalking Horse refused Pam and Jim's invitation to spend some time at their ranch as their guest, and after a scant twenty-four hours, he departed for Portland, leaving White Elk with the Randalls.

Immediately after breakfast the following morning, Pamela adjourned with White Elk to the chamber that was used both as the boy's classroom and play area. She sat him at a desk and, taking her place opposite him, said, "Let's see how much you remember of our alphabet." She handed him a blank sheet of paper and a pencil.

White Elk was not only exceptionally bright but very industrious as well. He wrote the complete alphabet in capital letters and then did the same in small letters. Without being asked, he printed Arabic numbers from one to twenty and then repeated them in Roman numerals. He had not lost his reading ability either and read aloud through several paragraphs of a novel by Charles Dickens that Pamela handed him.

Equally important, his deportment had not suffered during the months he had spent with Stalking Horse. He still used "please" and "thank you" extensively and properly, and he remembered to stand aside in order to allow Pamela to precede him in and out of a room.

He passed every test in the basics that Pamela devised, and she introduced him to the first fundamentals of a new course, a study of American history.

By now, noon was approaching, and White Elk's concentration began to break. From time to time he gazed out the window at the rolling hills of Idaho and paid scant attention to what Pamela was saying.

Realizing that his mind was wandering, Pamela felt an irrational stab of disappointment. Perhaps her model pupil was less than perfect, after all.

"What's the matter?" she asked him, trying to conceal her irritation. "Don't you like history?"

"I like it just fine, ma'am," he replied obediently, and his gaze drifted to the windows again.

"You don't look all that interested," she said in frustration.

"I guess I'm hungry," the boy admitted.

"We'll go directly to the table for our noon dinner the moment that Mr. Randall comes home," she said. "He's off somewhere on the ranch right now, but he ought to be here any minute. What else is bothering you?"

The child hesitated. "Well, ma'am," he said at last, "I've been learning how to track and hunt from Stalking Horse, and I've been looking forward to tracking deer or elk through the wilderness here. Big animals like elk and moose are all gone from the forests of Oregon, but from what Stalking Horse says, there are many still to be found here in Idaho, and I've hardly been able to wait to try my luck at finding one or more of them."

In spite of herself, Pamela laughed. She realized that she had set standards far too high to be realistic. White Elk was eager to learn and excelled at what he did, but she was losing sight of the fact that he was a boy, and an Indian boy, at that. He needed the time and opportunity to develop interests other than the academic, and it was her place to encourage him.

"You've done very well for one morning," she said, "and I think you've had enough schoolwork for today. Go and wash up for dinner, and we'll see if we can't persuade Mr. Randall to take you tracking this afternoon. I think it's very important that you find an elk or a moose."

The *Big Muddy* sailed steadily downstream from Bismarck, and on the second morning after leaving the city, Edward Blackstone realized, for the first time, that the stern-wheeler was being followed by a small vessel. Edward mentioned the matter at the noon dinner table to Tommie Harding, who, as usual, was taking her father's place there during the daylight hours.

"You're far less observant than you sometimes appear," Tommie answered, making an obvious reference to the encounter she'd had with Edward in the cove. "That ship appears to have been following us ever since we left Bismarck."

"Why?" he demanded.

"I have no idea," Tommie replied, shrugging, and then said, half under her breath, "Papa's been wondering the same thing, but he has no answer."

Later that same day, when the *Big Muddy* ended her day's run and pulled up to anchor for the night on the left bank of the Missouri, Edward noted that the smaller vessel had closed the gap and was anchoring nearby.

Feeling uneasy, Edward went to his cabin for his custom-made English repeater rifle, and slipping several cartridges into his jacket pocket, he went straight to the wheelhouse.

"I don't want to alarm you, Captain, but there's something very odd about that ship that keeps shadowing us."

Isaiah Harding lowered the binoculars he'd been using. "I've just been studying her," he said, "and I can't figure her out. She appears to have a crew of ten or fifteen men, and there are another dozen or more who are passengers. All of them are heavily armed, and I'd say they're looking for trouble. Whether they're river pirates or whatever they may be remains to be seen."

He began to speculate on the possible identity of the ship, her crew, and passengers when Tommie burst into the wheelhouse. "Papa!" she cried. "There's a delegation heading this way from the stranger."

Captain Harding looked toward the shore and then remarked calmly, "Sure enough." He reached for his rifle and rose to go down to the main deck and meet the delegation as it approached.

"I'm coming with you, if you don't mind, Captain," Edward said firmly, and fell in with Harding. Tommie followed close behind them.

The captain halted. "Thomasina," he said severely, "you will oblige me by staying in the wheelhouse. You keep watch on the proceedings from here, and if anything goes amiss, I'm sure you'll know what to do."

Giving her no chance to reply, he started out again, with Edward at his heels. "That confounded daughter of mine," Harding muttered when he was out of earshot of the wheelhouse, "doesn't know the meaning of fear. She's always getting into trouble, and then I've got to bail her out!"

Edward smiled and kept his own increasingly favorable views of Tommie to himself.

A few moments later, the pair stood at the rail, awaiting the arrival of the heavily armed trio of strangers who were walking along the riverbank. Edward was uneasy, and he sensed that Captain Harding, behind his tranquil façade, was also tense.

"What can I do for you, gentlemen?" the captain called.

The three men halted, and one of their number said, "We got no quarrel with you, Captain, but we're anxious to have some words with a feller who supposedly is on board this here ship of yours. Do you have a passenger, name of Luis de Cordova?"

"It's possible," the captain admitted cautiously.

"We want some words with him," the man said. "Me and some of my friends been havin' some little talks since he came ashore the other night with a lady friend of his, and by puttin' two and two together, we discovered he cheated us all out of a good many thousands of dollars. Like I said, Captain, we ain't holdin' you or any of your people responsible for what de Cordova done, but we aim to get our money back from him. Pronto! Either he pays us, or we have a little tarrin' and featherin' party before night falls tonight. I'll be much obliged if you will fetch him for us."

"Let me make my position very clear to you, gentlemen," Captain Harding said. "I hold no brief for Luis de Cordova. I have no admiration for him, and if you say he's cheated at cards, you're probably right. On the other hand, he's paid cash for his passage to St. Louis, and he deserves exactly the same protection that I afford all my passengers. I'll be glad to give him your message, and if he's willing to talk to you, he'll come down to the deck himself. If he refuses, however, let me warn you, you'll have to use force in order to remove him from this ship."

The trio exchanged long looks. "Fair enough, Captain," the spokesman said. "You understand our position, and you've made yours clear to us. I'll just say that we ain't foolin'! We didn't hire this here boat to be turned down by de Cordova."

"I'll deliver your message right now, if you'll be good enough to wait," the captain said, and promptly went to the stairs. Edward remained on deck, keeping an eye on the strangers.

After an absence of only a few minutes, Captain Harding returned. "I'm sorry, gentlemen," he said, "but Mr. de Cordova has refused your request. He claims that he did not cheat at cards, that your gaming with him was all honest and aboveboard, and he says that under no circumstances will he return the money you lost to him. He also refuses to subject himself to your threats."

The spokesman listened in wooden-faced silence, as did his associates. Without speaking another word, they began to trudge back to their own vessel.

"I'm going to stop off at my cabin," Edward said evenly, "for my pistols. I'll meet you in the wheelhouse in a few minutes." He turned away and mounted the steps two at a time while Captain Harding, who was close behind him, continued all the way to the top deck.

Edward was so preoccupied that he failed to close his cabin door tightly behind him after strapping on his six-shooters. As a consequence, the door opened a crack, and Robin Hood, the little monkey, went out on the deck. The smell of food being prepared in the galley on the opposite side of the deck attracted the animal, and he hopped into the galley unnoticed by the chef, who was busy preparing supper for the first-class passengers. Climbing to a window ledge, Robin Hood concealed himself behind a large metal pot in which vegetable scraps and other refuse were being thrown.

In the meantime, as Edward mounted to the top deck, he realized that the *Big Muddy* was being moved to a place in midriver, where Tommie directed the roustabouts in the lowering of the anchors.

"I decided to reduce our risks to a minimum," Captain Harding said without preamble as Edward joined him. "We'll be much harder to board in midstream than we were on the bank."

"Do you want your cannon loaded with scrap metal?" Edward asked. "We can make life uncomfortable for the men who are seeking revenge against de Cordova."

"I thought of using the cannon, but then I decided against it," the captain said. "We're in a most peculiar situation. The men who are threatening us have no legal right whatsoever to bring action of any kind against this ship, her passengers, or her crew, regardless of how much they believe that Luis de Cordova may owe them. At the same time, I want to keep our record straight and our skirts clean in the event that we are attacked. Loading the cannon with scrap is a sure way to cause serious casualties and to lose public sympathy in the event there's an investigation."

Edward cut swiftly to the core of the problem. "Suppose we're attacked, Captain," he said. "A fairly likely supposition, in the face of what's been happening, I should think. What do we do to protect ourselves?"

"We engage only in defensive fire," Isaiah Harding said firmly. "I realize this compounds our problem and makes the task that awaits us much more difficult to perform, but I've already requested Tommie and the crew to obey my injunction in this. I'll have to exact the same promise from you, Mr. Blackstone. My good name and the safety of my passengers come first."

"I'll do whatever you say, Captain Harding. It's your ship."

"I've asked Tommie to go from cabin to cabin after the anchor is lowered fore and aft and request the passengers to stay out of the open until this incident is resolved. I don't want anyone hurt by stray bullets."

Edward nodded as he examined his rifles and pistols to make sure they were properly loaded. He was still inspecting his weapons when the crackle of gunfire started emanating from the other ship.

"They're shooting high," he said. "Every shot is going far overhead."

Captain Harding nodded and smiled sourly. "They're no doubt opening fire overhead in the hope they can frighten us into turning Luis de Cordova over to them. I wish we could get rid of him that way, but I'm afraid it's impossible."

Another fusillade sounded, and this time the shots were aimed much lower. In fact, one bullet barely missed the glass of the wheelhouse and buried itself in the wooden window frame.

"I reckon the time has come," Captain Harding said, "for us to begin to discourage them a mite from shooting too freely at us." He moved to the open window, rested his rifle on the sill, and, taking careful aim, squeezed the trigger. "I winged one of them," he announced in quiet triumph. "Got him square in the shoulder. That's one man who won't be letting loose any more fire at us tonight."

Edward grinned, nodded, and placed the barrel of his own precision-made English rifle on the sill. Then he, too, took aim and fired. Captain Harding, who had been watching the exhibition in curiosity, couldn't help blinking in astonishment. Either deliberately or by accident, the Englishman had duplicated his own feat, putting a bullet into the upper arm of a man on the deck of the other boat. Either Edward had been lucky, Harding thought, or he was a superb marksman.

He made it obvious that he was the latter when he fired again and incapacitated but did not seriously injure another of Luis de Cordova's pursuers.

A hail of gunfire erupted again from the other boat, and shots whistled overhead. This time, however, they were even closer to the wheelhouse, and Captain Harding became apprehensive. "They may be shooting at us in earnest now," he said. "I reckon it's time we leave this goldfish bowl and hie us to a safer position." He quickly led the way to the main deck, nimbly climbing down the stairs in spite of his advanced years.

There, crouching behind the protective bulk of the firewood piled high on the deck, were reinforcements— two of the ship's officers and four crew members, all of them armed with rifles, and all of them peering at the enemy from behind their protective shield.

The enemy shrewdly guessed the destination of the pair they had seen descending the ladder, and a volley of shots plowed into the firewood, doing no damage. Thanks to good fortune and inspired planning on Captain Harding's part, he and his men enjoyed protection much greater than that afforded by the bare, open deck of the boat the men were firing from.

"You know what to do, boys," Isaiah Harding said. "Knock 'em out, but do your best not to kill any of them. Fire whenever you're ready."

His subordinates opened fire immediately. Edward, meanwhile, made himself comfortable behind his makeshift palisade and peered out at the other boat. Seeing two figures outlined on the deck, he squeezed his trigger twice in succession.

Both of the men promptly disappeared. He knew he had wounded them at the very least, but he had no idea whether he had been able to obey the captain's injunction and refrain from killing them.

Bullets continued to pound steadily into the thick shield of firewood, but the men concealing themselves behind it remained unscathed. The battle raged unabated for the better part of an hour, and then as dusk fell, Captain Harding bellowed, "Tommie!"

His daughter appeared two decks above him and began to descend the stairs, crouching low in order to spoil the aim of those on board the boat who were taking pot shots at her. Continuing to crouch low, she ran the final yards to her father's side behind the wall of firewood.

"Tommie," Captain Harding said, "collect some of the roosters and weigh anchor when I give you the signal. I'm going up to the wheelhouse now, and as soon as I'm ready, we'll make a run for safety in the river, nighttime or no nighttime." White-faced, the young woman nodded.

"I've been keeping count of the injuries on board the other boat as best I'm able," the captain said, "and if my figures are anywhere close to being accurate, they've got a lot of wounded men, and they're hurting for personnel. They'll have the devil's own time getting together enough of a crew to chase us down the river. With any luck, we should be able to get away clean."

Edward, who had overheard the conversation as he continued to observe the upper decks of the other boat, wondered whether the risk that Harding was taking was worth the possible loss of his ship.

Isaiah Harding answered his unspoken query. "Man and boy, I've sailed this river my whole lifetime," he said, "and if I can't guide a ship a few miles downstream to get away from a band of thugs, even though it's after dark, I deserve to be caught high and dry on a sandbar. I'll make out just fine."

Tommie had complete confidence in him. "I'm sure you will, Papa," she told him.

The captain turned to Edward. "Mr. Blackstone," he said, "I wonder if you could oblige me by taking charge of the sharpshooters here. It'll be especially important once we're getting under way to keep the enemy fire to a minimum, so I'll appreciate it if you can keep her deck clear of riflemen during the ten to fifteen minutes that we'll be engaging in delicate maneuvers."

"I shall do my best, sir," Edward replied crisply.

Captain Harding was the first to make an appearance in the open. Taking advantage of the growing dusk, he mounted the steps two at a time until he reached the wheelhouse.

Tommie breathed a deep sigh of relief when her father reached his destination safely. Then, at his signal, it was her turn. Calling for the assistance of roustabouts, she went to the hoists fore and aft to raise the anchors.

In the meantime Edward quickly gave new instructions to the riflemen. "Suspend your fire for a time, gentlemen," he said. "I hope to mislead the enemy into believing that we're devoting our total energies and attention to weighing anchor and moving the *Big Muddy* out of here. If they fall for the deception, they're likely to take far more exposed positions on the deck, and they'll be that much easier for us to pick off. If Captain Harding is right, every man we put out of action will impose a terrible burden on them."

The men who comprised his little core of sharpshooters held their fire as Tommie directed a group of roosters in the weighing of the anchor. As they hauled the anchors up onto the deck, the ship began to swing around in the tide. Captain Harding neatly intercepted that movement with the steering wheel, and the *Big Muddy* began to move slowly downstream. The captain, peering intently at the dark, swirling waters below him, maneuvered in such a way that the big ship stayed in the center of the channel.

Those on board the enemy boat belatedly became aware that their quarry was escaping, and an intensified flurry of rifle shots sounded from her deck.

But the strategy that Edward Blackstone was employing proved to be accurate. Men on the other boat's deck were openly exposing themselves now, not bothering to take cover as they directed their fire at their escaping foe.

"Open fire at will, lads," he called softly, and suited action to words, taking careful aim and squeezing the trigger of his own rifle. Once again, he succeeded in wounding a sharpshooter on the deck of the other boat.

The crew members at his command promptly followed his example and fired three volleys at the upper decks. Four or five men had been stationed there, but when the smoke cleared away, no one was to be seen.

Peering hard through the swiftly gathering darkness at the enemy's deck, Edward could find no sign of any marksmen. "You may cease fire for the moment, lads," he said, "but keep your powder dry. We'll let them have another volley or two if they prove they haven't had enough yet."

The ship's second officer chuckled. "I reckon that's one hound dog that'll go creepin' back to Bismarck with his tail between his legs," he said.

Edward had to agree with him.

Little by little, those on board the *Big Muddy* realized that the hostilities had come to an end and that they had emerged the victors. But Captain Harding took no needless risks and guided the ship downriver cautiously for an additional three-quarters of an hour before finally becoming convinced that he was no longer being followed. Only then did he draw up to the far shore of the river and anchor for the night.

Edward was momentarily alarmed when he discovered that Robin Hood was missing from his cabin, but a hasty search revealed that the little monkey was safely ensconced on a window ledge in the galley, where he had become a faithful friend of the cook. The chef, who was still busy preparing supper, gave him choice tidbits of food, which the monkey, chattering incessantly, hastily and happily devoured.

Edward promptly took Robin Hood off to his own cabin. Anytime he found the animal missing in the future, he would know precisely where to search for him.

Supper in the first-class dining room predictably became a celebration that evening. Several passengers ordered wine for the entire company, and the chef outdid himself in honor of the occasion. Captain Harding was toasted repeatedly for his cunning and valor, as was his daughter, who looked unexpectedly appealing in a simple cotton dress. Edward received a fair share of praise and was made uncomfortable by the realization that he had achieved the questionable status of a celebrity.

What disturbed Edward even more was the strange attitude adopted by Luis de Cordova, who was responsible for the incident. He had been saved, prevented from suffering a tarring and feathering at the very least and perhaps even being severely beaten and executed, but he pretended that he had no part of the altercations. He thanked no one, taking no notice of the exchanges of congratulations. His attitude made it plain that he had removed himself completely from the entire affair. Indeed, he continued to engage other passengers on the ship in games of high-low, and he even had the audacity to suggest a game to Edward, who of course curtly rebuffed him.

Millicent Randall said nothing about the clash with the other boat, either, but Edward, observing her as best he could from a distance, became convinced that her ignorance was not deliberate or feigned. De Cordova appeared to have told her nothing about the cause of the fight, nor of the developments that had taken place during the course of the battle, so she knew less than anyone else present that evening.

Later that night, as Edward retired, he reviewed the incidents of the day and decided that they had been all to the good. First and foremost, Luis de Cordova's true nature had been revealed, and no one on board could find even the semblance of an excuse for his despicable, cowardly behavior. Also, the ship's officers and men had learned to work under duress and to fight together; they had been strengthened immeasurably for any future crises that might arise.

At dawn the following morning, the *Big Muddy* resumed her voyage as though nothing out of the ordinary had taken place. The battle had one additional lasting effect, however: Edward and Captain Harding had achieved an enduring mutual respect for each other's abilities.

VI

The previous night's battle proved to be the start rather than the end of the *Big Muddy's* troubles. The steamer had moved into that portion of the Dakota Territory that was occupied by the Sioux Indians, the largest Indian nation of the West. The tribe had lost much of its land to settlers, and the Sioux were now engaged in striking back, conducting raids and creating havoc wherever there were settlers. They had adopted the policy of driving the settlers from their territory, and as a consequence, Dakota was in turmoil.

On the average of two or three nights each week, the *Big Muddy* stopped at one or another of the small army forts along the river to deliver weapons, munitions, and food supplies. On these occasions the ship, spending the night under the protection of the fort's big cannon, was safe, and no one dared to attack her.

On the other nights, however, when she drew up to the bank of the Missouri somewhere in the wilderness, she was subjected to extreme danger. It became a common practice for Edward and other sharp-eyed passengers to note the presence of lone Indian braves sitting on their ponies some several hundred yards from shore, observing the anchoring of the ship.

The significance of such sightings was impossible to gauge. Did the presence of a silent Sioux observer on the shore mean absolutely nothing? Or did it presage an Indian attack?

Isaiah Harding personally mounted guard whenever he saw a Sioux keeping the *Big Muddy* under observation. In order to relieve the captain and give him an opportunity to rest, Edward Blackstone volunteered his own services and began to alternate night duty with the ship's master. Gradually he learned that eternal vigilance was the price of peace.

One night shortly after supper, while the chef baked bread for the following day and Robin Hood kept him company in the galley in return for the usual delicacies that he was fed, Edward slowly mounted the stairs to the wheelhouse. He placed his rifle within easy reach on a table, opened the windows, and then peered out in the darkness toward the Dakota hills, looking for some sign of Indian presence.

The task was at best daunting. The hills of Dakota melted into the landscape and became one with the sky and the horizon. When the clouds were heavy overhead, as they were that night, the moon and stars were not visible, and the entire landscape seemed to be blanketed in darkness. Rather than trying to detect an alien presence on shore, a task that was virtually impossible, Edward followed the advice of Captain Harding and tried to make himself sensitive to any sign of movement, which could indicate the presence of other humans nearby.

He saw nothing, however, and settled down to a long, lonely vigil. The weather was cool and damp, a perfect night for sleeping, and Edward remained alert only because he realized that the Sioux were inclined to take advantage of a night like this to launch an attack.

Over the course of the next hour, he found himself repeatedly growing drowsy, and in order to keep himself awake, he resorted to brisk walks on the little cleated deck around the wheelhouse. Back in the cabin, however, sleep threatened to overtake him again.

Suddenly he heard a low moaning sound from below. Oddly, the sound seemed to diminish in intensity, and finally it died away. Snatching his rifle, Edward bolted out the door and raced down to the main deck. There he found the common rooms dark, with the exception of the galley, where oil lamps were burning. Taking a firm grip on his rifle, he pushed open the door and found the chef standing beside the open window, staring down, while Robin Hood perched on the man's shoulder, chattering volubly.

"What goes on here?" Edward demanded.

The chef made no immediate reply but continued to peer down at the water below. Robin Hood chattered even more rapidly and intensely.

Edward was growing impatient when the chef finally turned to him. "This here monkey," he announced fondly, "is the smartest feller I know. He's a real genius, that's what he is!" He handed the monkey a candied cherry and a mushroom fashioned of marzipan. Robin Hood snatched the treats from him and stopped jabbering while he ate them.

"He was settin' right there on the ledge, bold as you please, next to the jar where I keep my kitchen slops before I throw 'em out," the cook said. "I swear I didn't hear a sound, nothin' that would make me suspicious, but all of a sudden, this here smart little rascal pushed over the slop jar, and all of a sudden, it landed on a Sioux brave who was climbin' up the hull of the ship aimin' to come in the window and put a knife into me. That brave would've killed me for sure if it hadn't been for this little monkey!"

Edward moved to the window and looked down toward the water but could see nothing.

"He's drowned and dead by now," the chef said. "When the slop jar hit him, it knocked him out for sure. He fell into the water, and I watched him drown." He grinned in satisfaction, then gave Robin Hood another candied cherry. Patting the monkey, he said, "From now on nothin' is too good for him—nothin'!"

Concealing a desire to laugh aloud, Edward went back out on deck and looked down at the quiet, dark river. There was no sign or sound of anyone. If the warrior had any accomplices, he had failed to signal them, for they did not put in an appearance. Thanks to the ingenuity of Robin Hood, quiet reigned for the rest of the night.

An incident very much out of the ordinary took

place two days later when the *Big Muddy* pulled up to a dock at Fort Pierre in the Dakota Territory. The fort, complete with a riverside log fortress and a large, wind-swept parade ground that permitted cavalry maneuvers, was a typical army post.

The colonel in command came to the docks to greet Captain Harding, who had been bringing him arms, supplies, and medicines for years, and the officer was joined by a large number of off-duty troops, who gathered to ogle the women passengers.

As always during stops at army posts, Luis de Cordova remained in his suite. Taking no chances, he also made certain that Millicent Randall kept out of sight, too.

A scant half hour after the *Big Muddy* tied up at her berth, as the cargo was still being unloaded, a dashing captain of cavalry came down to the dock, driving a small carriage pulled by two magnificent black geldings, which he handled with ease. As he climbed on board the *Big Muddy* and began to mount her stairs, he greeted two of the ship's officers boisterously, obviously having known them from previous voyages. As Edward watched from below, the stranger and Captain Harding exchanged warm greetings on the little cleated deck outside the wheelhouse, and they were interrupted almost immediately by the arrival of Tommie.

The captain instantly took the woman's hand, which he held, in Edward's opinion, far longer than politeness dictated. They talked at some length, and Edward, who could not tear his gaze away, was glad that he couldn't hear what was being said. He was forced to admit, too, that he had never seen her look so animated.

Then she went off to her own cabin, returning in short order wearing a becoming, blue silk dress and a pair of high-heeled slippers that Edward had never before seen. She looked exceptionally attractive.

Tommie kissed her father lightly, then went ashore with the captain, who handed her into the carriage. The young cavalry officer sat beside her and, with a flick of the reins, rode off, disappearing shortly behind the palisade of Fort Pierre. Tommie failed to reappear for the evening meal, and her father went ashore to dine with the colonel commanding Fort Pierre.

That evening Edward felt very much disgruntled. He had no appetite for the attractive meal that the chef had prepared, and the talk of his fellow passengers struck him as being particularly inane. Bored and finding it increasingly difficult to carry on a conversation, he excused himself early from the table and retired to his cabin. He was greeted by a chattering Robin Hood, whom he silenced curtly.

He tried to read but found he could develop no interest in a magazine article in *Harper's Weekly*. He found two books equally dull.

Craving fresh air, he went outside and began to pace the deck. He saw Captain Harding returning from his supper engagement, and that made him all the more anxious to see Tommie, but she did not appear. Not wanting her to think he was spying on her, however, he retired to his own cabin and locked the door behind him for the night.

His transom and his outer window remained open, however, and unable to sleep, he strained for the sound of Tommie's voice, which would alert him that she'd come back from her engagement. At least once every quarter of an hour, Edward looked at the pocket watch resting on the bedside table and realized that time was almost standing still. Never had he known it to creep by so slowly.

In spite of his repeated efforts to drop off to sleep, he remained wide awake, but he refused to allow himself to look at the watch again.

Eventually, too restless to remain in bed, he got up, put on his dressing gown, and began to pace the confines of his cabin. Suddenly he was electrified by the sound of a woman's laughter, Tommie Harding's laughter.

He stopped pacing at once and, hating himself for eavesdropping, nevertheless strained to pick up her conversation.

She was standing somewhere in the vicinity of the gangplank, talking in low tones with the cavalry officer who had been her evening's escort. The sound of her light, melodious voice mingled with his deeper tones, and from time to time, both of them laughed.

Edward broke into a cold sweat, and although he didn't know it, he clenched his fists tightly. In his mind he saw the captain taking Tommie into his arms and kissing her good night. The kiss was passionate, tender, and prolonged, and a sheet of red flame seemed to envelop Edward.

He struggled for self-control, and by the time he achieved it, the conversation at the gangplank had ceased. All was quiet, and he was forced to assume that Tommie had boarded the ship and gone to bed while the officer had returned to the fort.

At last Edward went back to his own bed, but sleep did not come to him for a long time. He slept poorly for the rest of the night, waking up frequently from dreams of Tommie Harding. Had anyone told him, however, that he was suffering from a case of acute jealousy, he would have vehemently denied the charge.

The threat of attack by the Sioux became as constant as the possibility that the *Big Muddy* would go aground on an underwater sandbar in the Missouri River or that her hull would be punctured by an uprooted tree trunk.

As before, wherever in the wilderness the *Big Muddy* halted for the night, a Sioux warrior appeared shortly before sundown, sitting his pony silently and keeping the ship under surveillance from a distance of several hundred yards. There was little doubt that these braves were Sioux because a look through Captain Harding's binoculars revealed that all of them wore the same distinctive headgear, a series of eagle feathers that trailed down their backs. Although these scouts invariably were armed with old-fashioned rifles, they made no overt gestures against the ship or her company.

Content to let these warriors watch him as long as they made no attempt to attack, Captain Harding left them alone and did not try to drive them from their observation posts. "It's better to know where they are and what they're doing than to engage in guesswork," he told Edward, who was rapidly emerging as his military lieutenant. "I know the Sioux, and they never waste their time. Sooner or later, they're bound to let loose an attack on us. Until then, we can keep watch on them while they're watching us."

Edward and the captain continued to alternate nights on sentry duty, and the young Englishman, with Robin Hood perched on one shoulder, became a familiar sight as he scanned the shore, his rifle close at hand. He had known very little about Indians and their ways when the trip began, but he learned quickly, and he marveled at their patience. Every night a different warrior appeared to keep the ship and her company under observation; the same brave never appeared twice. Their behavior was identical, however: They sat their mounts, unmoving and silent, for hours on end and usually did not vanish into the distant hills until the small hours of the morning.

The earth gradually became flatter as the *Big Muddy* drew closer to the area known as the Great Plains, and Captain Harding predicted that the period of quiet was about to halt abruptly. "We've got to keep our eyes open and be more alert than usual," he said. "I feel it in my bones that the time is fast approaching when the Sioux are going to attack us."

Edward spent a day pondering the matter, and that night he broached the subject to the captain and his daughter at the supper table. "I can't for the life of me see why we should be required to let the Sioux strike the first blow."

Captain Harding looked somewhat bewildered. "There's no valid reason except tradition," he said. "That's the way we've always treated them. I suppose it's been a reluctance to start hostilities when they might be postponed for a time longer."

"But you're sure there will be hostilities?" Edward asked.

"Dead certain," Isaiah Harding replied, and Tommie nodded in corroboration.

"Do I assume correctly that we'll suffer some casualties in the fighting that's to come?" Edward asked.

The captain nodded solemnly. "I'm afraid that's the price that we inevitably have to pay."

"I have an idea," Edward said, "that well might cut our casualties to a minimum, while increasing our chances of winning a major victory."

Captain Harding and Tommie leaned forward in their chairs with interest.

"I propose that we plan a surprise for them," Edward said.

"What kind of a surprise?" Tommie interrupted.

He glanced at her for a moment before he replied. "Suppose, Captain, that you and I stop making ourselves conspicuous every night as sentries. Suppose we keep a hidden watch instead, from the curtained windows of a cabin on a lower deck."

Captain Harding nodded impatiently. "What then?" he demanded.

"I assume," Edward said, "that if the Sioux believe they're no longer being watched, they'll become much bolder far more quickly. It's the same strategy we used with the strangers who were after de Cordova, and I have every reason to believe it will also work with the Indians."

"A reasonable assumption," the captain murmured.

"Actually," Edward went on, "we'll be keeping a very sharp watch on them, and if it's at all possible, we'll time our move as precisely as we can. When we think they're readying an attack—but before they have the chance to strike—we attack first. We hit them with everything we've got. We have a rifle corps prepared, ready, and waiting, and we'll coordinate their fire with that of the cannon you have mounted on the prow, which we'll have filled with scrap metal. That will discourage even the most courageous of warriors."

Captain Harding was lost in thought while he weighed the proposed action. "I don't see where we have anything to lose, and we stand to gain a great deal," he said eventually. "By all means, let's try out your idea."

"I want a part in all this!" Tommie said eagerly.

Edward was annoyed. He was willing to admit that she was exceptionally efficient in doing the work of a man on board the *Big Muddy,* but her desire to participate in active combat with a savage foe was going a step too far. "What can you do?" he asked rudely.

Color rose to Tommie's cheeks, but she replied quietly, "I'm not exactly a stranger to armed combat."

Her father intervened quickly. "Of course you can help out, Tommie," he said flatly. "Even if some of the passengers are passably good marksmen and volunteer their services, along with those of the crew, we're going to need all the help we can get."

She looked pleased and did not glance in the direction of the young Englishman again.

Edward had to admit to himself that the captain's thinking was sound, even though he himself was opposed to Tommie's participation in the coming action.

"I suggest," Isaiah Harding said, "that we assign

various responsibilities right now and that we begin our preparations accordingly. Will you take charge of the riflemen, Mr. Blackstone?"

Edward was pleased by the request. "I'll be honored, sir," he replied.

"Good, that leaves me with the swivel cannon. She's a balky, temperamental little dragon, but I'm familiar with her moods, and I'm probably the only person on board who can handle her properly. So I'll take charge of loading and firing her, while you arrange your rifle corps in any way you see fit, in order to make them effective."

"We'll pass the word to the passengers and crew tonight, asking for volunteers," Tommie said. "This is going to be exciting."

Regarding her sourly, Edward told himself they were neither playing a game nor planning a lark. They were intending to engage in a grim contest of strength with warriors of a savage nation. Much would depend on the outcome of that engagement, including the future of river steamers, which were responsible for carrying the lifeblood of the settlers to every point within reach of the vast Missouri River.

The strategy for dealing with the Sioux was effective from the outset. Captain Harding and Edward Blackstone disappeared from their usual sentry post, and the Indians, after spending evenings cautiously observing the ship, decided that for some reason the captain had abandoned his customary vigilance. Thereafter, the number of warriors who appeared nightly not far from the western bank of the Missouri River multiplied greatly.

By this time Edward's rifle corps consisted of two of the ship's officers, three crew members, and two passengers who were familiar with firearms and had volunteered their services. In addition, he was burdened by the presence of Tommie, who remained enthusiastic about the chore that awaited them. She explained her stand briefly one day when she said that she had spent years on the defensive in relations with the Sioux and that she was looking forward to reversing the situation and taking the initiative at last.

One evening, at least thirty Sioux braves gathered in the distance, and when they edged somewhat closer to the shore, Edward felt certain that they intended to launch their attack at any moment.

"Not yet," Captain Harding said. "They're still building up a head of steam, but they're not ready to launch an assault yet."

"How do you know that?" Edward demanded.

The captain's reply was as blunt as it was surprising. "I don't, really," he said. "I have no information one way or the other that leads me to a conclusion. All I'm going on is my instinct, which dictates the savages are still in a preparatory stage and don't yet intend to launch their assault, at least not tonight." His hunch proved to be right, but late the very next afternoon, after the ship had tied up for the night, the Sioux began to congregate in the largest group they had yet assembled.

"I think the time is growing closer," Captain Harding said, and quietly loaded his little cannon on the ship's prow with scrap metal, making ready for firing.

Edward quickly assembled his sharpshooters, gathering them behind piles of lumber and cargo on the main deck. There, he and his comrades, all of them carrying rifles, settled down to wait, and at Tommie's instigation they were served sandwiches instead of going indoors for supper.

By the time they finished eating, Edward counted at least seventy-five mounted braves only a hundred yards from the shore and saw that the number was still increasing. Concealing himself as best he could from the sight of those on land, he went down to confer with Isaiah Harding in the prow of the ship.

"It looks as though we have no choice in the matter and must start the battle for the sake of our own self-interest," he said.

"I reckon you're right," Captain Harding said, sighing unhappily. "It goes against the grain to start a fight with the savages, but I don't think they're giving us much choice. If we postpone action much longer, we run the risk of being overwhelmed."

"We're ready to move right now," Edward told him.

The older man shook his head. "No," he said, "I think we'll be wise to wait until after nightfall. The operation that we've planned will be most effective after dark."

Edward rejoined his comrades. He was grim and silent, and he found that they were also far from talkative as they waited for the action to begin. The tension mounted steadily.

The atmosphere was unexpectedly relieved by Tommie Harding, who showed a surprising talent for light banter that made her colleagues forget the imminence of battle. Edward was forced to admit to himself that, so far, she was proving herself an asset rather than a liability.

Before the sun even began to set, the bulk of the mounted braves seemed to move even closer to the shore. Edward anxiously looked toward the prow, and Captain Harding, becoming aware of his gaze, sent him a brief signal.

Tommie, kneeling beside him on the deck, interpreted her father's message. "Wait!" she commanded.

Edward grimaced impatiently. If he had been in charge of the operation, he would have launched an attack immediately and would have thrown every resource into it. He could see no reason for delaying the start of the action any longer.

Tommie put a hand on his arm, her expression indicating her sympathy for his stand. A surge of anger welled up within him. She knew nothing about fighting; he neither wanted nor needed her sympathy.

Dusk came, and the mounted Sioux braves maneuvered still closer to the *Big Muddy*. Watching them closely, Edward was convinced that they intended to launch a strike at any moment. Then it occurred to him that they, too, were waiting for dark to fall, and the only question in his mind was whether he and his comrades could strike the first blow.

Tensions continued to build steadily. Passengers and crew members who were not part of the fighting force remained indoors.

By now it had grown so dark that the figures on shore had been reduced to shadows.

Tommie Harding caught sight of a signal from her father that Edward missed. She put a hand lightly on the young Englishman's arm and murmured in a barely audible voice, "You're free to fire whenever you wish."

"Fire at will, gentlemen," Edward called softly, and suiting action to words, he initiated hostilities by taking aim as best he could in the half-light and squeezing the trigger. The reverberation of his shot across the flat prairie marked the start of the battle. The members of his little corps discharged their own weapons, adjusted their sights, and then fired again.

The Sioux, although taken by surprise, were professional warriors and recovered swiftly. Several of their number had been struck in the first volley, and two or three of their horses also had been hit, but they rallied at once with no urging from their chiefs and gave as good as they received.

When Edward emptied the rifle of its round of cartridges, he had no opportunity to reload. His rifle was lifted from his grasp, and Tommie Harding handed him another in the same motion; it was loaded and ready for immediate use.

"Lower your sights a notch," she told him, "and fire several inches more to your left. The ship's movement is causing you to fire slightly to the right; you've got to compensate for that."

He was startled but nevertheless followed her instructions. He was rewarded by a scream of terrible anguish from the shore as one of his shots struck home.

As he fired the last round, Tommie smoothly handed him his own rifle again, which she had reloaded. He noted that she was doing the same thing for the other members of the corps and was not trying to engage in the gunfire herself. Apparently, he thought rather condescendingly, she recognized their marksmanship as superior to her own and was content to reload their spare weapons. He had to admit to himself, however, that Tommie was rendering the group extremely valuable assistance. He had had no idea that she could be so helpful.

The Sioux, disorganized and disoriented, fought back as individuals but appeared incapable of taking concerted action, which was what Edward had hoped when he had thought of his battle plan. Gradually, however, in spite of the heavy losses they were suffering, they regained their equilibrium.

Unable to see their enemies on board the ship clearly, they waited until the flash of a rifle indicated the location of a foe on deck, and then they let loose at the spot, firing their guns or shooting their arrows. But since the members of the rifle corps were well hidden behind piles of firewood and lumber, they continued to remain safe.

The battle gained in tempo and intensity. Edward, peering through the dark night toward the shore, was dismayed, even though he was personally protected from enemy fire. To his surprise the Sioux were gaining, inching ever closer to the steamer. His one mistake had been to miscalculate the number of warriors who would take part in the struggle. The Sioux had gathered at least one hundred fighting men for their purpose, and they were continuing to exert pressure against those on board the steamer, who, in spite of their accurate fire, were badly outnumbered. Edward realized the need to adopt some new tactics, but even though he racked his brain, his mind refused to come up with anything new.

Suddenly, with a bright flash and loud roar, the brass cannon in the bow of the *Big Muddy* obliterated all other sights and sounds. The small cannon, which had been filled with nails and scraps of metal, had been fired by Captain Harding point blank at the Sioux.

The results were devastating: The ranks of the warriors and their ponies were immediately decimated. For once Edward forgot his staid English manners and found himself cheering as lustily as his comrades as the enemy faltered.

As Captain Harding quickly began to reload the cannon, Edward realized that this was a crucial period that should be used to the best possible advantage. Urging his comrades to redouble their rate of fire, he, too, shot repeatedly at the braves.

Somehow Tommie Harding kept pace with the unit, although neither then nor later did Edward know how she managed to do so. She wasted no motion as she filled the empty rifles with new rounds of cartridges and handed them fully loaded back to the men.

To Edward's astonishment she lost neither her poise nor her sense of humor, and her attitude helped the little unit keep up its high spirits as they maintained their steady rate of fire.

The cannon roared a second time, its flash of light illuminating the shore and again taking a deadly toll.

Edward, seeing that the tide of battle was turning in favor of the *Big Muddy*'s crew and passengers, realized what had to be done to bring the fight to a successful conclusion.

"Listen carefully," he told his comrades. "After Captain Harding fires a third round at the enemy, we're going to go ashore and rush the Sioux. We're going to take advantage of their temporary loss of cohesion, and we'll strike down every warrior we can reach. Hold your ground when they begin to retreat, but under no circumstances follow them and under no circumstances cut yourself off from immediate access to the ship. If they draw us any distance from the shore into the wilderness, we'll be lost, so be careful of where you go and don't allow yourselves to fall for the ruse of following them. We're going to take advantage of their retreat to intensify it and make it complete, but we're not going after them. Is there anyone among you who doesn't understand?"

There was a moment's silence, and then a passenger from northern Wyoming, a ranch owner, growled, "Let's go!"

"Wait!" Edward said sternly, and pointed to the prow, where Captain Harding had just begun reloading the brass cannon for the third time.

They watched in fascination as Isaiah Harding once again loaded the cannon and touched a long sulfur match to it. The explosion seemed to rock the entire waterfront. "Let's go, lads," Edward shouted and, leaping to his feet, he lowered the gangplank and sprinted toward the shore. His companions were close behind him, and his blood froze when he recognized Tommie Harding, carrying a rifle, running in her man's attire toward the position occupied by the Sioux. Obviously she had grown weary of assisting the members of the rifles corps and wanted to participate directly in the climactic action of the battle.

There was nothing he could do to prevent her

participation in the advance. All he could do was to ignore Tommie as he called to his comrades, "After them, lads! Keep up a steady fire!" Heeding his own advice, he squeezed the trigger every time a Sioux appeared in his gun's sights.

Showing no fear and not hesitating for an instant, Tommie followed in his wake, relishing every minute of her experience. She was taking part in the battle as a full-fledged fighter, and as she repeatedly pulled the trigger of her rifle, she gave no quarter.

In spite of the fury of the attack, Edward remained conscious of the proximity of the young woman, who was a short distance behind him to his right. Not once did she slow her pace; not once did she falter. She demonstrated courage and skill equal to that of any man in the corps, and she handled herself faultlessly.

The assault of the rifle corps, combined with the deadly cannon fire, took a heavy toll, and the Sioux began to retreat. They did not engage in an ordinary withdrawal, however. Edward was stunned to see that every warrior who was unable to escape from the enemy was put to death on the field of action by his comrades before they drew back. Similarly, any pony that was disabled was shot, too, rather than being left for the white man to take possession of it. Consequently the bank of the river was lined with Sioux and animals that had been killed.

The remnants of the Indian force withdrew from combat smoothly and expertly, the war chiefs extricating their subordinates with great skill and sending them inland out of reach of their foes. Only one fact was certain: The warriors' losses had been appreciable, so heavy that they were unable to continue to fight and had to retreat. Without strong reinforcements to bolster them—and none were available—they were forced to abandon the field and give up the fight.

Therefore, the *Big Muddy* had won a significant victory. As Edward wearily made his way back to the ship, he heard his equally tired companions congratulating Tommie Harding, who was barely able to place one foot before the other.

Edward did not speak until he reached the deck of the steamer. Then he turned to Tommie and said, "If I had my way, I'd spank the daylights out of you for subjecting yourself unnecessarily to danger!"

Her unfeigned laughter floated clearly in the now-silent night air. Edward had the uncomfortable sensation that she was laughing at him.

VII

Rob Martin paid an unexpected visit to Boise, which he had last seen as lieutenant governor of the territory of Idaho. He had combined his work for the Southern Pacific with a personal errand. Going straight to the ranch of Jim and Pamela Randall outside Boise, Rob explained the situation to them over predinner drinks.

"Toby Holt," he said, "wanted to come here himself to attend to this errand, but he couldn't get away from Portland. He's accepted a new assignment from his stepfather, and this responsibility is keeping him with his nose pressed very close to the grindstone."

"Are we permitted to know the nature of his assignment?" Pamela asked.

Rob knew the best way to handle such a situation was to feign ignorance, so he shrugged. "I have no idea," he said apologetically. "Toby is very closemouthed about matters of business, and General Blake is even worse." The Randalls nodded, taking his word.

"In any event," Rob went on, "Stalking Horse is ill. My father, who has been his physician for many years, says that he has an enormously strong constitution, but at his age, you never know what to expect from one day to the next. Toby's decided that White Elk should be near at hand in case Stalking Horse has a flare-up."

"Of course!" Jim said instantly.

Pamela nodded, but her agreement was muted. Her days had been filled by White Elk, and with that support removed from her life, she was afraid she would be tempted to renew her unwise relationship with Randy Savage.

"Toby said to assure you that as soon as Stalking Horse is mending again, we'll return White Elk to you. From what my father indicates, I suspect that will probably be sometime late summer."

"Don't worry about the little fellow coming back to us," Jim said. "The important thing is for Stalking Horse to get well again. Is there anything we can do for him?"

"You're doing plenty," Rob said, "by allowing me to take the boy back to Portland."

Rob lost no time and left with White Elk for Oregon early the following morning. White Elk was deeply concerned over his adopted grandfather's health and was anxious to be reunited with him. At the same time, however, the boy was genuinely sorry to shorten his visit with Pamela, of whom he had become exceptionally fond. He was already adept in the Indian art of concealing his emotions, but nevertheless, tears came to his eyes when he hugged and kissed her good-bye.

As for Pamela, life lost its meaning without the presence of the child. Time seemed to stand still, with each day exactly like the one that preceded it, and after a week she was bored to distraction.

On two afternoons she went into Boise, but the bustling frontier town had little appeal for her. She attended quickly to her errands and then rode back to the ranch, dissatisfied with the way she had spent her day.

Had Jim known of Pamela's state of mind, he might have provided her with some amusement, but she told him nothing, and he was so busy after his winter of inactivity that he failed to take note of her absentminded silences.

He had bought one hundred additional acres of land during the winter, which had to be fenced in with his adjoining property. Cattle had to be moved from one pasture to another for better grazing, and there were calves, born during the winter months, to be branded. The outside of the ranch house and of many auxiliary buildings needed to be painted, and a new well had to be dug. In all, this was his busiest season of the year, so he failed to observe his wife's restlessness and discontent.

Pamela made strenuous efforts to overcome her malaise. She ordered several dozen books from a San Francisco bookseller, and she initiated an ambitious knitting project, a large afghan for her bed. In addition, she forced herself to go outdoors and spend an hour or two in rigorous horseback riding as daily exercise.

One day she was indulging in her morning canter when, in the distance, she caught sight of a number of dismounted ranch hands who were extending the fence that marked the boundaries of the ranch to include some of the newly purchased land. She rode closer in order to see more of what they were doing.

As Pamela drew near, the men removed their hats in a gesture of respect, then replaced them and went on with their work.

Her heart beat faster when she caught sight of Randy Savage at the far end of the group. She had been deliberately avoiding him since the day she had gone too far and had kissed him. Now, however, it was impossible to prevent a confrontation.

Randy retained his composure. "How do, ma'am?" he said as he tipped his broad-brimmed hat.

Pamela returned his greeting with a distant smile but was annoyed with herself when she felt color rising to her cheeks. Not only was she spoiling the effect of indifference that she was trying to create, but she was reacting like a schoolgirl.

Randy busily decided the location of several more postholes and put a number of the men to work digging them. Then he moved closer to Pamela's mount.

"You haven't seen the completion of our work on the bunkhouse, ma'am," he said. "Seeing as how you were directly responsible for the whole project, me and the boys have been anxious to show it off to you."

She no longer cared that her cheeks remained crimson. "I—I've been terribly busy lately," she said lamely.

He accepted her flimsy excuse as though he believed it. "Well, ma'am," he said politely, "anytime you happen to have a few minutes to spare, I'd like very much to show it to you. By the way, the reading and writing room is in constant use, just the way you said it would be."

She felt trapped. "If I can arrange it," she said, "I'll try to stop in after noon dinner today."

"You're welcome there any time, ma'am," he told her earnestly.

At a loss for words, Pamela spurred her horse and rode away quickly, trying without success to put the pending meeting out of her mind.

When Jim joined her for midday dinner, he could talk only of developments in Boise, where he had spent the morning. He had been appointed to an advisory council by the new governor to seek ways and means to promote the territory rapidly, in order that it could achieve statehood at the earliest possible time, and he was enthusiastic about the opportunity.

"I'm sure there'll be enough going on to keep you busy, too," he said.

The vague promise didn't sound very encouraging. "Really?" she asked indifferently.

In his own enthusiasm, Jim failed to note her indifference. "The governor," he said, "is interested in far more than developing agricultural pursuits and starting up industries in Idaho. He's hoping to put on a big cultural campaign as well. That means he wants to encourage things like the theater and music as best he's able on all levels here. I told the governor in so many words that you're exactly the right person to serve on such a commission. He was very interested, and I'm almost positive that you'll be hearing from him."

Here, at last, was something she could do, she thought excitedly. "How soon?" she asked.

He had no idea how thoroughly he would dash her hopes. "I'd guess," he said, "that you ought to be getting a letter from him in the next six to eight months. The commission for agriculture and industry has to take off first, and the commission for transportation needs to be on safe footing before the administration can begin to think in terms of culture."

Within another six months, Pamela reflected, she could die of boredom. "I'm grateful to the governor for thinking of me," she said dutifully, and her mind slid to the approaching meeting in the bunkhouse.

Jim explained that he had to ride back into Boise after dinner, in order to attend the organizational meeting of the commission to which he had been appointed. "Being the first, it will probably be a long meeting because everybody will want to put his pet ideas on record," he said, "but I'll be home by nightfall, you can bet on that. I'm not going to take any risks on the open road after dark, at least not until they've established a better constabulary system than they have at present."

"That's good," Pamela said, realizing that with her husband absent from the ranch for the entire afternoon, she would be free to do whatever she pleased.

After they finished their dinner, Jim immediately rose to his feet and went off into Boise for his meeting. Pamela, meanwhile, mounted the stairs to their second-floor bedchamber and there sat down at her desk, intending to add to a letter that she was writing to Edward

Blackstone, to be sent to St. Louis to await him there. So far she and Jim had heard nothing from him about his search for Millicent.

Now she told her old friend in detail about White Elk being recalled to Oregon because of Stalking Horse's illness, and then, suddenly, she ran out of things to write about. Incapable of concentrating, she gave up her effort. She wandered around the room for a time, absently lowering her neckline by opening the top button on her shirt, and then she sat down in front of her dressing table. There, scarcely aware of what she was doing, she began to fix her hair. Then she began to apply makeup. When she was done, she sat back, examined her reflection critically, and was satisfied.

Horses' hoofs and a wagon's wheels sounded below, and Pamela glanced quickly out the window, seeing several of the ranch hands on horseback or driving the wagon, in which had been piled posts and digging equipment for the building of more fences. She swiftly scanned their ranks and saw that Randy Savage was not among them. She wondered if he was waiting for her in the bunkhouse.

She had no appetite for guessing games and went resolutely to the stairs, then descended, intending to go straight to the bunkhouse. As she drew near to the bottom of the staircase, however, her resolution wavered.

Was she wise to be seeking Randy's company? Definitely not! Was she being indiscreet, flirting with danger because she had nothing better to occupy her time? Brusquely, she told her conscience to stop pestering her. Was the relationship she was subconsciously intending to have with Randy beyond her ability to control? The thought overwhelmed her, and she stopped short, grasping the newel post at the ground-floor level and taking a moment to steady herself.

Regardless of the consequences her actions well might cause, she had to take the risk and relieve her tedium, or she would surely go mad.

She had made up her mind. Not bothering to don an overcoat for the short walk across the yard, she left the main house by the side door and walked quickly to the bunkhouse. As she approached it, the door opened, and there was Randy Savage, standing in the frame to welcome her. It was quite obvious that he'd been waiting for her.

Pamela smiled and extended her hand in greeting.

The young foreman's wooden expression remained unchanged, but he held her hand for a long time. "I'm glad you came," he said bluntly.

"So am I," Pamela replied.

Randy was beet red, and he moved stiffly as he said, "I'll show you the reading and writing room now."

Pamela fell in beside him and was silent as they moved down the long corridor of the bunkhouse. In spite of her urgent desire to keep up a sparkling conversation, she could think of nothing to say.

He, too, was conscious of the heavy silence between them, but he was incapable of relieving it.

At last they came to the library, a room that may have been unique in ranch bunkhouses of the West. At one end of the chamber stood a stone fireplace flanked by small writing tables. The room was filled with easy chairs, and the walls were lined with shelves of books, most of them volumes that Pamela had accumulated in the time she had been in Idaho.

"Here it is," Randy said, halting abruptly.

Pamela looked around her and was enormously pleased. "I think the room looks just wonderful, don't you?"

Randy nodded. "There's two or three of the boys in here just about every night of the week. And blamed near every day, a couple of the boys come in here to write letters. I was dead wrong, and you were absolutely right when you said the boys would get a lot of use out of this place."

Pamela felt a rush of sympathy for him and unconsciously reached out, grasping him by the lower arm. "I take no satisfaction whatever in knowing that I guessed correctly, Randy," she told him. "I felt there was a need for this room, and since I was right, I'm very pleased that that need has been met."

"I've got to hand it to you, Mrs. Randall," he said. "I've been dealing for almost twenty years now with men who work on ranches, but you understand them a blamed sight better than I do."

"I don't know about that," she murmured.

All at once, he planted his feet apart, hooked his thumbs in his belt, and looked at her without flinching. "It makes me wonder sometimes, whether you know what I'm thinking," he said. "And if you do, why you don't tell Mr. Randall to get rid of me right off?"

Pamela knew what he meant, of course, but chose to sidestep the issue. "I'm not a mind reader, Randy," she replied firmly. "And I'm not foolish enough to suggest that my husband discharge the best foreman this side of the Rocky Mountains!"

He stared at her for a moment, and then he chuckled. "Well, now," he said, "you're not slapping my face either, which is a pretty sure sign that you're not reading my mind!"

Once again the color in her face betrayed her. "I'm relieved to say," she told him, "that you're a far better foreman than you are a mind reader, yourself. If you had any idea of the thoughts that are going round and round in my head, you'd run from me as you'd run from someone with the bubonic plague."

Again he chuckled and then suddenly challenged her. "I'm not so sure about that," he said, eyeing her boldly. "Try me!"

Pamela knew beyond all doubt that the time had come to stop playing with fire. Meeting his gaze was too unnerving, so she lowered her eyes becomingly. "It's a lady's privilege," she said, "to keep certain thoughts confidential. Of course, if you were to guess—and guess correctly—I couldn't deny the truth of what you said. Or if you chose to tell me what *you* were thinking, I couldn't very well stop you."

"Here it is then," he said, his face twisting into a pained grimace. "I dream every night of my life about hugging you and kissing you. I go to sleep thinking I'm making love to you, and I wake up all through the night convinced that I'm holding you in my arms. I know you're married and that I don't stand a ghost of a chance with you, but that doesn't stop me from dreaming and wishing!"

His outburst was so unexpected that Pamela was

startled. Her instinctive reaction was to laugh and make light of his declaration, but she knew she could not. He was a serious, intense man, and she knew he meant every word. Moreover, her own thoughts were startlingly similar to his.

The situation had gotten completely out of hand. What to her had started out as a passing interlude, an amusing pastime to while away idle hours, suddenly assumed too great an importance, and she had to deal with the problem immediately before her marriage was severely jeopardized.

Pamela faced him resolutely, not even realizing that what she was doing took integrity and courage on her part. She spoke slowly. "Randy, we've got to stop seeing each other. This whole thing is getting out of control, and we've got to put a stop to it."

Giving him no opportunity to say anything more, she turned on her heel and walked back through the bunkhouse to her own dwelling. She felt greatly relieved, as though a terrible burden had been lifted from her.

Randy stood unmoving, confused by her sudden change of mood. Watching her as she departed, his expression was a blend of defiance and hopelessness.

The course of young, true love was not running smoothly at Fort Vancouver. The trouble began one morning when Cindy Holt went into Portland on a brief shopping trip with her mother while Hank Blake engaged in a fencing match at the fort's armory with Lieutenant Hoskins. It was imperative that Hank keep in trim for the day when he would return to duty at the military academy, and the lieutenant, who had been a champion fencer of his class during his own stay at West Point, was glad of an opportunity to practice with an opponent worthy of him. Hank and the lieutenant had thrust and parried for almost two hours, and both were near exhaustion as they called off their match and sat down on a bench in the armory, mopping their faces with towels.

"You're good, Blake," Hoskins said. "It's no wonder that you're on the varsity team at the academy. I didn't make the team until my senior year."

"I don't know how good you were before all that, sir," Hank told him, "but you've sure made up for lost time." They grinned at each other, and a feeling of mutual comradeship and respect bound them together.

Still, Lieutenant Hoskins enjoyed an advantage other than his military superiority. He knew that Hank, the stepson of General Blake, was secretly engaged to marry Cindy and that the news was not being made public because cadets at the academy did not reveal their intentions to marry until they became first-classmen, or seniors. Hank, however, was totally unaware of Lieutenant Hoskins's strong interest in Cindy. The young officer had not mentioned her name in Hank's presence, her parents had sidestepped trouble by keeping away from the subject, and Cindy herself had carefully avoided mention of Lieutenant Hoskins.

But Eric had no intention of taking advantage of his knowledge. He genuinely liked Hank and discussed with him only what they had in common, their West Point background. "There were many times," Eric Hoskins said, "during my four years at the academy, when I was ready to give up and quit."

"I know what you mean, sir," Hank told him, briskly drying his hair with the towel. "Just about everybody in my class has had the same experience."

"It's a universal feeling among cadets, Blake. When you eventually graduate and the people in the classes ahead of you speak frankly to you because they are now the same rank as you, you'll find out they had identical feelings. The pressures are so great that there are times when you think you can't stand them for another minute."

"When that happens," Hank said, and grinned, "I go out for boxing and for track. I need physical exercise to get rid of the feeling that I'm going to explode."

"I don't know your father all that well," Eric told him, "but from what I've seen of him, I sure don't envy you. It can't be any fun to be the son of a perfectionist two-star general."

"There are easier ways to get along in the world," Hank answered with a slight smile, "but there's nothing I can do about it—and nothing I want to do, really." Thinking of what he might have become had he not been adopted by the Blakes, Hank shook his head. "At the risk of sounding smug, which I'm not, I think that everything in life is working out for the best, and I have no complaints."

Eric reflected that Cindy had made a wise choice. Never had he encountered someone of his generation who was as well balanced as Cadet Henry Blake.

While the two young men chatted, Cindy and her mother arrived home from their shopping expedition. They paused in the front hall of the mansion to look at the basket of mail, which had been brought to the house by General Blake's master sergeant. Eulalia took the letters addressed to her without comment and then went on into another part of the house. Then Cindy began to leaf through the mail that was left in the basket, and suddenly she stopped short when one communication in particular caught her eye. It was a large, square envelope made of expensive stationery, and the writing was in a bold, obviously feminine hand. It was written in purple ink, and when Cindy raised it experimentally to her nostrils, she smelled the very strong odor of perfume.

What bewildered and outraged her was that the letter, which bore a Baltimore postmark, was addressed to Cadet Henry Blake.

Who on earth would be writing such a provocative letter to Hank? Cindy knew no one in Baltimore, and to the best of her knowledge, Hank had never mentioned any girl there.

She dropped the envelope into the basket as though it had a live coal burning in it. It was wrong, she told herself as she flounced off to her own room, to judge Hank prematurely. She owed him the courtesy of waiting until he had an opportunity to explain who had written him the provocative-looking letter. She would not raise the subject with him herself because she might be accused of prying. But if she knew Hank, it would be unnecessary for her to speak a word on the subject; he would tell her everything.

Attired in his academy uniform—that of an officer but without any insignia of rank on the shoulders or elsewhere—Hank arrived home with General Blake shortly thereafter for noon dinner. General Blake was patiently explaining a complicated military matter to his son, and Hank was listening carefully, interrupting occasionally with a question. He seemed totally absorbed.

They continued their discussion even when they sat down in the dining room. Eulalia knew better than to interrupt, and Cindy followed her mother's example. As the housemaid served them the roast beef and potatoes, the two women sat silently at the table, waiting for a change of topic.

At last Lee Blake looked apologetically at his wife and stepdaughter. "I'm terribly sorry, ladies," he said. "We get carried away sometimes, and we appear to be monopolizing the conversation with shop talk. That's enough of it for one mealtime." He immediately began to question them about the morning's shopping.

As they ate, Hank made no mention of the letter. Perhaps, Cindy thought, he was waiting to discuss it with her in private.

The young couple adjourned to the parlor for afterdinner coffee, but Hank still remained silent on the subject. Cindy continued to say nothing, thinking that quite possibly he had not yet seen the letter.

Before long Hank had to go off to the fort's rifle range. He had agreed, as a favor to an instructor, to put on an exhibition of marksmanship to a company of recruits.

Hating herself for being nosy, Cindy nevertheless couldn't restrain herself from going to the front hall and examining the mail basket. It was empty; the provocative letter addressed to Hank had been removed.

She fretted for the rest of the afternoon, telling herself repeatedly not to allow such a trifling matter to build itself into a major incident. She knew she was giving in to an unreasoning sense of jealousy, but she was incapable of controlling her feelings.

Hank did not return until late afternoon. Cindy stayed in her room and did not see him until the family gathered in the parlor before supper. Just before they were called to the dinner table, Cindy excused herself and filled with self-loathing, she nevertheless hurried to the front hall, where she looked in the basket. There, among the pieces of outgoing mail, was a letter in Hank's handwriting, addressed to a Miss Alice Snyder in Baltimore. At least she now knew her rival's name!

So jealous that she was incapable of thinking clearly, Cindy told herself that he had answered the communication he had received with extraordinary promptness—as rapidly as he replied when she herself wrote him at the academy. She was outraged because he apparently had lacked the decency to tell her about this Alice Snyder.

Throughout supper, Cindy was exceptionally silent and withdrawn. Hank had no idea what was troubling her, but after making several futile attempts to draw her into the conversation, he desisted. For whatever her reasons, she was out of sorts; he was sure she would recover in due time.

Certainly he had not mentioned his exchange of letters with Alice Snyder to her. He had been very much annoyed when he had received the communication earlier in the day from her. She was pursuing him blatantly, and his reply to her was brief and blunt: As he had told her when he had last seen her, he was seriously involved with a wonderful girl on the West Coast and saw no point in pursuing a relationship with anyone else.

Having written the letter that would put Alice in her place, Hank promptly dismissed the entire subject from his mind. He had no intention of wasting time, thought, or energy on her again.

Had he known what was going on in Cindy's mind, he would have been shocked. Her suppositions bore no semblance to reality. She would have been equally disturbed had she realized that her conduct was unbecomingly adolescent, that she was allowing her infantile jealousies to get the better of her. In brief, she had created an entire incident out of a supposition.

That made the consequences no less real, however. There was a tangible hurt in the air, and for the first time, a serious rift separated Cindy and Hank. Supper proved to be an ordeal for everyone. Cindy totally ignored Hank, even when he addressed her, and she made it plain that she was having nothing to do with him. After being rebuffed a number of times for no ostensible reason, Hank became silent, his own pride getting the better of him. General and Mrs. Blake were forced to carry the brunt of the table talk, which they managed with aplomb, and at the meal's end when the family adjourned to the parlor for coffee, Cindy disappeared into her own room and did not return.

Eventually Eulalia said, "What's come between you and Cindy, Hank? Not that it's any of my business."

"I don't mind your asking, ma'am," Hank replied, "but I can't answer you. I have no idea what's going on with Cindy."

Lee Blake felt a wave of sympathy for his confused, angry son. "Don't take her attitude to heart, Hank," he said. "Remember, you're dealing with a woman, and with all due respect to your mother, who's unique, other members of her sex sometimes have emotional ups and downs that no mere man can ever fathom. Trying to follow their thinking is like trying to find your way through an uncharted forest."

Eulalia gave her husband a penetrating look. "Thank you, dear, for your kind words about me, though I think you may be speaking a little unfairly about the female sex in general." Having said her piece, she smiled, then turned to Hank. "In due time, Cindy's behavior will become clear. For now, I advise you to hold steady, and eventually the problem—whatever it may be—will straighten itself out."

"That's good advice, ma'am," Hank said, trying to smile. "I'll do my best to follow it." He tried to enliven the atmosphere by discussing his preference for service in the cavalry after his graduation from the military academy, and General Blake picked up the topic eagerly.

"If you maintain your present academic standing until graduation," the general said, "which I fully antici-pate your doing, you'll qualify for service in the Corps of Engineers. Don't be too hasty in turning them down. The entire West is opening up, and the whole country is in a state of transition and growth. There are dams and bridges to build. There are rivers whose courses will be changed. There are whole mountains that will be moved to make way for brand-new roads that will connect metropolitan centers. It's going to be an excit-ing time to be in the corps."

"I'm sure it is, sir," Hank replied politely, and then his jaw jutted forward at a stubborn angle. "All the same, if I have a choice, I'm going to pick the cavalry.

There's nothing like it for pure excitement or for the exercise of military strategy and tactics. Why," he went on, warming to his theme, "just look at the great cavalrymen who served in the recent Civil War. We had nobody in the North to equal Phil Sheridan, and Stonewall Jackson was unique in the Confederacy. Cavalry leaders stand out in every great army of European history, all the way back to antiquity, for that matter—"

Lee Blake raised both hands and interrupted him. "I surrender, Hank," he said, chuckling. "It so happens I agree with you. I've always been partial to the cavalry myself, but I felt it only fair to make you understand that there are magnificent opportunities awaiting you in the engineers. Far more than you will find in the cavalry."

"I'm sure you're right, sir, and I guess I ought to wait and see what happens," Hank told him. "But I lost my heart to the cavalry long before I ever entered the academy."

The general knew it would be a waste of time and effort to persuade him to think seriously about entering the Corps of Engineers, and so he let the subject drop. Hank was so committed that he undoubtedly would become a fine horse soldier, but if forced to serve as an engineer, he would be a mediocre officer at best.

After a time Eulalia and Lee went off to bed, leaving Hank in the parlor reading a book. They mounted the stairs to the second floor, and Eulalia noted that a light was shining under the door of Cindy's room.

The pressure of their feet caused the floorboards to squeak, and as they were about to pass Cindy's door, the oil lamp burning in her room was hastily extinguished.

No, you don't, Eulalia thought, and opened her daughter's door. "Cindy?" she asked tentatively.

"I'm here, Mama," the girl replied in a remote voice.

Eulalia stood in the doorway, waiting for her eyes to adjust to the darkness. At last she made out the figure of her daughter, sitting upright and unmoving in a rocking chair near the window. "Aren't you feeling well, dear?"

"I'm just fine, Mama, thank you," Cindy replied coolly.

"What's wrong, then?"

"Wrong? Not a thing in the world!"

"It isn't at all like you to sit alone in the dark, brooding."

Cindy replied quietly, but there was a strident undertone in her voice. "I just felt like sitting alone and doing some thinking, that's all."

Eulalia did not press the matter. "Very well, dear," she replied, and was silent for some moments. "Are you and Hank having a fight—an argument—over something?"

The girl's light laugh sounded almost convincing. "I can imagine nothing," she said, "that could possibly cause a dispute between Hank and me." She sounded as though the very idea of such a disagreement was vastly amusing.

Eulalia knew better than to press for further information. When Cindy, like her brother, Toby Holt, and her late father, Whip Holt, wanted to keep silent on a subject, wild horses could not drag information from her. "Good night, dear," Eulalia said firmly, and closed the door behind her.

Early the next morning, when she and her husband came downstairs to the dining room for breakfast, with Eulalia dressed in a wrapper and Lee, who had bathed and shaved, dressed in his uniform ready for a full day of work, they were mildly astonished to find Cindy already there. She waved cheerfully, her mood having improved noticeably overnight. She was eating an enormous breakfast that the cook had made, and her parents noted but did not comment on the fact that she was wearing riding breeches and boots.

General Blake held his wife's chair for her, then moved to his own place at the head of the table. He asked the housemaid, who came into the dining room from the kitchen to pour them their coffee, to bring two servings of melon and toast. Then he turned to Cindy and smiled. "I see you're going riding this morning," he said.

"I sure am!" she replied enthusiastically. "It ought to be glorious on the river road at this time of morning. Want to come with me, Papa?"

"I wish I could," he replied regretfully, "but I'm starting things off this morning with a staff meeting in my office, followed by individual conferences with regimental commanders. Toby will be coming across the river for an important business discussion. In all, I'll be very busy today. However," he added, smiling again, "I'll deputize Hank to take my place."

Cindy looked as though she were encountering difficulty in recalling the identity of the person he had just mentioned. "Oh, Hank," she said, and shook her head. "He's sound asleep, I'm sure. Cadets are required to drag themselves out of bed at such ghastly early hours at the academy that when they're on furlough, they need all the sleep they can get. I daresay Hank won't wake up much before noon."

Eulalia loyally leaped to her adopted son's defense. "I'm sure Hank will be disappointed," she said, "when he learns you've gone for a canter without him."

"He'll recover," Cindy said abruptly, her manner indicating that the breach that separated her from Hank had not yet been healed. Then, saluting her parents with her riding crop, she departed.

Lee and Eulalia exchanged a glance.

"Can you interpret for me?" he asked.

She laughed helplessly. "Cindy drove me crazy for weeks," she said, "actually counting the minutes until Hank came home on leave, and now that he's here, she no longer knows that he exists. She's too much for me."

"Me, too." They sipped their coffee in silence.

"I was about Cindy's age," she said, "when my father, my brother, and I joined the first wagon train to Oregon. Tell me honestly—was I as impossible then as Cindy is now?"

Lee exhaled slowly, shaking his head. "You were spoiled and headstrong," he said. "You always knew what you wanted and went after it, but there any resemblance to Cindy stops abruptly." He paused a moment, then continued. "What always impressed me about you and Cathy was that, in spite of your youth, you both had ample common sense, which you unfailingly showed in emergencies—the same common sense that Cathy displayed again and again through the years we were married, and the same quality that you now show so abundantly. I'm afraid that quality is sadly lacking in Cindy's personality."

"I'm afraid it is, too," Eulalia confessed.

"Whether it's a characteristic one acquires gradually as one matures or whether it's an innate quality that is either present or absent in an individual's makeup is something I don't know."

"I don't know either," she said, sighing. "For Cindy's sake—and for Hank's, if they manage to overcome their present difficulties—I hope she acquires common sense, and wisdom, too, as she matures—if she matures."

The sun glistened as it rose above the rushing waters of the Columbia River, and it shone, too, on the palisade road that followed the riverbank to the west, where the great river poured into the Pacific Ocean. Riding at a slow canter on the smooth surface of the road, which had been built by the Army Corps of Engineers, Cindy Holt told herself that she was not only enjoying her freedom but was having a marvelous time. Thinking exclusively in melodramatic terms, she also told herself that she had shaken off the shackles of a relationship with Hank Blake that had threatened to confine and choke her. Now she was truly free, and she intended to make the most of it.

As she rode, she occasionally twisted in her saddle and stared off down the long, winding road. Ultimately her patience was rewarded, and she caught a glimpse of another solitary rider, whom she recognized instantly, heading in the same direction. Smiling archly, almost smugly, she slowed the pace of her mount.

Gradually the other horseman drew nearer, and when he recognized her, he spurred his horse to a gallop and pulled up alongside her. "Good morning," Lieutenant Eric Hoskins said. "You're—alone?" he asked a trifle hesitantly.

"Of course," she replied.

"When I first caught a glimpse of you on the road ahead," Eric said, "I quite naturally assumed that Hank Blake would be riding with you."

"Oh, no," she replied quickly, and then added, "What leads you to such an assumption?"

He glanced at her through narrowed eyes but was unable to determine whether she was playacting or whether she meant what she said.

"Hank," she said distinctly, "is my parents' stepson, so when he comes home on a visit, he quite naturally lives at our house. But we go our separate ways—naturally."

He stared hard at her. What she was saying now was a far cry from her impassioned declaration on New Year's Eve, when she had told him that she was in love with Hank and intended to marry him.

The memory of that earlier occasion swept over her, too, and she knew that some explanation was needed. "When I first mentioned Hank to you," she said loftily, "we imagined ourselves to be in love with each other. That was some months ago, but for all practical purposes, it could have been years. We were adolescents then, and since that time, we've grown up. As we've grown, we've drifted apart. He has his interests, and I have mine. All that we have to bind us together now are the family ties that we'll have as long as we live."

Eric Hoskins couldn't help showing his surprise.

"Best of all," she went on, "we discovered this new relationship when he came home from the military academy on furlough. But there's been no need for us to discuss our amended relationship. He accepts it, as do I, and that's the end of the matter."

"Are you quite certain," he demanded, "that Hank Blake feels as you do, that the romance between you is dead?" Cadet Blake had become his friend, and the lieutenant did not want to interfere in the private life of one whom he regarded as a close colleague.

"Of course I'm sure," she said with finality. "Why, Hank even has a girl back East somewhere, in Baltimore, I think." The memory of the envelope written in purple ink caused her to see red for a moment.

"This certainly does change things," Eric murmured.

Cindy hoped she wouldn't have to be so forward as to ask him for a social engagement. "Would you like to race along the riverfront?" she asked politely. "We can race for a dinner."

He shook his head. "You'll win anyway, so why waste the time? Suppose that you go out for dinner with me this evening, and we'll forget all about racing."

"Done!" she said, her goal accomplished.

That same evening, as the family drifted one by one into the parlor before supper, Cindy failed to put in an appearance. She had told the cook in private that she did not intend to be present for the evening meal, but she made no mention of it to her parents. Thus both of them were mildly surprised when she failed to appear.

"Where is Cindy, do you happen to know?" Eulalia asked her son.

"No, ma'am," Hank replied. "I've scarcely set eyes on her all day, she's been moving around so fast."

"Well, if you'll excuse me for a moment, I'll see what's delaying her." Eulalia rose and went off up the stairs.

There was barely time for Lee to pour a drink for himself and a nonalcoholic beverage for his son before Eulalia returned looking somewhat bewildered.

"Is she all right?" the general asked.

His wife nodded. "Yes, she seems to be just fine." His wife's confusion was mirrored in her tone of voice. "She was sitting at her dressing table just now, primping, and she said that she'd be down in a few minutes."

General Blake shrugged and promptly dismissed Cindy from his mind. He had other, weightier problems to think about.

Hank, however, was deeply concerned, feeling a sense of foreboding that he could not readily identify. All he knew for certain was that Cindy's behavior toward him had been strange for more than twenty-four hours. He suspected that she had no intention of keeping him in the dark forever, that she was leading up to a definitive action of some sort, and he dreaded that moment.

The front doorbell sounded, and he immediately rose to answer the summons. Opening the door, he found Lieutenant Hoskins on the threshold, wearing his dress uniform. "Hello, Eric," he said, mildly surprised.

The young officer appeared genuinely pleased to see him. "How are you, Hank?" he asked. Hank took his uniform cap and cape, hanging them up in the vestibule, and by the time he followed Lieutenant Hoskins into the parlor, the general and Mrs. Blake had recovered from their own surprise.

Lee offered the younger officer a drink, which was readily accepted, and then he sat back in his chair, waiting to learn the reason for this unexpected visit.

Cindy made an entrance, posing on the stair landing. She looked older than her years, due to the fact that she was wearing makeup and her hair was piled high on the crown of her head.

"Hello, Eric," she trilled, and then turned to her parents, her expression apologetic. "Mama, Papa," she said, "I'm terribly sorry, but I just this moment realized that I neglected to tell you I won't be home for supper tonight. Eric has asked me to go to a restaurant in Portland with him."

The Blakes took the belated revelation in their stride, concealing any confusion they may have felt. Eulalia smiled steadily, indicating neither disappointment nor dismay. The general went a step farther and actually murmured, "Splendid! I hope you have a fine evening!"

Hank felt as though he had been punched in his stomach. Fortunately, no one noticed his reaction. His parents were busy concealing their own feelings, and Cindy took great care not to glance in Hank's direction. As for Eric Hoskins, he was so busy looking at Cindy that he failed to take note of anyone else in the room.

The couple departed in a flurry of farewells. Those

whom they left behind sat in silence, listening to the sounds of the carriage receding into the night.

Eulalia glanced uncertainly at her son. His face showed the hurt, bewilderment, and rage.

"What do you know about this engagement?" his mother asked.

"Nothing, ma'am," he replied, his voice inadvertently grating. "As a matter of fact, I didn't know that Eric Hoskins was even acquainted with Cindy until a couple of minutes ago."

The full import of her daughter's date made itself evident to Eulalia. "Oh, dear," she murmured.

General Blake was a firm believer in delving to the bottom of so-called mysteries. "Hank," he demanded, "did you two have a quarrel or a dispute of any sort?"

"No, sir," Hank replied firmly, his jaw jutting forward pugnaciously. "There wasn't one quarrelsome word that passed between us on any subject. If you ask me, Cindy just plain got tired of me and chose this way—a not very subtle way—to let me know it, which is perfectly fine with me!"

Lee looked at his wife and nodded. "Perhaps we were wiser than we realized when we insisted that Cindy keep up an active social life."

"I'm afraid you're right, Lee," Eulalia said. "She's too young to know her own mind. How does all this strike you, Hank?"

"I'm glad I found out where I stand now," Hank said vigorously, "instead of a year from now when we would have announced our betrothal. This way, there's no harm done, and no one is embarrassed."

"You're sure you don't mind?" she persisted.

"Mind? Why should I mind?" Hank's laugh was hard, brittle. "It's a girl's privilege to change her mind about a fellow, and it's his place to accept her decision. And why shouldn't I? There are plenty of other fish in the sea." He thought fleetingly of Alice Snyder and decided he would write to her again to indicate that he had been premature in breaking off his relationship with her.

VIII

Running Bear, riding his spirited pony, made his way swiftly to the rendezvous in the Idaho wilderness near the base of Jersey Mountain. There, on the appointed day, when the new moon was scheduled to appear in the sky, he settled down to await the arrival of Luis de Cordova's aide.

It was late afternoon when Tom Brennan finally reached the rendezvous. He was saddle-sore and weary, having been delayed repeatedly by the spring flooding of rivers caused by the melting of snow in the mountains. Furthermore, he had scant hope for the success of his mission.

When he arrived at the meeting place, he and the Nez Percé went through the interminable ritual of a full Indian greeting, and then to Brennan's infinite relief, he was able to take several long swallows of whiskey from the bottle that he always carried with him in his travels. He did the polite thing and offered the Indian some of the liquor, but Running Bear refused.

Brennan was totally unprepared for what took place next. Running Bear removed a pouch of buffalo hide from his belt, laboriously opened it, and withdrew a fat wad of paper money. Smoothing and flattening it, he counted out for the white man twenty-five dirty, dilapidated one-hundred-dollar bills. The rest of the money General Blake had given him, which served as additional bait, he returned to the buffalo hide pouch.

Brennan was overwhelmed. He fingered each of the bills, holding them one by one up to the sunlight, squinting at them, and even sniffing them. To the best of his ability to judge, they were genuine.

Running Bear waited placidly for him to complete his examination. He knew the money was good because it had been provided to him by the finance officer at Fort Vancouver.

"These are the funds that you have requested," Running Bear said calmly, "which my people have taken from the white men who trespass on our land. Now I shall expect delivery of ten of your magic rifles as soon as possible."

Brennan smiled. Things were working out even better than he could have hoped. The Nez Percé had found the money to pay in full for ten of the new rifles. He thought quickly, telling himself that delivery could be made far more rapidly if the Indians could pick up the weapons closer to their present hiding place in Portland. "If you will come," he said, "to a place of your own choosing in the wilds of the Washington Territory, where other of your people have their villages, you may have delivery of them there."

"Let the arrangements be made as you have directed," Running Bear said. "At the same time, my nation wishes to have additional rifles—all you have available."

Brennan's head swam. There were four hundred stolen rifles in all, and the sum of money involved in such a sale, of which he would get a share, was astronomical. Clearly the Indian had the funds—or had access to the funds—to pay for all the rifles, and Brennan rejoiced. In his wildest flights of fancy he had not anticipated a success this overwhelming. Luis de Cordova would be enormously pleased and would trust him with even bigger missions in the future.

"It is good," he said, "that we are able to do business with each other."

Running Bear looked at him long and hard. "It is very good," he said. "The council of my people has authorized Running Bear to tell you that we will pay for our new order when the total delivery of weapons is made."

"We want to do our best to satisfy you," Brennan said. "How soon do you want this delivery made?"

"As soon as possible!" Running Bear was following Toby Holt's instructions to complete the deal as rapidly as he could without arousing the suspicions of the rifle thieves.

Brennan was equally eager to facilitate the exchange. He was anxious to get as much money as possible from the transaction and to get rid of the incriminating evidence. "There are four hundred rifles in all," Brennan said. "Would it suit your nation's purposes if we delivered all of the rifles at one time? By that I mean those for which you've just now paid me and those for which you will make payment when the final delivery is made."

"It will be best," the young warrior said solemnly, "if we receive all of the weapons at one time."

Brennan was relieved. "That is what we'll arrange, then," he said.

"When will you deliver the total number of weapons?" Running Bear demanded.

Brennan engaged in some rapid mental calculations. It was imperative, he knew, to allow ample time. Great secrecy and care would be required in the transfer of four hundred rifles from the civilized area of Portland to the wilderness of Washington. "Suppose," he said, "that we deliver the rifles to you in ten days. That will give us time to move the weapons at night without calling attention to them."

"Ten days will be good," Running Bear said, reasoning that that would give Toby Holt enough time to prepare to take the guns from the thieves by force.

"Where do you want them delivered?" Brennan asked.

Running Bear had already decided on the area for the rendezvous, one that would suit Toby's purposes, but he pretended he was dreaming up the location on the spot. "In the eastern portion of Washington," he said, "there lies a great basin, or valley, that has thousands of magnificent trees soaring toward the sky. This is a wilderness that is almost totally uninhabited. In the midst of the region, the great Columbia River is joined by the Spokane River. Running Bear proposes that we meet in ten days' time at a small clearing beside that meeting place of the rivers and that the transfer of weapons for money takes place at that location."

"It is agreed," Brennan said, "that the meeting will take place at the location you have picked, ten days from today. We'll meet there one hour after the setting of the sun. Even though no one lives in that area, it is best that the meeting take place at night."

Running Bear rode his horse directly to the Portland area, where he reported to Toby Holt on the arrangements he had made for delivery of the stolen weapons. Toby made plans to meet Running Bear and some additional Nez Percé braves at the appropriate place in the wilderness, twenty-four hours prior to the time for the scheduled rendezvous. As soon as the young Nez Percé departed for his village, where he would first report to the elders of the tribe, then enlist the braves to go back with him to Washington, Toby went to Fort Vancouver for an interview with his stepfather.

"So the thieves have taken the bait," General Blake said.

"It looks like it," Toby replied. "The strategy of sweetening the pot with an immediate down payment for the rifles made them greedy for a much larger sum."

"You're all ready to greet them accordingly, no doubt?" Lee Blake smiled.

Toby shook his head. "That's why I'm here right now, sir. I wanted to discuss the arrangements with you. I don't know how big a band the thieves will employ, but common sense tells me that they're unlikely to use more than a dozen men, at the most. The more men they hire, the more they'll have to split the loot they believe they're going to collect."

"Are you saying that you don't want to meet them with an overwhelming force?" the general asked.

"The fewer effectives I employ," Toby said, "the better I can control them, and thus the battle. I'm hoping to take some of the ringleaders alive because I'm very anxious to learn every aspect of the operation."

"The full facilities of Fort Vancouver are at your disposal," his stepfather said. "Use them in any way you see fit."

"Thank you very much, sir, but as I see it, we're going to enjoy a far greater success with certain civilians I have in mind rather than a military operation. So the help I'll want and need from your force is minimal. I'll come to that in a moment."

"Who do you have in mind?" Lee demanded.

"First of all, Stalking Horse," Toby replied promptly. "He's just recovered from his illness, and though I don't think he's capable of sustaining any protracted periods in the field, there's no one on earth like him for a brief campaign."

"I don't think there's any question of that," the general said.

"Next," Toby said, "I'll want Rob Martin. We've worked together on so many projects over so many years that we know each other's methods of operation intimately. Rob knows without being told what I'll do next, just as I understand what he's going to do before he does it."

"That kind of teamwork can't be taught," the general said a trifle wistfully. "It's the sort of relationship I enjoyed with your father in battle when both of us were young."

"Here's a list of a lieutenant and three sergeants, all of them from the infantry, whom I'll want to borrow from you for a few days. All of them know what they're doing in the wilderness, and all are first-rate shots. They should fit in very well with my little corps of marksmen."

"They'll report to you before you leave the post this afternoon," his stepfather promised.

"Also, Running Bear will be accompanied by some of the Nez Percé, and that should make our force just about complete." Toby hesitated. "There's just one more person I want," he said, "and I seek your personal permission, not your official permission, to recruit him."

"I'm afraid I don't understand."

"As long as he's staying in the area and is available," Toby said, grinning, "I want to avail myself of the services of my adopted brother, Hank Blake. Hank is a positive genius with a rifle. He's the best shot I've ever known, military or civilian. I've had to exert myself on the few occasions when I've engaged in a shooting contest with him, and I've been lucky enough to win those bouts, but I'm not at all sure that I'm in Hank's class."

"I won't argue that point with you," Lee Blake said. "You're each in a class by yourself. The reason I think it would be a good idea to include Hank in your war party is because he's been at loose ends for things to keep him occupied ever since he and Cindy came to a parting of the ways."

"I didn't know they'd broken up," Toby said. "What happened?"

"I don't know," the older man said, "and I'm not sure I'll ever find out. Let's just say it was a case of galloping immaturity, perhaps on both sides."

"Fortunately," Toby said, "Hank's ability to hit a bull's-eye has never depended on his emotional state. I have your permission to speak with him, then?"

"By all means," the general said, "but don't talk to him in your mother's hearing. She's still inclined to think of him as a little boy."

Toby grinned warily. "I know," he said. "I'd accumulated a dozen notches on the butt of my rifle before Mother ever admitted that I'd become an adult. I'll speak to Hank in private."

When he left the army headquarters, Toby went directly to the commander's big house. There he found that his mother was attending a tea at the house of the wife of the colonel who was her husband's deputy chief of staff. Cindy had absented herself, too, as was her new custom, and he found Hank at home alone. Considering himself fortunate, he suggested that Hank accompany him on a walk.

The young cadet agreed, and they strolled together toward the long stretch of woods that adjoined the rifle range and athletic fields.

"I was surprised to hear from the general a little while ago that you and Cindy are moving in opposite directions these days," Toby said.

"If it's all the same to you," Hank said stiffly, "I prefer not to talk about her."

"You bet," Toby said cheerfully. Ever since she had been an adolescent, Toby had known his little sister was going to grow up to win many admirers—and break many hearts.

They walked in silence for some minutes. "When are you due to report back to the academy?" Toby asked.

"Unless something more interesting turns up," Hank answered, "I'm planning on leaving in a few more weeks."

This was just the opening that Toby sought. "I wonder," he said quietly, "if I could interest you in a venture on behalf of the U.S. Army?"

Hank's eyes reflected his surprise, and his expression became animated for the first time in many days.

"The army," Toby said, "wants the mission to be kept secret, so I'm afraid I can't tell you about it unless you agree to serve. I'll just say that the general knows I intend to speak to you, and he approves, if you elect to join forces with me. But please understand you're under no obligation to do so."

"Can you give me any idea—" Hank began.

"I want to be fair to you," Toby told him, "so I can tell you this much. It's possible that this is going to be a cut-and-dried operation that will be over almost before it begins, but I'm inclined to doubt it. I'm more likely to believe that there are going to be plenty of fireworks and that there's going to be a considerable risk involved by everyone who takes part on our side. We're up against a band of hardened criminals. They haven't stopped at murder to gain their ends before now, and I see no reason to think they'd hesitate to kill again."

"Count me in," Hank said. "You referred to our side. Who's on it?"

"You and I, Rob Martin and Stalking Horse, as well as a few army sharpshooters, a Nez Percé warrior named Running Bear, and some of his braves."

"I gather," Hank said, "we're going to use firearms."

"We sure are!" Toby told him. "Now that you've agreed to join us, I can explain the whole mission to you."

Hank's spirits rose, and the feeling of desperation that had enveloped him because of Cindy's strange behavior began to dissipate. "It's enough for me to know," he said with a lilt in his voice, "that you and I are going to go into battle together! I reckon there's nobody who can handle firearms like we do; the battle is half won before it even begins!"

Luis de Cordova was nettled. His plans were not materializing as he had anticipated. Granted that Millicent Randall was providing him with a substantial bonus, earning for him many thousands of dollars of income in return for very little effort on his part. But his major scheme of acquiring the *Big Muddy* and the other remaining ships of the Harding Line was achieving no results, even though he had handed over the documents to Captain Isaiah Harding demanding either a vast sum in cash or the release to him of the large Missouri River steamer.

De Cordova did not know it, but Captain Harding's

spine was stiffened by the advice he received from Edward Blackstone.

"Basic finance," Edward argued, "is the same in every country in the world, Captain. You borrowed ten thousand dollars from Luis de Cordova, and you've more than repaid him. I claim there's no way that you are now indebted to him for another penny, documents alone the amount of fifty thousand dollars. He's tricking you by charging you outrageous interest."

"You're saying, then, that when he comes to me and demands a huge sum of money, I give him nothing?"

Edward nodded. "If I were you," he said distinctly, "I'd reply to de Cordova's demands by tearing his letter into pieces and returning them to him. I'd be damned if I'd pay him one red cent!"

Tommie, who was present during the discussion, nodded emphatically. "That's good!" she said. "Listen to what Mr. Blackstone says, Papa, and take his advice."

"De Cordova has threatened to haul me into court, and I don't know that I can take that risk," Isaiah Harding replied. "It sounds courageous to stand up to the man, but if a court rules against me, I'll lose my ship, and with it, our livelihood. I'll have spent more than forty years on this river in vain."

"It strikes me," Tommie said, "that there comes a time in every situation when it's necessary to take chances. I think such a time has arrived in our relationship with Luis de Cordova. I'll tell you this much, he's been giving me many strange looks lately, and I have a feeling he's going to start pestering me again about marrying him. Well, let me just say that the next time he even *looks* at me funny, I intend to let him know exactly where I stand!"

Her opportunity came two evenings later after supper. One of the passengers, an elderly woman, halted Tommie with a question as she was about to leave the table, and she paused to reply. Therefore, her father, Edward, and others who sat near her were on their way out of the dining room when the incident took place.

Luis de Cordova, gripping Millicent's arm, suddenly came face to face with Tommie.

He released his hold on Millicent, took a small step forward, and murmured something to Tommie, speaking so softly that only she could hear what he said.

Color drained from her face, and then quite suddenly she reddened. Her fury exploded, and she reached out and slapped de Cordova across the face with all the strength she could muster.

"If you ever come near me again," she said clearly, "I'll kill you!"

De Cordova's eyes flashed, and he glared at her menacingly. One hand stole toward the six-shooter he carried in his belt.

Edward, viewing the incident from the far side of the saloon, took no chances and instantly drew his own six-shooter.

It was difficult to determine whether de Cordova was aware of the gesture or whether his own common sense intervened. Regardless of the reason, he recovered his aplomb, and grasping Millicent roughly by the arm, he dragged her from the cabin.

Edward materialized at Tommie's side and guided her into the open, then mounted the stairs with her to the wheelhouse, where he continued to stand near her while her temper simmered. Her father, like Edward, knew better than to comment, and remained silent.

At last she grew calm enough to become articulate. "Thank you very much," she said to Edward, "for your willingness to intervene on my behalf. It was unnecessary, however."

"I thought," Edward said, "that he was intending to brandish his pistol."

"Maybe so," Tommie replied fiercely, "but if he had, I would have knocked it from his hand."

Edward grinned. She could be a formidable opponent, he thought.

Her father, treating the incident lightly, asked in a casual voice, "What was it that de Cordova said to you that so infuriated you?"

"I don't care to repeat his words," Tommie said firmly, "but nobody speaks to me as he did!"

Captain Harding sighed gently. "Well, one thing is sure," he said. "You've cleared the air, Tommie. You've made it plain what we think of him, and I reckon that he'll start to take stronger action against us."

The throbbing of the *Big Muddy*'s engine was felt in every part of the ship as she slowly made her way down the Missouri. The river spread out over an area of more than half a mile, and it was swollen by snow runoff and heavy, late-spring rains. Twisting and churning interminably, the great river was now more treacherous than ever, and the captain had slowed the ship's pace to a crawl. The reason for caution was plain, as Edward Blackstone fully realized. Standing at the prow on the main deck of the vessel, he looked down at the muddy brown waters of the river and marveled at what he saw.

The ship appeared to be moving through a forest of uprooted trees. Some stood right-side up, others were upside down, and still others floated on their sides, but the dangers from all of them were apparent. Their larger branches and sturdy roots formed a sea of spikes on which the *Big Muddy* could founder. It was easy to imagine a catastrophe in which one of the floating dangers would rip through the hull of the ship, making a gash that could permanently cripple the vessel and endanger its passengers.

The uprooted trees did not constitute the only menace to the *Big Muddy*. One of the reasons the river had spread out to such a broad area was because of shifting sandbars, which had gathered in the vicinity. Edward, peering down at the water, had no way of knowing or determining where the underwater sandbars might be located. All he knew was that they were present in large numbers and that, with the uprooted trees, they created serious obstacles to the progress of the *Big Muddy*.

The safety of the ship depended exclusively on Captain Harding, who stood at the wheel, seemingly relaxed and at ease as he navigated down the river. Only because Edward had come to know the captain did he realize that Isaiah Harding was far from relaxed.

The skill that Captain Harding demonstrated was extraordinary, and Edward could scarcely believe his eyes. The *Big Muddy* drifted on the current a few feet to the right and then, under power, slid a short distance to the left, like a dancer on a smooth, slippery floor. Variations of these seemingly simple tactics, repeated endlessly, preserved the steamer from harm.

The captain seemed to have a sixth sense regarding the location of underwater sandbars. As far as Edward could distinguish, nothing on the surface indicated the menace of sandbars, but the captain somehow recognized their presence and deftly managed to sail around them. A score of roosters lounged on the deck waiting for an emergency call from Tommie, who stood at the rail near the spot where Edward had stationed himself, but the call never came. Occasionally a harsh, grinding sound emanated from beneath the ship, indicating that the *Big Muddy* was striking the edge of a sandbar, but at no time did the vessel become beached on one.

Luis de Cordova paid scant attention to the maneuvers of the *Big Muddy*, however. He continued to be jarred by his seeming inability to call the bluff of Isaiah Harding and was now afraid that his financial scheme would not hold up in a court of law. He knew he had to rely on more direct means in order to gain control of the ship.

Pondering the matter from every angle, he was drawing nearer a solution when he was distracted by the *Big Muddy*'s approach to Yankton in the Dakota Territory.

There was a natural demand for a trading center in this region, and that center became Yankton. River steamers, moving up and down the Missouri, carried merchandise for sale and transfer at Yankton, and there was serious talk of extending the railroad to the city in the near future. Indeed, Yankton was one of the busiest ports on the Missouri River. Its population was greater than that of any community in the states of Iowa or Nebraska, which lay to its south, and it was spoken of as the most significant of the growing centers in the West.

Yankton had all the characteristics of a big city: restaurants and huge warehouses; docks along the waterfront lined with ships; and brothels, gambling halls, and saloons to support a community of this size. The streets, which were cobbled, were full of carriages and riders, and even the side streets were choked with pedestrians.

What Yankton lacked was an industrial base. There were virtually no major industries in the area, and consequently, the town was enjoying its greatest boom as a trading center. Never in its earliest history or in the years to come did it have the significance it enjoyed when the river steamer traffic was at its height.

The *Big Muddy* would spend two days and two nights in Yankton, and Luis de Cordova put all other thoughts from his mind as he prepared to make a killing, using Millicent once again as his helpless accomplice. "We're going to work in a couple of hours," he told her, "when we get to the city of Yankton. It's a rich town, so get yourself dressed accordingly. We're going to strike some gold mines in the place." He laughed unpleasantly.

Millicent felt ill. She was tired of being paraded as a sex object in front of scores of strange men. She was weary of being used by Luis to cheat men out of large sums of money. She knew by now that Luis had no intention of marrying her, that he used her sexually only to amuse himself, and that she was valuable to him only because of the great amount of money that she brought to him. There were times when she was tempted to go to her cousin Edward, but then shame overtook her, and she couldn't. Still, she could at least stand up to Luis.

"I—I don't think so," she said faintly.

Luis looked at her in openmouthed astonishment. "What did you say?" he asked incredulously.

Gathering her courage, she reminded herself that she was Millicent Randall, a woman with a glowing reputation as a flutist and as a composer and a person of some consequence, both in Boise and in her native Baltimore. Her voice gathered strength. "I see no reason for me to go ashore in this new town. I've gone with you wherever you've wanted, and I have nothing good to show for it. My pride has been hurt, I've been shamed in front of total strangers, and I've been used as a means of making you large sums of illicit money. I've had to turn my head and close my eyes while you've cheated men out of thousands of dollars at cards, and I won't do it any longer."

He stared at her coldly. "Would you prefer that I let them beat me at cards and take you off for the night?"

"At least that would be honest!" she flared.

Color drained from Luis's face as he stared at her in silence. Then he marched to a cabinet against a wall of their cabin, removed something, and returned a moment later with a silver-handled riding crop grasped in his right hand. Before Millicent could do anything, he ripped off her dress with his left hand and struck her with all his might across the buttocks with the riding crop. She gasped in surprise and pain.

Now that he had launched an attack, he was determined to see it through to the finish, and advancing closer to her, towering over her, he struck her repeatedly across the buttocks and upper thighs.

Millicent was helpless, unable to protect herself. She refrained from crying out because she was ashamed to have others on board the *Big Muddy* realize what was going on. She lacked the physical strength to throw herself at Luis and force him to desist, and there was no place where she could run and hide.

Luis struck her again and again, his arm rising and falling rhythmically, his teeth clenched, his eyes blazing. Gradually his anger dissipated, and when Millicent collapsed on the bed, burying her face in a pillow and sobbing, he desisted, his right arm hanging listlessly at his side.

For some moments there were no sounds in the cabin but those of Luis's labored breathing and Millicent's racking sobs.

At last, he broke the silence. "I hope you've learned your lesson," he said harshly. "When I tell you to do something—do it!"

Somehow Millicent found the inner strength to murmur, "I refuse to dress and make up like a whore so that you can earn money by cheating at cards."

Totally exasperated, Luis lost all self-control. He dropped to one knee on the bed beside her, and twisting one arm hard behind her back, he pushed her face into the bedclothes in order to stifle her screams.

She moaned, kicking and thrashing, but Luis was relentless and did not ease the pressure, maintaining it so long and with such force that she was sure that he had wrenched her arm from its socket.

Eventually, he eased the pressure slightly. "Will you obey me," he demanded, "or must I cripple you for life?"

Her pain was so intense that she capitulated. "All—right," she said, "you win. I'll—do as—you've ordered me—to do." Only then did he release her wrist.

Luis glanced at his pocket watch and smiled in satisfaction. There was still ample time for Millicent to get ready before the ship arrived in Yankton. Nothing was lost by her demonstration of rebellion, and as a matter of fact, he was glad that the incident had occurred. They had cleared the air, and henceforth she would be much easier to manage. All that surprised him, really, was that despite the effects of the drug, which he continued to put in her drinks from time to time, she had refused to do his bidding. Well, now the situation was straightened out, drug or no drug. She would be useful to him in Yankton and again in St. Louis, and thereafter he would let her fate take care of itself. Certainly he did not intend to worry about it.

For the present, he congratulated himself on his temperance. Even when he'd been his angriest, he had not struck her with any blows where they would show. No one in Yankton who saw her and lusted for her would realize that her body was crisscrossed with strap marks and that her wrist and shoulder were black and blue.

When the *Big Muddy* reached Yankton at noon, Millicent and Luis were the first passengers to leave the ship, the woman looking stunning in a cheap, flashy way in a low-necked blouse and a snug-fitting skirt that concealed the marks left by de Cordova's riding crop. Luis, smiling and nodding genially, was a picture of affability, and he had no reason to look otherwise. He had won his first battle—his only battle—with Millicent, and he had no reason to anticipate that she would flout his will again.

Suspecting that the potion he had been surreptitiously giving Millicent was losing its potency, Luis made up his mind to make as much money as he could from her while he still had a hold over her. Therefore, he drove her endlessly, forcing her to go to one gambling establishment after another while he made his customary wagers with the patrons.

Millicent lacked the will to resist; she was emotionally and physically beaten. For hour after hour she played her role like an automaton, smiling at the strange men who ogled her, striking provocative poses for their benefit, and then drifting off to repeat the process for the next group of strangers whom Luis had elected to fleece.

She enjoyed her respite when they stopped for dinner at one of Yankton's gaudier restaurants. Without her knowledge, he gave her yet another dose of the Hungarian potion. Thereafter, she could not refrain from responding when he stroked and petted her, but she came alive without joy, and as soon as he took his hands from her, she lapsed into a half-lethargic state again.

His pockets bursting with thousands of dollars that he had won in his gambling ventures, Luis was in rare spirits when he returned with Millicent late that night. Never before had the woman won him so much money in such a short time. She was so tired, so discouraged, however, that lines of weariness showed in her face, and Luis consequently made no attempt to make love to her.

She climbed into bed, her body movements stiff, thanks to the severe beating she had received hours earlier. She was at least grateful to him for leaving her alone as she dropped off into a deep, melancholy sleep.

When Millicent awakened, sunlight was streaming into the cabin, and she realized that the *Big Muddy* was still tied up at her dock. Slipping into one of the absurdly revealing negligees that Luis insisted she wear, Millicent discovered a container of hot coffee on her dressing table and gratefully sipped it.

She was still drinking it when Luis came into the cabin. His dress was immaculate, as always, and he was in high spirits. "I figured you needed some rest, so I was letting you sleep," he told her cheerfully.

"Thank you," she replied, her manner cold, stiff, and unyielding.

"We're going ashore again today, but you can take your time getting ready," he said. "I've discovered that Captain Harding has gone ashore and is off somewhere attending to business, and I have an important errand that will keep me on board the *Big Muddy* for a time."

She was vaguely curious and waited for him to continue. Luis, however, acted as though he had already said too much and hastily dropped the subject.

"We're going to the best jeweler in Yankton," he told her, putting an arm around her, pulling her close, and kissing her. "I want to buy you the most expensive chunk of jewelry I can find. You deserve it after the money you made me last night, not to mention what you're going to earn today." He continued toward the door and was gone again.

Wondering what his important errand could be on the *Big Muddy*, Millicent began to dress. It was second nature for her by now to wear the outlandish clothes that he had selected for her in Fort Benton, and she dressed and applied makeup absently. Scarcely bothering to study the effects she created in the mirror, Millicent did her best to empty her mind. Experience had taught her that she would best survive the hours in town if she tried not to think about what she was doing.

When she had finished her preparations, Luis had not yet returned for her, and Millicent wondered what was keeping him. Going to the door of the cabin, she opened it partway to determine if she could see any sign of him on board the ship.

To her surprise, she caught a glimpse of him farther down the deck, coming out of a cabin located at the corner. Several seconds passed before it dawned on Millicent that Luis was emerging from Captain Harding's cabin.

Not only that, but he looked like a man who didn't want to be caught coming from a place where he had no business to be. Luis halted along the bulkhead adjacent to the door, flattening himself against it and looking uneasily first to the left and then to the right. Seeing no one, he quickly regained his poise and sauntered off as though he didn't have a care in the world.

Millicent hastily closed the door. Certainly she knew better than to ask Luis what he'd been doing in Captain Harding's cabin. It was best to let the entire subject drop and to bring it up again at some future time, but only if circumstances warranted it.

A moment later, a smiling Luis came into the cabin, obviously pleased with himself. He went directly to the desk in their cabin, and Millicent saw him stuffing something into a cubbyhole. She did not dare to ask him what he was putting away. Instead, she moved to the door, waiting to go ashore. He joined her a moment later. "Let's go," he said. "This is our lucky day!"

His prophecy proved accurate. Carefully guided by Luis's unerring gambling instinct, the couple made a small fortune in wagers with the unwary, the naive, and the foolish. Their success was even greater than that which they had enjoyed the previous day, and Luis kept his promise and bought Millicent a rather gaudy sapphire ring. Then they went to supper, and by the time they finished, Millicent was exhausted. She stumbled as they left the restaurant, and Luis had to catch her arm to prevent her from falling. He took pity on her and returned to the *Big Muddy* with her, not because he felt compassionate, but because he was anxious to protect his investment.

"You're tired," he told her. "I suggest that you go straight to bed and get a decent night's sleep. I'll join you shortly, perhaps in a quarter of an hour, and we'll let our lovemaking wait until we wake up when the ship is under way, tomorrow."

She was grateful for the respite but nevertheless wondered about his intentions. "Thank you," she said, "but where are you going?"

"I have a business matter I've got to attend to first," he replied blithely. In truth, he intended to take a quick stroll about the ship's decks, to see if there was any sign that Captain Harding had discovered what was missing from his cabin.

Millicent made no comment, acting as though it were normal for him to have an errand connected with his business, to be performed after midnight. They parted, with Luis looking after her as she slowly began to move down the outside passageway that led to their cabin.

After giving her a head start, Luis hastened in the other direction. He noticed at once that no light was burning in Captain Harding's sleeping cabin but that the captain was seated in his wheelhouse, poring over some charts that he had acquired in Yankton. *Good*, Luis thought. The old man didn't know anything was amiss and wasn't raising a ruckus. Not that it much mattered. Luis's hold on the captain and his daughter was now much too strong for them to do anything about it.

Meanwhile, as Millicent was making her way rapidly to her cabin, she passed Edward Blackstone's cabin and noted absently that a bright light was plainly visible under the doorjamb. Without thinking, forgetting about any feelings of shame or embarrassment, she tapped softly on the door, her heart beating rapidly. Edward, wearing a heavy silk dressing gown, opened the door and peered out. He was astonished to see his cousin Millicent and was equally surprised by her appearance. She resembled a tart in her overly revealing dress, black net stockings, and shoes with spiked heels. Her makeup was heavy, and deep smudges streaked her face beneath listless eyes. She looked tired and dispirited, years older than her actual age.

He recovered quickly from his surprise. "Millicent!" he exclaimed. "Please come in!"

She shook her head and spoke breathlessly. "I can't," she said. "I don't dare. Luis will be joining me at any moment, and I've got to be in the suite when he arrives, or he'll tear the place apart. I—I just wanted you to know that I realize now I was badly mistaken when I refused your offer of help shortly after we boarded the ship. I want and need your help desperately, and I need to escape from Luis's clutches. Please, in the name of our family relationship, help me."

"I'll do everything in my power to help you, naturally," Edward said, "but why can't you just walk out on this chap, de Cordova?"

Before Edward finished his question, she fled down the passageway and disappeared from sight. A few minutes later he heard slow footsteps that indicated Luis de Cordova was coming down the passageway, and he closed his door.

Pondering his unexpected, brief encounter with his cousin, Edward tried to figure out what to do next. He was at a complete loss. It was obvious to him that the man had a hold over her of some sort, but he had no idea what it might be or how she could overcome it. All he knew was that his cousin needed his help, and he had promised it to her. Now he had to make good on that promise.

Unable to decide on a sensible course of action, Edward made up his mind to wait until morning, when he would tackle the problem anew. Then, in one way or another, he would determine how to proceed and decide what needed to be done in order to rescue Millicent.

The *Big Muddy* sailed at daybreak in order to clear the harbor before the river became crowded with the arrival and departure of many other boats. The throbbing of the ship's steam engine awakened Edward, who dressed quickly and was about so early that he was alone in the dining room at breakfast. He ate quickly and then went up to the wheelhouse, where he found Tommie Harding, who had brought her father a mug of coffee and a large jelly roll from a Yankton baker. The captain ate with one hand and, steering with the other, kept his eyes fixed on the swirling waters of the river below.

"What's on your mind, my friend?" he asked.

Edward told him the story of the previous night's encounter with Millicent. Tommie listened carefully, too, but refrained from comment.

When Edward finished his brief recital, Captain Harding turned to his daughter. "What do you think, Tommie?" he demanded bluntly.

"It's quite apparent," she said, "that de Cordova has a hold of some kind over Miss Randall. He could be blackmailing her in some way—I wouldn't put it past him—or his hold may be financial. If you forgive a purely personal observation, I'd be inclined to guess that his domination is based in some way on a sexual hold. Don't ask me to define it any more closely than that. Perhaps he dominates her out of fear. I wouldn't put it past him to beat her into submission and to make her so terrified of him that she obeys him in all things.

That's just guesswork, however, based on what I know of Luis de Cordova. I can't pretend to understand your cousin at all. But another reason I think there's a sexual factor involved is the blatant way that she advertises her femininity. For someone who was reared as a lady—as you say she was—she certainly makes no attempt to be discreet or modest in her appearance."

"Let's assume," Edward said, "that everything you say is true. I still have no clear idea of what to do, how to act, or how to help her."

"I'm sorry," Tommie said, "but I don't think anyone is capable of advising you. All you can do is learn whatever you can of your cousin's situation, depending on what she's willing to reveal to you, and then to base your judgments accordingly."

Edward thanked her and went off to his own quarters, as confused as before.

Tommie was sorry she hadn't been able to offer him more specific advice, and she was somewhat surprised to find herself thinking of him not only with sympathy but actually with affection. But though her interest in Edward Blackstone was aroused, it did not occur to her that these feelings could be reciprocated. In her opinion, he was too wealthy, too cosmopolitan, too experienced a world traveler to show an interest in a woman who lived on a Missouri River boat and spent the better part of her life in men's clothes, fighting the river and the elements.

She would have been astonished had she known that he treasured her advice and that he regarded her as both wise and shrewd, unusual qualities in a young woman as dynamically attractive as Tommie Harding.

Since first coming to the United States—indeed, in the years that had passed since he had been a subaltern in the Royal Army in India—Edward had found only one other woman as interesting and attractive: Margie White, whom he had met in Boise. But Margie White was living in Boston now, making her own life for herself. Tommie Harding, on the other hand, was right here, very much a part of the present.

After Yankton, the Missouri River flowed through territory that left the frontier far behind. This was still the West, but it was the "tame" West, virtually unrelated to the wilderness lands that lay to the north and the west. The river formed a boundary line between states; to the east lay Iowa and to the west was Nebraska, both of them lands where farms of hundreds of acres were the rule, not the exception. The soil was rich and black, and fields of corn and wheat extended all the way to the horizon in every direction.

Buffalo by the thousand and tens of thousands had roamed these vast plains, but now the land was divided, cut off by the neat fences of man, and the buffalo had been replaced by domesticated animals, chiefly the cow. Where deer and antelope had run freely, chickens and hogs were now confined in pens, and the land itself was yielding bounteous quantities of food to a nation that was growing more rapidly than any other on earth.

These new, rich farmlands were true to their heritage, however, and the spirit of freedom that had prevailed throughout the West was still very much alive here. Men had come to these lands from all parts of Europe, and here they had sunk their roots—roots of liberty, which had been denied them in the old world. There were Scandinavians and Germans, Russians and Austrians, Bohemians and Yugoslavs, men and women from the Low Countries—all of them united in their yearning for freedom, in their desire to create new lives for themselves and for their children as equals under God.

Few Indians were seen in the towns through which the *Big Muddy* now passed. As the tide of civilization rolled westward, combining the best qualities of the New World and the Old, the more primitive communities of the Indians vanished, to be swallowed up and replaced by those of the white men, who were dominant.

Just as the log cabin had been the original symbol of the coming of the immigrant to the American frontier, the schoolhouse and the church were the symbols of the civilization that the newcomers were building. Schools proliferated in the territories and new states, and land-grant universities were springing up everywhere as newcomers sought the right of all Americans to a free education. Houses of worship of every denomination sprang into being, too, and men and women freely exercised their right to worship as they pleased. A new spirit truly was abroad in America, a spirit based on accomplishment.

On this stretch of the Missouri River there was no fear of underwater impediments slowing traffic. The Army Corps of Engineers, in cooperation with the states of the region, was hard at work removing sandbars and uprooted trees. It was no longer necessary to keep a night watch for hostile Indians, and the dangers posed by river bandits decreased dramatically.

Eventually the *Big Muddy* came to Omaha, a meat-packing and agricultural center, a growing city of consequence. Enough of its citizens had come from the older, established communities on the Eastern Seaboard to give Omaha a conservative, staid quality. Brothels and saloons were discreetly located, advertising their wares quietly and catering to a discriminating clientele. The influence of religiously oriented groups was strong in Omaha, and visitors were not encouraged to carry on in public or make exhibitions of themselves.

Luis de Cordova knew well before the *Big Muddy* slipped into her berth on the waterfront that Omaha was not a town in which he could freely advertise the charms of Millicent Randall and earn large sums of money by placing crooked bets on her. Making the best of the situation, he told her as he changed his cravat and waistcoat, prior to going into town, that she should remain on board ship. "You're tired, and you've earned a rest," he said indulgently. "Stay on board the entire time that we're in Omaha and don't even bother to come ashore."

She was grateful for the respite. "Thank you, Luis, but what of you? Are you going into town, regardless?"

Luis nodded. "I have some business affairs to attend to in Omaha," he said, and offered no explanation. Actually, he intended to send telegrams to his attorneys in St. Louis, instructing them to meet the *Big Muddy* when she reached the terminal point of her voyage and to be prepared to take possession of her at that time. His latest plans had been carefully made, and he saw nothing now that would impede his taking charge of the valuable steamer. To the best of his knowledge, the way was clear for him to move, and he intended to act decisively.

A few of the passengers went ashore in Omaha, but the majority, including Millicent, remained on board. She waited until she saw Luis go down the gangplank and engage a carriage to drive him to town. Only then did she make her way to Edward Blackstone's cabin. He had asked Tommie Harding to dine with him at one of Omaha's better hotel-restaurants, and she had accepted, so they were intending to go off in about two hours. Until then, he planned to remain on board.

"Thank goodness you're here, Edward," Millicent said faintly. "I don't know what I'd have done had you gone ashore."

"Sit down, Millicent," he said, indicating the one easy chair in his cabin.

She obediently sank into the chair.

"A few days ago," he said to her sternly, "you asked for my help, but I'm unable to aid you in any way unless I have some idea of what I'm doing. You'll have to tell me more about this fellow, de Cordova, and about his interests, not to mention his hold over you. Only then will I be in a position to assist you."

Millicent nodded slowly. "I know," she said, smiling wanly and shaking her head. "I realize that I was hysterical when I came to you to ask for help and that there's nothing you can do for me unless you know something about Luis's business."

He nodded, telling himself that perhaps the situation would not be as difficult to handle as he had feared.

"The most important thing," Millicent said, "is the

existence of some valuable papers that came into Luis's possession at about the time that we docked in Yankton. I don't know how he got them. I suspect that perhaps he stole them from Captain Harding. I realize that it's a serious matter to make an accusation like that, especially when I can't prove it, but I'm just telling you what I think."

"Go on," he urged her grimly.

"I've watched him," she said, "when he goes to the desk in our cabin. He thinks I'm reading or asleep and has no idea he's being watched. His conduct is always almost exactly the same."

"What do you mean?"

"He keeps some papers in a cubbyhole of the desk," she said. "First, he rummages around and takes out the papers. Then he opens them one by one and actually chuckles and laughs aloud as he looks at them. There's something about them that just delights him, and he rubs his hands together and makes a great fuss over them. Eventually he grows tired of looking at them and ties a string around them and puts them away. That's about all that I know."

"What do you suppose is in those documents that he finds so amusing?"

"If I know Luis, and I've come to know him all too well, those documents concern something that is going to stand him in good stead to the detriment of someone else. He feels he now has an advantage over someone, and he's gloating. I've been petrified to go to the desk myself and look through his papers, in case he has them marked in some way and catches me at it, but I don't need to see them to know what's going on."

"We'll return to the question of those papers," Edward said, "but there are other, more important things that I've got to know in the meantime. How did you happen to meet Luis de Cordova, and what's the nature of his hold over you?"

Millicent turned scarlet, and twisting a tiny lace handkerchief in her hands, she stammered an inaudible reply.

Remaining calm, Edward waited for her to continue.

Finally, Millicent overcame her embarrassment sufficiently to go on with her recital. She related her first meeting with Luis and her subsequent seduction by him, which had opened a whole new world to her. Thereafter, she confessed, she had been putty in his hands. She had allowed him to dress her and make her up extravagantly. She had accompanied him on trips to gambling establishments where he had used her as sex bait while he cheated men at cards, and he had maintained his tight hold over her.

"Why don't you tell him now," Edward demanded, "to go to the devil and walk out on him?"

Millicent spread her hands helplessly. "I can't," she murmured in shame. "You don't realize the strength of the hold that he has over me." Blushing and stammering, she related how she had recently refused to accompany him on one of his gambling expeditions and that he had beaten her severely. "I—I'm afraid of him and ashamed of myself," she murmured. "Also, our—our relationship is so wonderful when we become intimate," she added, in spite of herself. True, she had been relieved on recent occasions when Luis had avoided

239

making love to her, but she couldn't help remembering the other times.

Deeply incensed, Edward wanted to shout that she was spouting rubbish, like a romantic schoolgirl. Instead, he nodded silently, aware of the need to tread lightly until there was an opportunity to straighten out his cousin's delicate feelings. "I'll put the information you've given me together," he said, "and perhaps we can figure out what to do with it." He smiled encouragingly, and Millicent was heartened as she went off to her own quarters.

Edward, however, felt anything but heartened. When he met Tommie Harding a short time later, they took a hired carriage and went into Omaha for supper. Reluctantly Edward related his talk with his cousin, taking care to speak gently as he explained her apparent sexual infatuation with Luis de Cordova.

"I can't pretend to know the significance of these documents that have come into de Cordova's possession," Tommie said. "They could be enormously important, or they could mean nothing. It's useless to speculate."

"Of course," Edward agreed.

"As for her infatuation with him, surely she's old enough and wise enough to overcome her feelings, but I've heard that people don't always behave sensibly when they imagine themselves in love. You say she already sees through de Cordova and recognizes him for what he is, though, so that's a good sign. If you'll just be patient for a little longer, perhaps she'll overcome this spell he seems to exercise over her."

"I hope so," Edward said, and dropped the subject.

Thereafter, he tried to discuss her own life and

future but got no further than her love for life on the Missouri River and her devotion to her father's fleet of riverboats. She appeared to have no interest in leading a normal life, and the idea of marriage and a home somewhere away from the river were apparently furthest from her thoughts. It was remarkable, Edward thought, that such an attractive girl could be so single-minded.

In actuality, Tommie told him what she wanted him to hear rather than what she really felt. She was repeating her usual line to casual acquaintances who were threatening to become serious suitors. Thoroughly aware of her obligations to her father and of her need to help him maintain his fleet, she was determined to keep her personal feelings from intruding.

Believing all that she told him, while wishing he could change her attitude, Edward slowly walked back to the waterfront with her after dinner. It did not occur to him that she might be fooling herself because of what she regarded as her duty to her father.

After the filling meal, they decided to walk back to the dock rather than rent a carriage, and soon they came to the long, low-slung warehouses of the riverfront area. Here the streets were seemingly deserted, as the employees of the various establishments went home at sundown. Now Edward realized that perhaps he would have been wise to have hired a carriage. His and Tommie's very presence in the area would call the attention of any hooligans who might be in the vicinity, and what made them particularly noticeable was that both were well-dressed.

Three roughly clad men stepped into the open

directly ahead, from around the corner of a warehouse. One carried a large club, and the other two held knives in their hands. Indifferent to any risks he would be forced to take, Edward was furious. His carelessness had caused Tommie to be in danger, and he hadn't even taken the sensible precaution of carrying his six-shooters when they had left the *Big Muddy*. Lulled by Omaha's reputation as a staid, conservative community, he had stepped into a trap.

The menacing trio regarded the approaching pair steadily.

"We don't dare turn back," Edward said softly, "because the minute we take flight, they'll be certain to pursue us."

Tommie remained marvelously calm. "What do you suggest we do?"

"There's only one thing we can do," he told her. "We continue to press forward."

She nodded, then asked, "Do you think we can avoid violence?"

He considered the question for a moment and then replied honestly. "To tell you the truth," he said, "I don't think that's possible. In the event that a brawl breaks out, keep walking—rapidly—but under no circumstances break into a run. Continue toward the ship, and I'll try and keep the rogues occupied to give you a chance to get there safely."

In spite of the gravity of their situation, Tommie was amused. "How on earth do you propose to keep three thugs occupied single-handed?"

"It may not be easy," he admitted, shrugging, "but I'll try my best."

They were coming within earshot of the waiting trio, and Edward dropped his right hand into the outer pocket of his suitcoat. A conspicuous bulge promptly appeared, and Tommie was astonished. She had had no idea that he was carrying a gun.

"Remember," he told her in an undertone, "no matter what happens, keep moving!"

As they approached the trio, he suddenly called out in a sharp voice, "Raise your hands high over your heads and drop your weapons on the ground! Do as I say—now! Or I'll drill you full of holes!"

The three ruffians, seeing the bulge in the Englishman's pocket, promptly obeyed. The heavy club fell to the ground, followed by the two knives.

To Edward's extreme annoyance, Tommie Harding paid no attention to his instructions. Rather than continuing to walk rapidly toward the ship, which was tied to the dock about two city blocks away, she halted and picked up the discarded weapons.

Edward became very angry. He had to admit she was courageous, but her bravery was causing unexpected complications, and he didn't know quite how to proceed.

Tommie made matters still worse. She approached the thugs from the rear, and Edward could not see what she was doing. "What are you up to?" he demanded.

There was a strong hint of laughter in her voice as she replied, "I'm using their knives to cut their belts. I don't think they'll be nearly as ferocious when they're in danger of losing their trousers."

By the time she completed her chore, she was laughing aloud.

243

The thieves were in agony. Faced with the possible dilemma of keeping their hands raised above their heads and at the same time preventing their trousers from falling, each man tried to compromise by holding one hand upraised while clutching desperately at his waistband with his other hand.

Edward tried hard to keep his amusement from his voice. "Get out of our sight," he said, "in a hurry! Run for your lives! Now! In ten seconds, I start shooting."

The terrified thieves fled the scene, clutching their trousers as they ran wildly down the street and out of sight at the far corner.

Tommie and Edward exploded in laughter. Tears coming to her eyes, she handed him one of the knives and the heavy club, keeping the other knife for herself.

"You've exposed yourself unnecessarily to great danger," he said severely, after he had composed himself, "because you didn't do as I asked."

"I couldn't," she replied earnestly, laughter dying in her throat. "I couldn't leave you exposed to grave danger while I ran to safety. After all, you had nothing but your cabin key to protect you."

He regarded her sheepishly as he reached into his pocket and withdrew the large metal key that he had pretended was a firearm.

"I'm in your debt," he said simply.

"Nonsense. I'd hate to think what might have happened if you hadn't tried that bluff and playacted so convincingly. You even had *me* fooled for a time."

"I've learned my lesson," Edward told her as they resumed their walk to the ship. "I'll never go anywhere in the United States again without carrying my six-shooters. There's a tremendous difference between so-called conservative communities in Europe and America."

The experience they had undergone together united them, and they unconsciously walked close together as they boarded the *Big Muddy* and began to climb the outdoor staircase that led to the private sleeping quarters on the upper deck.

All at once, Tommie grasped Edward's arm. His instinct told him to say nothing, and he looked in the direction that she indicated.

Millicent Randall stood at the window of a cabin, her face pale. She was frantically gesturing.

As Millicent moved away from the window to allow Tommie and Edward to look in through the narrow opening between the curtains, something soft and light landed on Edward's shoulder, and he grinned. Robin Hood, who had been keeping company with the cook in the ship's galley, was aware of his master's return to the ship and chose to greet him by perching on his shoulder.

The smile faded from Edward's face as he peered in through the window. Inside the cabin that was furnished like a living room, Luis de Cordova was sitting in front of an open rolltop desk. A number of papers had been removed from a cubbyhole in the desk, and Luis was going over them, one by one. He nodded and chuckled as he read.

At last, with a show of reluctance, he began to gather the papers one by one, to tie them together with a string, and to stash them away in the cubbyhole.

His curiosity aroused, Edward knew better than to ask Millicent to steal the papers or to go through them and identify them. She lacked the courage, so he would need to rely on some other method to obtain the information he sought.

Meanwhile, Robin Hood had also been observing de Cordova through the window. Suddenly a daring notion occurred to the Englishman, and without bothering to weigh it, he murmured to the monkey perched on his shoulder, "Do you see the papers in the cubbyhole on the desk, Robin? Look at those papers! Remember them."

The monkey appeared to be staring at the papers; it was possible he would indeed remember them. Wasting no more time, Edward moved off down the deck with Tommie following close behind him. They did not bother to discuss what they had seen, even though both were curious regarding the identity of the papers that had given de Cordova so much pleasure. They bade each other good night, exchanging further thanks for the experience they had shared with the bandits, and Edward went off to his own cabin.

The evening that had just passed was something of a confused jumble in Edward's mind, but one fact stood out clearly: His interest in Tommie Harding was growing. He couldn't get her out of his mind.

Tommie was still on his mind when he awoke the next morning and went to breakfast. The *Big Muddy* was making splendid time as she sailed down the river toward her next port of call, St. Joseph, Missouri.

He was alone at the breakfast table, and so he ate rapidly. He had just finished pouring himself a second cup of coffee when Captain Harding and his daughter came into the dining room. Both appeared to be badly upset, and it was obvious they were not looking for breakfast companions. They came straight to Edward.

The captain lowered his voice and spoke softly in tragic tones. "I've been hit by the worst catastrophe I've known in more than forty years on the river," he said. "The papers that attest to my ownership of the *Big Muddy* are missing! So are the documents that identify me as the owner of the other three vessels of the Harding Line."

His catastrophe was so enormous that at first Edward could not absorb it and stared at him blankly.

"The claims to ownership of riverboats are like paper money or the shares issued by gold and silver mines," Tommie explained. "They're not made out to any individual by name. Possession of such documents is considered adequate legal proof of the ownership of property in every territory and state of the West. Whoever has those papers is the legal owner of Papa's Missouri River fleet."

Edward exchanged a long, hard look with Tommie and knew their thoughts were identical. Both were convinced that Luis de Cordova had stolen the ship's documents, which he was concealing in a cubbyhole in his desk.

"I don't know," Captain Harding said, "what impelled me to look in the little safe that I keep in my sleeping cabin, but look I did this morning, and to my consternation the documents of possession for every ship in my fleet were missing. I know the ownership papers were there when I last checked them in Yankton," the captain said, swallowing hard. "They were at the back of the safe—under an old pile of canceled bills. This morning they were just plain gone! My safe hadn't been cracked and was intact, which means that whoever took the papers used the combination to open the lock and then locked it again after removing the documents. It's all too clever for me!"

Sipping his coffee, Edward pondered at length in silence.

"I'm afraid you and I have the same idea, Edward," Tommie said. "I thought of it the very instant that I heard Papa's news, and it's evident to me that the same thoughts are going through your mind."

"Thinking something and proving it are two entirely different matters," Edward said. "Assuming we're right, as logic indicates, and obtaining sufficient evidence to prove it in court are separate and distinct matters. The best solution of all, obviously, is to regain possession of the documents without further fuss. In that way, a great deal of legal controversy can be avoided. But we're facing a diabolically clever opponent. If we were to march in and demand those papers—even if we were to sneak in and attempt to steal them back from him—we might wind up worse off than we are now. De Cordova would probably figure out a way to have *us* charged with stealing, with breaking and entering. But I think I may already have a plan that will give us the jump on him."

"What do you have in mind, Edward?" Tommie asked.

Edward looked at her, feeling his heart beat a little faster as he saw her lovely, appealing face, her imploring eyes. "Before I tell you," he said, "let me just say that we have to weigh our own position very carefully before we move, and to be sure that the action I'm thinking of taking is the right one. Fortunately, we have a little time before we reach St. Louis, and we've got to take advantage of that interlude to study every possibility and then to act accordingly!"

IX

Pamela Randall's conscience gave her no rest. Despite her earlier resolve to call a halt to her growing interest in Randy Savage, she found that she still relieved the boredom of daily living by engaging in erotic daydreams about him. These imaginings were so real to her that she enjoyed no respite from torment. She continually imagined in these dreams that, in a blaze of emotion and sentiment, she and Randy ran away together. Sometimes this flight was successful, and on other occasions, a posse, organized by her husband, caught up with them.

Either way, they failed to enjoy their experience. If apprehended, they were hauled back to Boise in disgrace by a posse to face a trial for adultery, and to live in shame for the rest of their lives. Happiness continued to elude them, even when they successfully avoided apprehension. Sometimes, in Pamela's dreams, they evaded the posse but lived the rest of their lives in its shadow, forced to take false names and to live in constant fear of betrayal.

Pamela lost weight and could not sleep. She knew that Randy was in much the same situation; a glance at his haggard face told its own story.

By unspoken consent the couple avoided all contact with each other. On days when Jim went into Boise on business or had to absent himself from the ranch for some other reason, Randy became exceptionally busy on the far reaches of the property, repairing fences and otherwise making himself totally inaccessible. He and Pamela became adept at making detours to avoid crossing each other's paths. In all, their situation was as painful as it would have been if they had been in close daily contact with each other.

Unable to tolerate the situation indefinitely, Pamela realized she would have to do something about it. One day, after Jim told her that he had to spend the day attending a cattle auction in Boise, Pamela waited until her husband had ridden off into town, and then she went directly to the bunkhouse in search of the foreman.

She found him as he was about to lead a party of hired hands into the fields for a branding session, and she announced in forthright terms that she found it necessary to confer with him at once. The foreman agreed because he had no choice, and after giving instructions to his subordinates, he followed Pamela into the bunkhouse's reading and writing room.

She seated herself in an easy chair that was slightly too large for her and indicated another chair directly opposite it for him.

"I'd—I'd rather stand, ma'am," he muttered.

"As you please," Pamela said to him bluntly, and looked at him without flinching. "I don't know quite how to go about saying this, other than to remark that you've been avoiding me lately."

Randy began to stammer some excuse, but Pamela interrupted him. "I've also been avoiding you, I know," she said. "We've both behaved very badly, as though we're frightened to death of each other."

"I'm not afraid of you," he said, gaining control of himself. "I'm afraid of me and of what I might do if I allow myself to be around you too much."

"That's well put," Pamela said. "And that's been my fear, too. So now we're going to have to put a stop to this silly infatuation once and for all, and the only way to do that is to talk honestly and get everything out in the open."

He nodded.

"I've been discontented," she continued, "not because I think badly of my husband. On the contrary, I regard him very highly. I realize more clearly than ever what he's doing not only for me but for this entire community. He's a wonderful man."

"He is that," Randy said, "and I haven't wanted to be the one to betray him."

"I haven't been accustomed to ranch life," Pamela said, "so frankly, I've been bored. You've offered me escape from boredom by being interested in me—for whatever your reasons."

"Those reasons are kind of obvious, ma'am," he said, smiling painfully. "You're the best-looking woman who's been in these parts for years; there's none in the area can hold a candle to you." He hesitated, then said in a whisper, "I've wanted you something awful."

"I appreciate those feelings," Pamela said, maintaining her composure, "but I wonder if you recognize their significance. If we were to run off together, I wonder how long you'd keep thinking of me as attractive and glamorous, just as I wonder how long I'd continue to regard you as handsome and dashing."

He was startled by the concept she presented to him. "I—I don't know, ma'am," he said.

"Neither do I," Pamela said, "but I have a dreadful suspicion it wouldn't be terribly long before we'd be tearing at each other's throats. We have too little in common to sustain a long-term relationship."

He looked dubious but said nothing.

"You're American and I'm English," Pamela continued, "but that's only the beginning of the differences between us. I've never had to work a day in my life, and you've known nothing but work since you were a small boy."

"I begin to see what you mean," he interjected.

Determined to drive home the point she was making, she did not stop. "I enjoy reading books, going to the theater, and attending the opera. I doubt if you've ever read a book in your life or sat in the theater. Your idea of a relaxing evening is to drink and play poker with ranch hands, and I can think of nothing that I would find more boring. I could go on indefinitely: what we like and don't like about food and clothing, and our ideas on scores of other subjects. If we ever ran away together, we'd be courting certain catastrophe. We could never admit that we'd been mistaken and go our separate ways. The pressures of public opinion would force us to stay together for the rest of our lives, and I can think of nothing more miserable than spending my entire life with a man to whom I'm temperamentally unsuited."

Randy grimaced. "You sure don't paint a very pretty picture, ma'am," he said.

"That's because the subject of the picture isn't very pretty to contemplate," she replied. "I'm trying to be a realist, but I can't do it alone. This is something that requires both of us to make an effort, and that's why I was so anxious to see you this morning."

"I don't know that I rightly follow what you mean, ma'am," he said.

"Both of us need to recognize that we're heading for trouble," she said. "We've got to acknowledge the fact that our paths lie in separate directions and to act accordingly."

"I reckon I'd better take off and get myself a job somewhere else," he said.

Pamela's jaw jutted forward. "No!" she cried. "That won't do at all. You'd just be running away from the problem. Both of us must stay where we are, accept our situations, and live with them to the best of our abilities."

"It'd be a blame sight easier if I took off somewhere and was never seen in these parts again," Randy protested.

She shook her head. "You're wrong," she said. "It

might seem easier at first if I persuaded my husband to sell this ranch, pull up stakes, and move back to Baltimore. He still owns a town house there, and we'd lead a life similar to what I've known in London, but that wouldn't do at all. I need to prove to myself that I can live successfully and happily with you as a neighbor— rather than as a lover—and I'm sure you have the same needs. Once we stand up to these temptations, we can manage successfully in relations with anything and anyone."

Randy absorbed what she said, nodded and, hitching up his belt, hung his thumbs in its width. "You're a heap smarter than I gave you credit for being, ma'am," he said. "You're right, and we'll tackle this problem your way. Don't worry: If you weaken, I'll be strong, and the same will be true the other way around. Together we're going to beat this problem!"

Pamela extended her hand, and as Randy shook it warmly, a feeling of great relief enveloped her. For the first time in months, she felt safe, secure in the life she had chosen for herself.

Traveling swiftly and inconspicuously through the great, untamed forests of northern Washington, Toby Holt and his small band of associates made their way to the rendezvous in the eastern part of the territory. All of them, from Stalking Horse, the oldest, to Hank Blake, the youngest, wore buckskin shirts and trousers that made them nearly invisible in the sea of trees. They avoided towns on their journey, and they went out of their way not to be seen by people who might recognize Toby and Rob.

When they reached the rendezvous twenty-four hours before the expected arrival of Luis de Cordova's subordinates, who were bringing the stolen army rifles, they found that Running Bear and a group of young Nez Percé warriors had already arrived.

There were twenty braves in the group, which Toby regarded as too large and unwieldy a band to be worked into his plan. However, he realized their presence was necessary because presumably they would be required to take possession of the weapons and move them into Idaho after they paid for them. So he made the best of the situation by arranging with Running Bear to let de Cordova's men see the braves but not to let the thieves come in close contact with them. In the meantime, of course, Toby's men would be completely hidden.

Toby's strategy depended on a lightning attack against the gun runners, conducted with great force and skill. Under no circumstances did Toby want the large band of Nez Percé warriors to come between his men and the robbers during the battle.

He explained the situation in detail to Running Bear, who agreed to keep his braves apart from Tom Brennan and his men at all times. At noon the following day, after the warriors and Toby's unit had shared a meal, they separated.

Toby withdrew deeper into the forest, and there he divided his party into two groups, one of them consisting of the military men, whom he put under the direction of Stalking Horse and Rob, and the other made up of only Hank and him. "When the thieves have camped for the night and are least expecting it," he told Rob and Stalking Horse, "open fire on them and give them as heavy a barrage as you can. You'll have the element of surprise in your favor, but a great deal will also depend on the accuracy of your fire. Keep up a heavy, constant fire to disguise the fact that you're small in numbers, but at the same time make every shot count. I'm relying on your ability to demoralize the enemy."

"What will you and Hank be doing?" Rob demanded.

"We'll keep ourselves as invisible as possible," Toby said, "and we'll pick off the enemy one by one. The longer it takes them to discover our presence the more effective we'll be. If we can destroy or incapacitate enough of them before they realize we're even present in the forest, we'll be that much closer to our goal. I hope to induce them into a state of panic and send any survivors fleeing for their lives."

"You mean you'll let them go?" Rob could not conceal his disappointment.

"By no means," Toby said firmly. "I'm sure none of them is as familiar with the wilderness as Stalking Horse is," Toby replied. "For that matter, I think you and I also have a large edge on them, Rob. So it will be an easy matter to round up the survivors. We'll take them prisoner, and one way or the other, we'll learn from them the mastermind behind this whole plot."

By midafternoon, a series of jolting crashes, echoing ever nearer in the endless forest, heralded the approach of Luis de Cordova's underlings. Peering through the thick foliage, Toby and Hank caught glimpses of a number of workhorses, each of which was pulling a wagon. In these sat large, cumbersome crates, obviously the stolen rifles. Ahead of the horses were two dozen workmen, cursing and sweating as they hacked a path out of the wilderness. Hank gaped at the procession; Toby, until this moment, had not realized the extent of the problems involved in the moving of the stolen merchandise to such a remote spot.

Running Bear appeared unexpectedly in front of the workers, and they, glad of the excuse, promptly stopped felling small trees and hauling away underbrush.

Tom Brennan came forward and conferred at some length with Running Bear. Then his men dragged all the boxes of rifles into one small area, where they piled them one on top of another and established a guard around them. Clearly, Brennan had no intention of releasing the weapons until he received payment in full for them, and Running Bear was under orders to procrastinate on making further payments until morning, by which time the rest of the plan would be in operation.

Following Toby's orders precisely, the braves made no attempt to fraternize with the new arrivals, and de Cordova's underlings were none too anxious to become friendly with the savages. Now that the actual transfer of the weapons was at hand, Brennan was extremely nervous. He knew it was a major federal offense to sell firearms to Indians, and he was afraid that if anything soured the transaction now, he would, at the very least, spend years in a federal penitentiary. As a result he became increasingly apprehensive.

And when Brennan became apprehensive, he drank. As the afternoon wore on, Brennan frequently went off into the underbrush, sometimes approaching close to the place where Toby and Hank were concealed, and then lifted a whiskey bottle to his lips. By the time his followers and the Indians had lighted their separate supper fires several hundred yards apart, he was well on his way toward becoming intoxicated. That was all to the good, Toby thought, because it deprived the enemy of competent leadership. Any minute now Rob would begin the attack.

Toby stole a glance at Hank Blake and was pleased that Hank appeared calm, certain of his own abilities as the hour of crisis drew near.

A sudden burst of gunfire erupted in the sector where Rob Martin's contingent was hidden.

Brennan may have been intoxicated, but the other men reacted in a disciplined manner to the emergency. No one bolted, no one deserted his post, and all held firm.

Rob was following orders precisely. Fire continued to pour from his sector toward the enemy. Meanwhile, Tob dropped to one knee beside Hank, squinted down the length of his barrel, and took aim.

De Cordova's men were so preoccupied with the fury of the fire directed at them from the direction of Rob's contingent that it did not occur to them that there might be other enemies in the field as well. Rising from the ground and blinking at the flashes of fire, one of de Cordova's men sought a target, not realizing that, in the meantime, he left himself vulnerable. Toby promptly put a bullet into his temple.

Enjoying the thrill of combat in which the penalty for a lapse of a single second meant certain death, Hank spotted a target of his own, a marksman who was firing from behind a tree at a sharpshooter in Rob's command. Hank raised his rifle and squeezed the trigger the instant that the butt nestled against his shoulder, and a second foe crumpled to the ground.

Whatever personal disappointments he might be experiencing in his relationship with Cindy, Hank put them completely from his mind. He was now involved in actual army combat for the first time in his life, and he was determined to make a good accounting of himself. This is what the army expected of him, what General Blake and Toby expected of him, and he would not let them down, would not let anything interfere with his duty.

It was not easy to keep count of the number of foes who had fallen. Toby brought down his fair share, easily doing away with as many of the enemy as Hank. He and his young companion were drawing virtually no attention to themselves as they decimated the ranks of the thieves.

Not until the survivors of the enemy force began to withdraw from the field, leaving their booty of stolen rifles behind, did it occur to Toby that his forces had won the day.

The task was not yet completed, however; the messiest stage of the battle, the "mopping up," was still to be accomplished.

Toby left this phase of the operation up to Rob and Stalking Horse. As de Cordova's men withdrew from the field, Rob's force in pursuit of them, they continued to fight courageously, perhaps because they knew that all was lost if they surrendered. They would prefer death to imprisonment.

The enemy was reduced to a small handful by the time that Toby came into the open, with Hank close behind him. The first person he saw was Tom Brennan, who was stretched on the ground, pressing his crumpled-up shirt against a gaping wound in one side.

"Are you the head of this operation?" Toby demanded.

"No," Brennan gasped. "I'm just a hired hand—like all the rest."

"Who is your boss?"

A cough racked Brennan, jolting him severely. "Luis de Cordova," he whispered. "He's on the Missouri, bound for St. Louis."

"Where did you hide the rifles after you stole them?"

In spite of the man's weakness, a sneer lighted his face. "Cemetery," he said huskily. "Luis and I . . . just too smart for you." He reached for the rifle that lay on the ground beside him, but his grasp was too feeble, its weight too great for him to hold, and it slipped from him as he died, the sneer still on his face.

Only three of the robber band survived the battle, and they knew nothing other than the little they'd been told. They received their pay, they followed orders, and they could contribute nothing to the information that Toby had accumulated.

The greatest problem Toby still faced was that of moving the contraband rifles to a civilized place and transferring them into the hands of the authorities. Fortunately, he still had the workhorses and wagons that belonged to the thieves, and his men now loaded the crates of guns back onto the wagons. The three surviving members of the robber band were handcuffed, and they would also be brought back to Portland in the wagons, to be turned over to the authorities.

Toby bid the Nez Percé farewell and gave them his thanks and the thanks of the United States government for their cooperation. Following the instructions of General Blake, Toby told Running Bear to keep the money he had been given as bait for the thieves. "This is your reward for your help in apprehending the thieves," Toby said. "May you and your people on the reservation always flourish."

As he and his braves departed for Idaho, Running Bear said to Toby, Rob, Hank, and the other men, "We are truly brothers. It is a great day when the white man and Indian fight side by side. By fighting together for what is right, we can live in peace together in this great land."

After spending two days in the wilderness, Toby sent one of his sergeants ahead to Fort Vancouver to inform General Blake of the success of the mission. A week later, the victors limped into the fort. General Blake listened to Toby's report in full, then thanked him and the other civilians for the significant roles they had played. He awarded medals to each of the army men who had participated, and saving his stepson for last, he finally summoned Hank to his office.

"Hank," he said, "as you know, since you're officially on leave from the military academy, you haven't been even temporarily attached to the Army of the West for the duration of this assignment."

"I realize that, sir," Hank answered, "but it really

doesn't matter. We got the job done, and that's all that counts."

His stepfather pretended not to hear him. "When you've served in the army as long as I have," the general said, "you learn there are all sorts of ways to skin a cow. I've written a long memorandum on the part you played in the recapturing of the stolen rifles," he said, "and I've included in it the pertinent sections of Colonel Toby Holt's report that relate to you and to your activities. I've requested the superintendent of the academy to include it in your file, and I've taken care to send a copy of the entire matter to the War Department and have called it to the personal attention of the chief of staff."

Hank shook his head, as if to clear it, and swallowed hard.

His stepfather tried not to smile but didn't quite succeed. "General Sherman," he said, "has expressed interest in your development from time to time, and I'm sure that he'll be quite eager to read this commendation."

Only one reply was possible. "Thank you, sir," Hank said. After saluting, he turned smartly on his heel and left the office. There was a time he would have been thrilled by the knowledge that the commendation could be a valuable asset to his career. Now that he and Cindy Holt had gone their separate ways, however, he found himself taking little joy in anything. He had hoped to get over his hurt during the mission in the Washington mountains, but he had not, and he actually no longer cared whether he won a favorable assignment upon graduation.

Lee Blake admired his self-control, without understanding the reasons for it. Then, putting Hank out of his mind, he returned to the urgent business at hand. Toby told him that the man responsible for the theft of weapons, one Luis de Cordova, was on board a river steamer called the *Big Muddy*, which was due to reach its destination, St. Louis, in less than a week. Thus, one major task remained. The general wrote a telegram, which he classified as secret and, summoning the head of his signal corps, sent the communication to the commandant of the U.S. Army post in St. Louis.

The message directed the commandant, by order of the commanding general of the West, to arrest Luis de Cordova on his arrival there on charges of stealing government property and subsequently reselling it to Indians. De Cordova was to be returned to Fort Vancouver without delay under heavy military escort.

The day of reckoning with Luis de Cordova was at hand, and Edward Blackstone made his final arrangements with care. Confiding only in Tommie Harding, he refined and altered his plans, and only when he won her approval did he agree that the operation was now set.

The *Big Muddy* put into Independence, Missouri. There in the town known as "the gateway to the West," most warehouses, docks, and retail establishments were owned by Sam Brentwood, who had supplied countless wagon trains that had traveled from Independence to either California or Oregon.

Tommie quietly went ashore in Independence to make a minor purchase at Edward's direction, but he remained on board the ship during the few hours that the vessel was in port. The town's reputation was such that Luis de Cordova made no attempt to go ashore with Millicent Randall. Independence had its fair share of saloons, but thanks to Sam Brentwood's influence, the police department was incorruptible, and the few gambling halls and brothels in operation there were closely watched.

Late that afternoon the *Big Muddy* resumed her voyage, sailing eastward toward St. Louis. That evening, Edward awaited his opportunity, then accosted de Cordova as he and Millicent were heading into the saloon for supper.

"De Cordova," Edward said to him, as the couple neared the dining room, "I've been thinking over the offer you made to me on this voyage. Are you still willing to bet in games of high-low against possession of this young lady's appreciable charms for an overnight period? And are you willing to increase the stakes to two thousand dollars a throw?"

An expression of astonishment appeared on Millicent's face, but de Cordova's smug smile indicated that he had reasoned all along that this unpleasant stranger would sooner or later succumb to the woman's quite obvious charms. As to the significantly higher stakes, de Cordova would be delighted to take as much money as he could from the foolish Englishman.

Edward allowed his gaze to flicker toward Millicent, and the stern look in his eyes conveyed the message to her that she was not to reveal that they were cousins.

She had an idea of what he had in mind, and she immediately played up to the image he was trying to create, flirting with him, batting her eyes, and giving him the benefit of a bewitching smile. Looking almost foolishly enamored, Edward blinked at her.

"I'm available for a friendly game of high-low at your convenience," de Cordova said. "Would you care to try your luck with the cards after supper tonight?"

"I'm tired tonight. I prefer tomorrow afternoon, after noon dinner," Edward replied, having worked with Tommie to settle the precise time of day that would be best for what he had in mind.

"Tomorrow afternoon it will be, then," de Cordova replied with a courtly bow and held out his arm to Millicent. As she took it and swept on to the supper table, she favored Edward with a dazzling smile.

At supper that night and in the hour following the meal, Edward was warned by a number of passengers not to be taken in by de Cordova's ruses. By now, all of them had become familiar with de Cordova's card game, and although they also suspected him of cheating, the only thing they could do about it was to refuse to play with him anymore. Edward, however, had his own part to play and cast aside the warnings as though they were of no consequence to him.

The next day the skies were clear, and the early summer weather was hot in the Missouri farmlands. After noon dinner, Edward found an excuse to pay a brief visit to his cabin before engaging in the card game with de Cordova. Going slightly out of his way, he was pleased to see that the weather was sufficiently warm that de Cordova had left each window of his cabin open by the better part of a foot.

Uncertain of what might develop, Edward took his

derringer, and after making sure it was loaded, he slipped it under his right sleeve. This particular derringer was a strange little weapon. It was a pistol with two barrels, each of which was fired separately. A half-squeeze of the trigger fired a bullet out of one barrel, and the firing of the other chamber required pulling the trigger the rest of the way. The weapon, concealed beneath his coat sleeve in a special harness that fitted over his right arm, was ready for instant use once he dropped it into his hand. It had done him yeoman's service in the past, and it made him feel much more at ease.

When he left his cabin, he was hastily joined by Tommie Harding, who accompanied him as he went down the stairs to the main saloon. She looked at him with a tight, worried smile.

When they reached the large saloon, the dinner dishes and tablecloth had already been removed from the tables. A half-dozen male passengers were gathered quietly, their curiosity aroused, and all of them were glancing in the direction of Millicent Randall.

It was small wonder that they stared at her. Her appearance was bizarre, outlandish, a caricature of sexual attraction. She was wearing so much makeup that she seemed incapable of assuming normal expressions, and only her eyes, heavy with kohl and mascara, reflected her deep concern. She was wearing a thin silk blouse, through which one could see the outline of her breasts and nipples, and she teetered on extremely high-heeled shoes. Her skirt was slit high on one side, revealing her legs clad in provocative black net stockings. A broad girdle-belt held in her waist so tightly that it seemed to threaten her ability to breathe.

She smiled tentatively at Edward when he entered the saloon, and there was a faint glimmer of hope in her eyes.

"Good afternoon," Edward said crisply.

Luis de Cordova, who was already seated at the table, with Millicent dutifully standing beside him, barely acknowledged the greeting by nodding stiffly. "You understand the rules, which are quite simple," de Cordova said.

"Indeed," Edward replied, enumerating on his fingers. "We each draw one card at a time. Any time you draw, and your draw is higher than mine, I owe you the sum of two thousand dollars. The very first time that I draw a higher card than you do, I take possession of the lady until tomorrow morning. Is that correct?"

De Cordova favored him with a cold smile. "Correct," he said. He waved the other man to a chair and, taking a deck of cards from his pocket, began to shuffle them expertly.

"That won't be necessary," Edward said, and nodded to Tommie. She took a brand-new deck of cards from her pocket and passed it to the audience. It was wrapped and still had the seal of the manufacturer on the box.

"I took the precaution," Edward explained pleasantly, "of getting a new deck of cards for the occasion. Miss Harding picked them up for me in Independence. As you can see, the deck has never been opened and is completely new."

Holding up his hands in a gesture used by card dealers to demonstrate that they were concealing nothing, Edward unwrapped the deck of cards and began to shuffle them. Occasionally his left hand would rise high into the air above his right, and the cards would flutter down in a shower, only to be quickly scooped up by his right hand. It was obvious to everyone present that he was no novice at card playing.

Luis de Cordova stared at him aghast, and then his dark eyes narrowed suspiciously. It occurred to him that he had been drawn into a match beyond his depth by someone who was far superior to him.

Edward smiled at him blandly. "You may care to examine these for yourself in order to be assured that they're legitimate and that no one has tampered with them." He dropped the deck in front of de Cordova.

Already at a disadvantage, de Cordova had no choice and examined the backs of the cards. He could find nothing amiss.

While he did, Edward busied himself, removing an elegant cigar case of ostrich leather from an inner coat pocket and taking a long, thin cigar from it. After clipping the end with a monogrammed silver clipper that he took from a waistcoat pocket, he lighted it with a matching miniature sterling silver tinderbox. Then, jauntily placing the cigar between his teeth in one corner of his mouth, he smiled coldly at de Cordova, simultaneously blowing a thick cloud of blue smoke that obscured his face for a moment. "I trust you're satisfied with these," he said, scooping up the deck.

De Cordova, falling behind in the battle of wits before the contest even began, nodded mechanically.

But his mind was busy at work, thinking how he could put an end to this unpleasant Englishman. He began to think of ways he could make it appear Blackstone was cheating; that should be easy enough for someone who knew his cards as he did. Then he'd see to it that Edward was disgraced in front of all the passengers on board. And if the Englishman didn't like de Cordova's accusations, he could challenge him to a duel. That, too, would suit Luis's purposes. He knew many ways to ensure he never lost, not only in cards but also in gun duels.

Edward resumed shuffling, deftly and swiftly, puffing again on the thin cigar. He casually glanced at Tommie Harding, who was standing beside him.

She reacted as though they had a prearranged signal. Moving quietly, without speaking a word to anyone, she made her way to the door and vanished onto the deck.

If anyone thought it strange that she was leaving before the competition actually began, no one mentioned it. In fact, Luis de Cordova and the male passengers who were witnessing the contest did not seem to be aware of her departure. Only Millicent looked in the other woman's direction and then glanced curiously at Edward. He looked innocent, but she knew him well enough to be convinced that he was playacting now and that Tommie Harding was acting in connection with a plan that had been carefully worked out.

Edward finished shuffling with a flourish, then placed the deck in front of the startled Millicent. "Cut!" he commanded.

Unaware of his specific purpose, but realizing that

he had decided she was to play a more active role than usual in the drama that was to follow, she obeyed his instructions.

"You've watched this game being played sufficiently often," Edward said pleasantly, "that you must be thoroughly familiar with the simple rules by now, so I'll ask you, young lady, to be good enough to draw for both of us."

De Cordova opened his mouth to protest but realized how bad he would look if he opposed a drawing by the woman who was the object of his wager. Therefore, he clamped his jaw shut again. In time he would get even.

Edward's face vanished for the moment in another cloud of blue cigar smoke.

Millicent's hand trembled as she reached out to the deck and drew a card. A groan rose from the spectators when they saw it was a four of spades. She looked apologetic as she placed it in front of Edward.

Scarcely able to breathe, Millicent drew a second time, her hand shaking so violently that she seemed almost certain to drop the card. She did not, however, and the terrible disappointment that was mirrored in her eyes told its own story when she placed the six of diamonds in front of de Cordova.

The spectators, who were rooting for Edward, moaned quietly. Luis de Cordova, however, could not hide his elation. His face creased in a huge smile, he reached up for Millicent, pulled her down, and kissed her soundly. In spite of her disgust with him, she acted as if she enjoyed the kiss.

Edward Blackstone was inscrutable. Looking as

though he didn't care whether he won or lost, he reached into his pocket and removed a wallet, made of the same ostrich leather as his cigar case. Then he counted out two one-thousand-dollar bills, which he withdrew and threw on the table in front of de Cordova. "You've won first blood, sir," he announced, laughing.

De Cordova was enormously pleased with himself. "You want a chance to get even, I take it?"

"Of course," Edward replied carelessly. "That's half the pleasure of this particular game." He looked toward Millicent and nodded, giving her the signal to draw again.

She was so much under de Cordova's rule, however, that she made no move until he had put away the money and gave his own approval with a curt nod.

The spectators stirred uneasily.

Edward removed his cigar from his mouth, flicked an ash into his ashtray, and winked solemnly at Millicent. The gesture took her completely by surprise, and she seemed to freeze.

"This time," Edward said casually, "suppose you reverse the procedure. Draw first for Mr. de Cordova and then draw for me. Is that satisfactory?"

Luis de Cordova, reasonably sure now that the new deck of cards had not been tampered with in any way, gestured expansively. "Have it your way, Blackstone," he said. "It doesn't matter in the least which of us draws first. The results will always be the same."

Edward smiled at him blandly but took notice of the man's cocky, impudent manner. Millicent, meanwhile, was badly upset by de Cordova's attitude. She had seen so much of his chicanery over such a long period of time that she felt certain he had found some way to adjust the deck of cards to suit his own purposes. She wanted to warn Edward but was afraid to say anything in de Cordova's presence. Her hands trembled as she drew a card and placed it in front of de Cordova.

The spectators murmured; the card was the king of hearts. De Cordova smiled slightly but made no comment. Edward's expression remained unchanged, and he was still genial and unconcerned.

Millicent drew again, then gasped in horror. She had drawn the jack of hearts for Edward.

De Cordova made no attempt to conceal his delight. He jumped to his feet, grasped Millicent, and kissed her soundly again. Then he went to a nearby sideboard, where he poured himself a strong drink of whiskey. "Can I get you some refreshments, Blackstone?" he asked cordially.

Still reacting genially, Edward shook his head. "No, thank you," he said, as he counted out two more crisp one-thousand-dollar bills. "If you're willing, I suggest we make this friendly little game more interesting."

De Cordova's smile faded. "What do you have in mind?" he demanded.

"You've already won four thousand dollars from me," Edward explained mildly. "I'm willing to double that sum on the results of the next draw. In other words, if I lose, I'll pay you eight thousand on the single draw."

A gleam appeared in de Cordova's eyes. "What must I bet?"

"To be fair," Edward said carefully, "you, too, will

273

double your bet. If I should win, I'll take possession of the young lady for a period of two nights."

The bet was very much to de Cordova's liking. Perhaps he should have become more wary, but he was too elated with his success to do so. He forgot all about caution, all about his plans to get even with Edward, and cried, "It's a deal!" He extended his hand across the table.

Forced to clasp it, Edward concealed his distaste. He was not surprised when the man's hand turned out to be damp and clammy.

The incredible bet caused Millicent to tremble. Certain that her future literally rested on the turn of a card, she braced herself by pressing against the table; then she drew a card, which she put down in front of de Cordova. It was the ten of diamonds.

He had obtained a solid card in the draw, and the spectators murmured to each other. They realized that his position could not be defeated easily. De Cordova was aware, too, that the odds were in his favor, and he smiled smugly. Edward, however, merely puffed on his cigar. His face once again was momentarily hidden in a cloud of blue smoke.

Millicent knew that her next draw was critical. She sucked in her breath, bit her lower lip, and reached for the deck of cards.

Tommie Harding made her way straight to the door of the cabin occupied by Edward Blackstone and opened it with her passkey.

"Come along, Robin," she said to the monkey, who

had been drowsing, curled up on a chair. "We have work to do."

The little monkey began to chatter and hopped up onto her shoulder.

"Shhh!" she said, scolding. "We've got to be very quiet today. We're going to be doing some work that we don't want anyone to know about."

Closing and locking the door behind her, she made her way down the deck to outside Luis de Cordova's cabin. There she went to the open window. Making certain that no one else was within sight, Tommie addressed the monkey again.

"You see the desk over there?" she asked the monkey gently, pointing toward the rolltop desk that stood opposite the window. "Look at it carefully. There, in the right-hand cubbyhole, you'll see a number of papers." She took a folded sheet of paper from a pocket in her trousers and showed it to the monkey. "Those papers in the cubbyhole are very necessary. I must have them. I want them. Will you get them for me, please?"

Robin Hood jumped up and down, chattering away as he stared at the desk, seeming to remember the previous time he had seen it. But he made no move to go inside the cabin.

Tommie was becoming frantic. Everything in the plan that she and Edward had worked out with such meticulous care depended on the help and cooperation of the little monkey, who would be able to retrieve the papers without the Hardings or Edward Blackstone being implicated in any way if Luis de Cordova attempted to press charges of robbery or trespassing. De Cordova was diabolical enough to have booby-trapped the door or to have devised other methods to catch human trespassers; thus, they had made the monkey an integral part of the plan. Edward had believed the animal would readily go to the desk and imitate what he had seen de Cordova doing with the papers the last time, but it now appeared Robin Hood didn't understand.

"Please, Robin," Tommie begged, realizing the absurdity of having to plead with an animal.

Again she took the paper from her pocket and waved it in front of the little monkey. He seemed to be paying no attention to it, only to the desk in the cabin.

Inadvertently Tommie folded the paper, and it crackled. The sound of crumpling paper immediately caught the monkey's attention. He listened intently and then gave a high-pitched squeak.

In desperation Tommie continued to crush and crumple the paper. "Get the documents, Robin," she murmured. "There's a good boy. Please get them quickly, and I beg you, do be quiet!"

The monkey could not have understood her, but in part, at least, he behaved as though he did. Snatching the sheet of folded paper from her, he proceeded to crumple it further and threw it onto the floor inside the window. Then, pleased with what he had done, he leaped into the room and bounded to the desk, where he began to reach for the pile of documents in the cubbyhole in the upper right-hand corner.

Not daring to speak again, Tommie held her breath.

The monkey reached into the cubbyhole, grunting as he pulled and tugged, and at last he pulled a package of papers free. Tommie breathed more freely when she saw that the pack had been securely tied together.

The monkey moved to the center of the desk, where he tried in vain to free some of the pages of the documents from the bundle in order to make the same crumpling noise that he had made previously. Afraid she might distract him, Tommie said nothing, but she prayed silently that he would bring her the documents.

As though responding to her prayer, the monkey moved slowly across the desk carrying the package of papers, which was so bulky that he had trouble managing it. Then he leaped to the windowsill, and an infinitely relieved Tommie reached for the bundle and took it from him.

Robin Hood was outraged and began to protest loudly. Paying no attention to the animal's objections, she started down the deck. Still protesting, the monkey jumped to her shoulder.

Ignoring Robin Hood's chattering, Tommie hurried down the deck to her own cabin. Not until she was safely inside, still clutching the packet of documents, did she again breathe easily.

Only then could she give Robin Hood the attention that he deserved. Praising him lavishly, she fed him a handful of roasted peanuts that she had obtained from the cook. Then, when the monkey had once again become quiet, she undid the string on the precious pack of documents and began to examine them.

Luis de Cordova, his eyes registering great shock, stared ashen-faced at the card that Millicent had turned up and placed before Edward.

Not only was it an ace, beating by far the ten of

diamonds that Millicent had drawn for him, but the fact that it was the ace of spades—the first-ranking card in the entire deck—seemed of great significance to him.

Millicent herself felt only infinite relief. All she could think was that she had been transferred from the possession of de Cordova into the custody of Edward, and that temporarily, at least, she would be safe from harm.

The spectators, unaware of the relationship between Millicent and Edward, were highly pleased to see de Cordova finally meet his match.

Edward revealed no joy, no sense of being satisfied with his victory. There was no way of telling what he felt. Nevertheless, he was keenly alert to any trouble that might arise. He well realized that a man of Luis de Cordova's temperament would not lightly accept a defeat of this magnitude without putting up some struggle or protest. Therefore, he sat with his hands resting on the edge of the table, bracing himself for any eventuality.

He was not mistaken in his analysis. De Cordova's shock turned to anger; his face reddened, and his eyes glazed. "Damn you, Blackstone!" he shouted viciously. "You've cheated me! This has been a clever plot to swindle me! Not only have you pulled some sleight of hand with the cards, but Millicent was in cahoots with you, and you've made all sorts of promises to her if she'd cooperate with you, which she's done. This so-called victory of yours doesn't count!"

One of the spectators felt compelled to intervene. "I'm sorry to have to tell you this, Mr. de Cordova," he said, "but this match was waged completely fairly. All of us can testify to that." His companions nodded and murmured their agreement.

De Cordova refused to listen and became even wilder. He had lost all his poise, all his self-control. "You're all parties to a conspiracy against me!" he shouted. "Every last one of you is working with the others to cheat me!"

Millicent uttered a muffled scream when she saw de Cordova reach into his belt for a double-edged knife, which he drew and held at chest height. "You're not going to get away with this, Blackstone!" Luis de Cordova cried.

Edward wanted to make certain that the onlookers realized he was being threatened. If necessary, he could call on them as witnesses in a court of law.

"I don't take kindly to threats, de Cordova," he said. "Be good enough to put that menacing weapon away. It's a sharp knife, and someone could be hurt with it."

Laughing wildly, de Cordova just sat there, looking like a madman. Then suddenly he rose from his chair and, leaning across the table, thrust the knife at Edward.

Edward was ready for him. Not only had de Cordova persisted in his threat, but he had made the first move, which, in a court of law, would be construed as just cause for Edward to take steps to protect himself. Reacting instantly, Edward shook his right arm smartly just once. The derringer dropped into his hand beneath his shirt-sleeve, and as his fingers closed around the pistol, his forefinger automatically found the trigger.

He squeezed it, and the bullet entered Luis de

Cordova's heart, killing the man instantly. He fell on top of the table, his expression one of utter incredulity.

Millicent Randall was the first to recognize the significance of de Cordova's passing. His death meant that she really was free at last. A feeling of infinite relief, infinite gratitude to Edward Blackstone, welled within her. It was almost too good to be true.

At the same time, however, she was overcome by a feeling of sadness and regret. She felt certain that with Luis's demise, a golden period in her life had come to an end. Having no idea why she had responded physically, she was convinced that never again would she enjoy lovemaking so intensely with any man.

Just then, Tommie Harding came into the saloon, a look of triumph on her face, and Edward rapidly told her what had happened.

She forgot her own news for the moment as she sprang into action. First, she raced to the wheelhouse to notify her father of de Cordova's death; he would stop the *Big Muddy* in the nearest small town so that he could wire ahead to inform the authorities in Lexington, Missouri.

Luis de Cordova was buried at sundown in unconsecrated ground, and no funeral service was held for him, nor was any marker left at the head of the grave to indicate his burial site. It was taken for granted that none would mourn his passing.

That same night Captain Harding invited Edward to eat supper with him and his daughter in the privacy of the wheelhouse. Edward had earlier been with Millicent in the cabin she had formerly shared with de Cordova, and he had made sure she was comfortable and had everything she needed. They had much to talk about, but it could wait until another day, after Millicent had gotten some rest. Edward arrived at the designated time to find the food already at hand and both father and daughter looking pleased with themselves.

"I've given your little monkey several handfuls of peanuts," Tommie said, "and as soon as we reach St. Louis, I'm going to see if it isn't possible to buy a bunch of bananas for him. Nothing is too good for him—nothing!"

The grinning Captain Harding handed Edward a packet of papers bound together with a strong string. "These," he said, "are the documents that were hidden in Luis de Cordova's cabin. The monkey secured them for us, just as you and Tommie had planned."

"And not a moment too soon, either," Tommie said. "Once you had killed de Cordova—strictly in self-defense, as you've now established under the law—all of his property had to be sealed and remain untouched until the police inspected it. Had we waited any longer, these papers, which were never the rightful property of de Cordova, would have had to stay in his cabin and would have been subject to exhaustive examination."

"Then," her father added, "it would have been our task to prove that he had stolen them from us. We might or might not have been able to accomplish that feat, and it certainly would have taken a great many months to go through the rigmarole necessary to assure us of regaining ownership. Thus, our gratitude to the monkey is boundless."

Taking the documents, Edward removed one, unfolded it, and began to scan it.

"With these papers back in our possession," Tommie told him, "no one is in a position to doubt or question our ownership. Had de Cordova arrived in St. Louis with them, he easily could have obtained a court order and dispossessed us. Then it would have been up to us to prove that the ships really were ours—an almost impossible task."

"Impossible," her father added, "because, as we told you before, the papers are not made out to any individual by name. Well, now the ships are safely in our possession again. And the death of de Cordova also puts an end to his outrageous claims of interest due him."

Their talk was interrupted by the arrival of two farmers who were selling firewood and produce. Isaiah Harding often made purchases from the pair when in the neighborhood, and he went off to see them, leaving his daughter and Edward to finish their supper.

"It's easy to satisfy Robin Hood," Tommie said at last, a wistful note creeping into her voice. "He's a little monkey, so he's satisfied with nuts and bananas and the like. What can Papa and I ever do to thank a benefactor like Mr. Edward Blackstone of England, who has all the money and position in the world that anybody could want?"

Edward smiled and shook his head. "I really hadn't thought about it," he said, "but I'm sure there are many things in the world that I don't possess and that I want badly. But I'm not sure that anyone can give them to me. Thanks all the same."

"Well," she said, somewhat stridently, a catch in

her voice, "I do hope that you and Millicent Randall find the happiness that you both deserve."

Edward was silent for a long moment, studying her. "I'm not sure," he said, "that I understand you."

Tommie took a deep, tremulous breath. "I said—"

"I heard what you said," he replied, interrupting. "But I'm still in the dark as to its meaning. I distinctly remember explaining to you sometime ago that Millicent and I are cousins."

Tommie's face reddened. "Indeed you did explain it to me," she said, "but I thought you were just, well, talking for the sake of—well, for the convenience—I mean to say, I thought you were trying to let me down easily. After all," she continued miserably, "she is an extremely striking woman, and I can't blame any man who loses his heart to her."

Edward continued to look at her, very much amused, and shook his head. "In that portion of the civilized world where I was born," he said, "the children of a sister and a brother are first cousins. I assume it must be the same on this side of the Atlantic."

She looked at him in embarrassment, opening her mouth to speak and then clamping her jaws shut again.

Edward quietly came to her aid. Rising from his chair, he crossed the cabin and put a hand on her shoulder. "I think we've said quite enough," he told her. "You astonish me. You cooperated completely with me, not knowing that you stood anything to gain and thinking the whole time that I was acting because I was enamored of Millicent."

"Something like that," Tommie admitted, blushing still more violently.

"I think," he said quietly, "that you and I need to straighten out our relationship."

She could not reply, and they sat and looked at each other in silence as the seconds passed. Since it was dark in the wheelhouse, with only two candles providing light, it was difficult for each of them to see and interpret the other's expression.

At last Edward felt it was his place to break the silence. "If I may," he said, "I'll speak to your father."

His commitment was so unexpected that he caught her completely off guard. She started to stammer a reply, and then, seeing her father mounting the stairs to the wheelhouse, she became panicky.

Hastily stacking the supper trays and piling the empty dishes on the top one, she murmured, "We've forgotten our coffee. I'll have to get it for us." Not waiting for a reply, she dashed out of the wheelhouse, brushing past her father and almost colliding head-on with him.

Captain Harding looked after her in mild surprise. "Well!" he said. "I wonder what that was all about."

"I think, sir," Edward replied, "that she may have lost her bearings because she knew I intended to speak with you."

Isaiah Harding walked slowly to his desk, sat, and busied himself for quite some time, stuffing and lighting an old pipe. "I would be stupid if I pretended not to know what you mean, Edward," he said, "and I must answer you with the greatest candor of which I'm capable. I'm in your debt. I'm indebted to you as I never have been and never will be to any other member of the human race. Thanks entirely to you and to your efforts,

I've saved one of the two things in the world that has meaning to me. You've preserved my fleet for me, and the Harding Line will continue to be represented on the Missouri River. You have no idea how much that means to me. Now we come to my other major concern in life, my daughter. My wife unfortunately died in childbirth, and I've had the task of rearing Tommie alone. Often I've felt I've failed at the task. She's seemed so much more masculine than feminine to me."

"I can assure you on that score, sir," Edward said dryly. "She's one-hundred-percent female."

"You are well qualified to look after her financially, and I have the greatest respect for you, especially after all that you've done for me."

"Then I have your permission to pay court to her?" Edward asked eagerly.

"Not yet," Harding said. "Hear me out. In the past few years, Tommie's had some ardent suitors, but they've been few in number and far between. You may have noticed when we stopped at Fort Pierre that she was courted by an army captain there, but she sees the man twice, maybe three times a year. Basically, she's inexperienced in the relationships of men and women. Now you've come into her life. She's almost overcome with gratitude, and you're in a position to sweep her off her feet. If you propose to her now, she's certain to accept, but would such an acceptance be fair to her and fair to you? I've seen enough of marriage over the years to know that a truly successful one depends on the depth of the feelings that a man and a woman have for each other. Each of them must want, first and foremost, to give rather than to receive; the greatest joy in life comes from giving. Marriage is the quiet, deep satisfaction that a couple feels with each other. It very definitely isn't the surge of romantic emotionalism that you and Tommie feel at this very moment. With all due respect to your feelings," he added.

They looked out the window and saw Tommie starting up the stairs carrying a tray laden with three cups of steaming coffee.

Captain Harding continued to speak, but now he voiced his thoughts far more rapidly. "Don't misunderstand me," he said. "I'm in no way rejecting you as a potential son-in-law or as a suitor for Tommie's hand. I approve of you as I could never approve of anyone else. But I think you've got to be fair to yourselves and to each other, and that means you've got to allow yourselves time to come to know each other better under normal conditions, when the threat of Luis de Cordova isn't hanging over your heads and when you're free to live as you both please."

"Very well, sir," Edward said. "I agree."

An instant later, Tommie came in the door. In total silence she placed the tray on the table and distributed the three coffee cups and saucers. "If one of you doesn't say something, and say it soon," she announced sweetly, "I shall scream."

Her father briefly told her of their conversation. To the surprise of both men, she became indignant. "Am I to be given no voice in my own future?" she demanded hotly. "Do I have nothing to say about what becomes of me?"

"Of course you do," her father replied soothingly.

"You have the last word in the entire matter, regardless of what may happen."

Edward knew her well enough to realize that she had adopted the belligerent stand because she believed that her interests were being slighted. He chose his own way of dealing with the matter.

"What your father is trying to tell you," he said, "is quite simple. If you want—or believe you want—a relationship with me, you can have it, but we should not become betrothed until we have had an opportunity to know each other better under more normal conditions. Certainly I agree with that point of view. Not that I think either of us is going to change, but in my opinion, we owe it to your father in order to set his mind at ease. On the other hand, if you prefer it, just say the word, and I'll disappear from your life as soon as we reach St. Louis, and I won't return. The decision is yours."

Edward had spoken so bluntly that Tommie was nonplussed. "What—what do *you* want?" she asked, much less sure of herself.

"I've already told you in so many words," he said, "and if that hasn't made my position clear, my attitude certainly should have done so by now. Since it also hasn't, I'm sure your father will forgive me if I express myself in unmistakable terms."

Without further ado, he took a single step forward, drew her gently into his arms, and kissed her at length. When their lips touched, both knew that the relationship was right. Isaiah Harding's fears for them were groundless, but they had to observe his wishes in order to allay his anxieties.

When they finally drew apart, both of them breathing hard, they found her father, sipping his coffee and smoking his pipe, seemingly busily engaged in charting a course on a map of the Missouri River by candlelight.

The couple instantly drew somewhat closer together again and held hands. Edward had promised not to rush matters, but all the same, he knew the future was bright. So did Tommie, who stood looking at him lovingly, her fingers interlaced with his.

X

Cindy Holt bent low in the saddle, urging her mount to attain greater and still greater speed as she raced around the practice track utilized by the cavalry at Fort Vancouver. Glancing back over her shoulder, she saw that Lieutenant Eric Hoskins, who had given her a handicap of one hundred yards in their race, was gaining rapidly on her.

She tried to drive the animal forward at a still greater speed, but she knew that the mare had reached her capacity, and reluctantly she had to allow Lieutenant Hoskins to pass her. He grinned at her as his gelding swept past the finish line.

"A good race," Eric commented as he fell in beside Cindy and they walked their horses around the track in order to give the animals the opportunity to cool off.

"Just remember," Cindy said, "I beat you in the past."

The lieutenant laughed. "That's true enough," he said, "and you would have beat me again, except that today I'm riding a special U.S. Cavalry gelding that's been trained for speed. If you can persuade General Blake to let you take a government horse from the cavalry stables the next time we race, I'm sure that you will again win the race."

"It's odd," Cindy said thoughtfully. "Why are you being so nice to me, Eric?"

"I suppose," he replied, laughing, "that my conscience is demanding that I engage in fair play and give you every chance to win."

"That's very sweet of you," she replied, smiling at him, "but I really don't see what difference it makes. Win or lose, you always take me to dinner."

"And that is my concept of what's eminently fair," he said.

"I'll make you a wager that's really fair," she said. "Suppose that Papa agrees to let me borrow a horse from the cavalry stables. I'll bet you the usual dinner against a picnic meal prepared by me. We'll take it out into the woods beyond the limits of the fort to eat."

There was no need for him to consider the matter. "Agreed!" he cried. "You're on."

"I'll speak to Papa this very evening, and I'll let you know when we race again tomorrow what he says. Remember, this bet is irrevocable."

"So much the better," he replied, as he removed his forage cap and held it in one hand while she rode off in the direction of the commanding general's house.

Cindy rode quietly toward home, knowing full well that her relationship with Eric Hoskins was becoming considerably deeper and more complicated. Still rebellious, Cindy told herself that she was glad she was becoming more involved with the young officer. The situation served Cadet Henry Blake right for daring to carry on a private correspondence with a girl who used perfumed, expensive notepaper and who wrote in purple ink. The evidence that he was carrying on a surreptitious romance was only circumstantial, to be sure, but Cindy nevertheless told herself that Hank deserved her scorn and neglect. Whether she would ultimately forgive him depended completely on his attitude, and so far, she was forced to admit, he had done nothing to encourage her to believe that their own romance was still alive. He was avoiding her as much as she was avoiding him, and their relations were at a standstill.

When she arrived home, Cindy mounted the stairs to the second floor, and on her way to her room, she passed the chamber that Hank occupied. The door was open, and the room looked strangely bare, with no sign of either his uniforms or his civilian clothes. Her curiosity aroused, she went to her mother's sitting room and looked in.

Eulalia Blake was seated at her desk, writing out the coming week's menus for the cook. She glanced up, smiled vaguely, and scarcely interrupted herself to say, "Hello, dear."

"Hello, Mama," Cindy replied, shifting her weight from one foot to the other. Then she tried to sound casual as she finally asked, "Where's Hank?"

"Oh, didn't you know?" Her mother continued to write busily. "He's gone back East."

Cindy was so shocked she could not speak.

There was no sound in the room but the scratching of Eulalia's pen. Finally she said, "He decided it was time for him to return to the academy. He left here about a half hour ago, I'd say, and he's picking up the stagecoach to San Francisco, where he'll take the transcontinental train to New York."

The girl was utterly crushed but was too proud to cry in her mother's presence.

"He asked me to say good-bye to you for him," Eulalia went on, "and he said to be sure and tell you that he wishes you every happiness."

Cindy's legs felt weak. She tottered into the room and sank onto the chaise longue near her mother's chair. "I just can't believe," she whispered, "that he could actually go traipsing off to the opposite end of the continent without even stopping to say good-bye to me."

Eulalia stopped writing and pushed her quill pen into a jar of sand. "Why on earth should he?" she demanded bluntly. "After all, you've ignored him cruelly."

Cindy tried to speak, but her mother had started and was not pausing. "As a matter of fact, even when he returned with your brother from the expedition on which they recovered all those rifles, you didn't offer him a single word of congratulations. He was a hero, but no one would have known it from your lack of reaction!"

"I had a good reason—a valid reason—for treating Hank as I did," Cindy declared defiantly.

The older woman's dark eyes were icy as they inspected her daughter. "I think, Cindy," she said, "the time has come for us to have a candid talk. It's long overdue." She folded her hands in her lap.

"Whatever you say, Mama," the girl replied in a surly tone.

Eulalia was able to control her temper only by reminding herself that Cindy was still very young, inexperienced, and if the truth be told, badly spoiled.

"All I know," Eulalia said, "is that you and Hank were as thick as the proverbial thieves until one day several weeks ago, when suddenly Eric Hoskins reappeared in your life. From that moment onward, you couldn't see Hank for dust. The general and I have wondered about it often—so has Hank, for that matter— but you've never indicated, by so much as a word to any of us, what's been bothering you. I think the time has come to speak candidly, right now."

"You make it appear that I'm completely in the wrong," Cindy said hotly. "Well, I'm not!"

Her mother looked at her complacently. "I'm listening," she said.

Breathless and angry, Cindy related how she had seen a letter addressed to Hank in the incoming mail basket, and she described the communication, its thick linen texture, its purple ink, its writing in an obviously feminine hand, and its strong scent. "If he had mentioned it to me," she continued, "I wouldn't have thought a thing of the matter, but not only did he say nothing, he actually answered her within twenty-four hours!"

"You foolish, stupid little girl." Eulalia laughed helplessly. "What a mess you've made, and for no reason on earth! If only you'd had the sense to bring your suspicions into the open, this ridiculous rift could have been avoided."

"How so?" Cindy demanded belligerently.

"It so happens," her mother said, "that Hank mentioned the matter to us at supper the very same night that you suddenly took off with Eric Hoskins. If I remember correctly, the girl is related in some way— she's a sister, I believe—of the girlfriend of Hank's roommate. She had her cap set for him, and he neatly avoided her, making it clear that he wanted nothing whatever to do with her. That's the whole story."

Cindy stared at her mother in horror, then moaned and sank forward on the chaise, covering her face in her hands. She was so young, so vulnerable, Eulalia thought, and obviously badly hurt by the revelation. Eulalia's heart ached for her.

"I'm such an idiot!" Cindy cried, rocking back and forth in agony. "Whatever am I to do?"

"If you hurry," Eulalia said pointedly, "I should think you'd be able to reach the stagecoach depot by approximately the same time that Hank gets there. It wouldn't surprise me if he listened to a reasonable explanation of your conduct."

"Do you think he would?" Cindy demanded. "Do you actually think he'd listen to me?"

"I'm inclined to suspect he'd listen with great interest," Eulalia said mildly.

The woman's words spurred her daughter into taking sudden action. Leaping to her feet, Cindy snatched her riding crop from the chaise and called over her shoulder, "Tell Papa I had to borrow one of his cavalry geldings. I'm sorry if I've broken any army regulations, but I'll try to explain it all when I come home for supper!"

She was gone before the older woman had an opportunity to say a word.

Leaping two steps at a time to the bottom of the stairs, Cindy ran to the stables. As she approached them, she called to the master sergeant in charge, "Sergeant Hormel! Saddle the fastest gelding you have in the place."

Ordinarily Sergeant Jerry Hormel would have demanded a written order for a mount from anyone but the commanding general himself. However, he was mindful of the fact that the command had been given by the general's daughter, so he hastened to obey her. In a few minutes, he had the gelding properly saddled.

"Thanks, Sarge!" she called as she spurred her mount to a canter. "If my father asks any questions, tell him I'll explain later."

Looking after her, the sergeant pushed his campaign hat onto the back of his head and shrugged. He had no idea what she was up to and devoutly hoped that he would not get into any trouble.

Swiftly increasing her speed to a full gallop, Cindy provided a hazard for the wives and small children of several officers who were taking the summer air on the parade ground. Taking a shortcut across it, she headed toward the main gate, then veered sharply toward the river and, within a few moments, pulled to a violent halt at the riverside station where her stepfather's boat and other small craft were kept. "Corporal Jonas!" she called to the noncommissioned officer in charge. "I need transportation for my horse and me to the Oregon shore—right to Portland—as fast as I can get there."

The rotund corporal pulled a pocket watch with a large face from a fob pocket in his uniform. "The next ferry," he said, "ain't scheduled to leave for another thirty-five minutes, miss."

"Thirty-five minutes?" Cindy screamed. "Thirty-five minutes from now I intend to be at my destination in Portland!"

Although she had no authority, it occurred to the corporal that he might be less than wise if he argued the matter with the general's daughter. "Yes, ma'am," he said, and waved a crew on board the tied-up ferry.

The crew made excellent time as they sailed across the vast Columbia River. When they reached the Oregon shore, two of the soldiers led the gelding to the dock, but Cindy did not wait for them to help her down the gangplank. She raced to her horse, mounted again quickly, and was off on the main road into Portland.

In the years since it had been founded, Portland had become a community of substantial size. It was not only an important port on the Columbia River, but it also served as a produce center for Oregon and as the financial hub for the considerable gold mining that was done in the southern part of the state. Consequently, the streets were filled, as they always were at this time of afternoon, with crowds of shoppers and farmers, businessmen and shippers going about their business.

Cindy Holt constituted a hazard for all of them. She rode at breakneck speed, dodging carts, carriages, other riders, and pedestrians indiscriminately. At two busy intersections she narrowly escaped collisions, and the constables on duty at both refrained from apprehending her only because they recognized her as the daughter of the fabled Whip Holt and the stepdaughter of General Blake.

As she rode into the stagecoach depot, Cindy was infinitely relieved to see ahead of her a blue-painted wagon belonging to the United States Army. Cadet Henry Blake was just alighting from the buckboard and was taking his luggage from the rear. He looked up, saw Cindy approaching, and his jaw dropped.

Quickly pretending to be unaware of his presence because she was afraid to face him, Cindy dismounted, tied her horse to a hitching post, and began to walk in the general direction of the depot.

All at once Hank loomed directly in front of her. "Fancy seeing you here, Mr. Blake," she said in simulated surprise.

Hank's surprise was genuine, but he intended to take full advantage of what he regarded as a chance meeting. "I might say the same thing to you, Miss Holt," he replied formally, removing his gray uniform cap and holding it under one arm.

Cindy decided it was impossible for her to lie. "All right, Hank," she said, and sighed. "I'm here because I've come to see you—and for no other reason. I've just had a talk with Mama, and I had to see you before you left."

Hank was wary, not knowing quite what to expect.

"Is there—someplace we can go to talk?" she asked helplessly.

He shook his head. "The stagecoach that's going to take me to San Francisco," he said, "is due to leave any minute, so I've got to stay right here. I can't risk missing it."

"I see." She felt completely helpless.

"What do you have in mind?" he asked.

"You. Only you. Oh, oh, Hank, I'm so sorry," she cried, putting a hand on his arm, "but I've been such a stupid, mixed-up fool. I've wasted weeks of your furlough carrying a grudge when I had no right to have any such feeling. I made you miserable, I know, because I was determined to get even with you."

Hank could face firearms without flinching, but the mere thought that this girl might break into tears in his presence and in front of all the other passengers filled him with sudden alarm. "Here, now," he muttered. "Here, now."

The words tumbling out in an unending stream, she told him in detail how she'd been inflamed by jealousy when she had seen the letter in the mail basket written by Alice Snyder of Baltimore and how her anger had redoubled when he had replied to the communication without so much as mentioning the subject to her. "I was wrong, totally wrong!" she said miserably. "And if you choose never to speak to me again, it's the least punishment that I deserve."

Hank could only stand and stare at her, shaking his head. "I must agree with you that you've acted like a damned fool," he said, "but I can assure you that Alice Snyder isn't worth your little finger. She—"

"I won't listen, I can't listen!" she cried, clamping her hands over her ears. "It's quite enough now, and for the rest of my life, that you give me your word, and I accept it on faith and faith alone. If you'll have me back, I swear I've learned a lesson that I'll never forget as long as I live."

"Well, now," Hank said, "it seems to me that we've already wasted quite enough time." He reached for her, unmindful of the throngs at the station and, folding her into his arms, kissed her long and soundly.

When they finally drew apart, there were tears in Cindy's eyes. Neither she nor Hank paid the slightest attention to the score or more of people who were grinning at them.

"I hate myself," Cindy said passionately, "when I think of the time we could have been together that I've wasted!"

"I don't think it was time wasted," Hank said. "There was a lesson there for both of us to learn. Of all the ties that bind people together, the most important of them is faith, trust in each other. That's more true in my business than in any other because a soldier's life so often separates him from his wife. You and I need to trust each other, not only now when I'm off at the academy, but for as long as I follow a career in the army."

"I've learned my lesson," she said. "I put my complete trust in you, now and always."

Hank moved closer to her and put an arm around her.

"I hope that over the years I'll earn your trust," she said, "and I must begin at once. I've used Eric Hoskins badly in all this, and I'm obliged to tell him the truth."

"What do you call the truth?"

"That I misled him into thinking that you and I

meant nothing to each other, and admitting to him that I was just using him to make you jealous."

"That brand of truth," Hank said, "is unnecessary because it will hurt an innocent person. Wouldn't it be easier and better to tell him simply that we rediscovered each other during this furlough of mine? It'll be much easier on his vanity, and far easier for him to bear."

"How does it happen," Cindy asked, looking up at him in wonder, "that you're so wise?"

"Ordinarily I'm not in the least wise," Hank said, "but you seem to inspire me to greater wisdom. It's one of a thousand good influences you have on me."

They stood together in complete peace and happiness as they awaited the departure of his stagecoach, the breach that had separated them completely healed.

The *Big Muddy* moved with her customary ease into the berth she usually occupied in Lexington, Missouri, the farmers' market and manufacturing town that was her last stop before reaching her destination, St. Louis. She was the first ship of the new season to sail down the river from Montana, and consequently, a small crowd was gathered at the waterfront to welcome her and to gape.

Standing in the midst of the group was a giant of a man, at least six feet three inches tall. He was broad-shouldered, his hair was sandy, and his eyes were a pale blue. He carried a pistol on his hip, which was unusual in this quiet, law-abiding town, and the instant the ship moved toward her wharf, he started forward. As soon as she was made fast to the dock, he went on board and sought Captain Harding.

"Sergeant Karl Kellerman, St. Louis constabulary," he said. "Be good enough, if you will, to ask all those who had any connection with the late Luis de Cordova to remain on board until I've spoken to them."

"I've already taken that precaution," Isaiah Harding told him. "You've been assigned to the case, I gather?"

"Yes," the sergeant replied. "I was assigned when the U.S. Army turned over to the constabulary the case of the stolen rifles."

Captain Harding shook his head. "Don't tell me de Cordova was mixed up in that, too! He seems to have been endlessly involved in illegal activities." He proceeded to relate his own problems with de Cordova to the police officer and then went on to tell him in detail of the incident in which de Cordova had lost his life.

The detective was efficient and took copious notes. "Your account can be corroborated, no doubt?" he asked.

Isaiah Harding summoned his daughter, the passengers who had witnessed the final scene with de Cordova, and Edward Blackstone.

Using the ship's wheelhouse, Sergeant Kellerman grilled them privately, one by one, and appeared satisfied with the results. Thorough in his work habits, he appeared to be very much at home and sipped the cup of coffee that Tommie had brought him.

"To be truthful with you, Mr. Blackstone," he told Edward, "I can't see the constabulary bringing charges against you for killing the man. Obviously you had just cause, and it's a wonder that he lived as long as he did. Do you suppose I could also interview your cousin, the woman who was involved with him?"

"By all means," Edward told him, "but if it's all the same with you, Sergeant, I hope you'll go easy on her. She's had a rough time since she left Idaho, and she needs some gentle treatment."

"Trust me," Kellerman said.

A few moments later, Sergeant Kellerman was seated in the cabin that Millicent had shared with Luis de Cordova. He was in no way prepared for her blatant sexuality, which she now knew how to enhance automatically with makeup and sensual clothes.

As for Millicent herself, she was no longer being fed the essence of the Hungarian mushrooms, but she knew nothing about all that. Their effect was long-lasting, even without continued usage, and as a result she was very much taken with Sergeant Kellerman's appearance. He was tall, handsome in a rugged way, and he exuded an aura of strong, positive masculinity.

Millicent flirted with the sergeant as she told him about her entire experience with Luis de Cordova. She flatly branded him a criminal and a cheat, and her testimony was the most damning of all. Sergeant Kellerman wrote out a statement for her, and she signed it with a flourish.

By that time the *Big Muddy* was under way again, and Kellerman, who was going on to St. Louis, escorted Millicent to the dinner table. After dinner it was only natural that they should retire to Millicent's cabin in order to continue their conversation. They stayed there for many hours and were still there when Edward Blackstone retired for the night. He thought it a little strange that the sergeant's interview with his cousin was taking so much time, but he did not dwell on it.

* * *

Wong Ke was one of the most distinguished of American citizens on the Pacific Coast. He and his partner, Chet Harris, owned real estate—hotels and office buildings, as well as private homes—several newspapers, and a variety of manufacturing plants. In addition, they managed the property and investments of others. Thus, wherever Wong Ke went, he was news.

Ke wrote to Toby Holt and to Rob Martin, informing them he would be arriving the following Tuesday to bring them their profits from the gold mine that he and Chet Harris managed for them in Montana. They looked forward to their meeting with him and, following the session, planned to have him out to the Holt ranch for supper.

On the appointed day, Toby and Rob prepared to go into Portland to his hotel to see him at four in the afternoon. They arrived separately, about a quarter of an hour early, and met in the lobby, where they expected Wong Ke to join them shortly. The appointed hour came and went, however, and he did not appear. They thought he had been delayed because of business and dismissed the matter from their minds.

But as five o'clock approached, they became concerned and went to the manager of the hotel, who took them up to Wong Ke's suite and let them in with the passkey. Toby and Rob, who were directly behind him, were stunned by what they saw.

Wong Ke was lying unconscious, stretched on the floor in a pool of blood. He had been badly beaten with a club of some kind, but significantly, there were still several bags of gold coins and unrefined gold in the room. Robbery definitely had not been the motive.

While Toby bound up Wong Ke's wounds and arranged for his transfer to a stretcher, Rob hurried to the Portland hospital to prepare them for the coming of an emergency case. His father was not on duty, but his first assistant, Dr. Anton Wizneuski, who had also been among the original settlers in Oregon more than a quarter of a century earlier, was there. He immediately took charge of the preparations.

A quarter of an hour later, when three men carried the unconscious body of Wong Ke into the hospital, Dr. Wizneuski took command. He disappeared into an operating room, and Toby and Rob paced restlessly outside the corridor for the better part of an hour. Finally the doctor joined them there, his white uniform flecked with blood.

"It is fortunate," he said in his distinctive Russian accent, "that you happened upon him when you did and that you acted so promptly. I've worked hard, very hard, and I think the odds are fairly good that he will survive, but I wouldn't swear to it yet. I've got to keep watch on him all night. Have you notified his family yet?"

"Yes, sir," Toby said. "I've sent one telegram to his wife and another to his partner, both of them in San Francisco. There's a stagecoach leaving this evening, due to arrive here day after tomorrow, and I wouldn't be surprised if both were on board."

Toby and Rob kept a quiet vigil through the long, silent hours of the night. Dr. Wizneuski frequently looked in on the patient, who had regained consciousness briefly and then fell into a sound sleep.

It was late afternoon of the following day when the

stagecoach from San Francisco finally arrived, and Mrs. Wong, escorted by Chet Harris, both of them bleary-eyed, hired a carriage to drive the short distance from the stagecoach depot to the hospital. When they arrived, Dr. Wizneuski met them and conducted them to the sickroom. There the wounded man's wife remained while the burly Chet Harris joined Toby and Rob in a small waiting room at the end of the corridor.

"How is he?" Toby demanded.

"To be honest," Chet replied, "he's not in good shape. I understand that he was in a much worse condition when you brought him in here and that your promptness saved his life. Between you and Dr. Wizneuski, he's still with us."

"Apparently," Rob said, "he took one terrible beating."

"So it appears," Chet said angrily. "Whoever attacked him really let him have it. Ke is elderly, and though he's far from frail, in no sense is he an athlete or a fighter. Whoever attacked him treated him unmercifully."

"Who could possibly hate him so much," Toby asked slowly, "that they would beat him half to death? It sounds almost inconceivable to me."

"In our type of business," Chet Harris said, "Wong Ke and I make scores of decisions—all day long—that affect the lives of other people. Some people are affected favorably, some unfavorably. It's virtually impossible to tell who bears him ill will unless you know every business transaction that he made from one day to the next, from one week to the next, for the past month or so, and even then we'd be shooting in the dark. I'm afraid there's no way we could really know."

A short time later police captain Peter Thoman, the son of boat builder Paul Thoman, another of the original Oregon settlers, arrived at the hospital on behalf of the Portland constabulary and sat down with Toby and Rob, as well as with Chet Harris, for a meeting.

Captain Thoman asked the same question that Toby had asked. "Does he have any personal enemies?"

"Not to my knowledge," Chet Harris replied.

"I don't want to bother his wife," Peter Thoman said, "when his life is still in danger, but I wonder if she knows of anyone who would want to attack him."

"I'm quite certain," Chet said, "that she has nothing to contribute. I raised the point with her on our long ride up from San Francisco and asked her to think hard of anyone she could possibly imagine who would seek that kind of revenge against Wong Ke, but she knew of no one. In fact, just thinking about it causes her to dissolve into tears."

"Well," the police officer said, "we'll spare her, at least for the moment. But I can't help wondering how many people knew of his arrival in town and that he was staying at the hotel here."

Toby laughed without humor. "I'd say that everyone in Portland knew it. Both the morning and afternoon newspapers printed articles on his arrival, and both of them made it very clear that he was a guest at the hotel here."

The young officer shrugged. "That makes the situation infinitely more complicated, does it not? It does," he answered himself emphatically. "It certainly does."

They agreed to meet again the next day after they

had had an opportunity to get some sleep and ponder the matter further.

Toby insisted that Chet stay with him at the ranch, and as they rode out, he slipped the catch off both of the six-shooters that he carried. Assuming that Wong Ke had been assaulted by an enemy he had made in business, Toby thought it was logical that Chet Harris could be subjected to an attack from the same source. He preferred to take no needless risks.

At long last, two months and ten days after leaving her home port in Montana, the *Big Muddy* sailed into St. Louis, on the Mississippi River. Here was the epitome of all the great river ports in the United States. Originally settled by French explorers, trappers, and traders, and subsequently by thousands of sturdy German immigrants, St. Louis currently boasted a racial stock of a dozen or more nations, as did almost every major American community.

Passing through this port by the millions of bushels were wheat and corn, rye and oats, and barley and rice. There were vegetables too varied to enumerate and sides of beef and lamb and hogs. There were poultry and ducks and venison. The world's finest timber, hardwood and soft, pure and straight and strong, came through St. Louis, as did wool and cotton without end. There were iron ore and coal, the raw materials for thousands of manufactured products, and there were the manufactured goods themselves, everything that civilized man wanted or could want, all gathered and sent on their way by barge down the Mississippi to New Orleans, and from there taken by steamers on the seven seas to distant climes.

The great seaports of America—New York, San Francisco, New Orleans, Philadelphia, Boston, Baltimore, Portland—all had an international flavor, but there was no sense of anything foreign in St. Louis. Here the atmosphere was strictly American in feeling. People spoke English, ate American fare, wore American-made clothes. Indeed, there was even a touch of the American frontier in St. Louis, as grizzled old miners, cowboys, and even latter-day mountain men who trapped for furs passed through the town.

Authorities were everywhere, and with good reason. St. Louis was a rough, tough town, and those who could not take care of themselves were as numerous, if not more so, than those who could. The U.S. Army maintained a powerful regional headquarters there, and a much smaller one was the center of U.S. Navy activities. There were police all along the waterfront, patrolling the harbor and docks as well as the huge warehouses that lined both banks of the river.

Shortly after the *Big Muddy* tied up, Edward Blackstone ventured ashore. He spent a busy hour or two attending to various errands, among them going to the post office to get Pamela Randall's letters and then writing her himself, to say Millicent was safe and sound. Returning to the steamer, Edward asked Tommie Harding to have supper with him. She accepted, suggesting one of the few respectable waterfront restaurants.

"This will come as a surprise, I know," he said when they were seated at their table, "but I've booked passage for New Orleans this afternoon on a side-wheeler called the *Mississippi Lady*."

"I know her well," Tommie said, concealing her

disappointment. "She has first-class accommodations and very good food. You'll enjoy sailing on board her."

"I suppose I will," he said, "but it's going to feel very strange not being on board the *Big Muddy* anymore. I've been on this ship long enough that she feels like home to me."

"She's been your home in every sense of the word," Tommie said solemnly, "and you've earned the right to call her your home. You'll be missed, sorely missed."

"By whom?" he demanded boldly.

Color rose delicately in her cheeks. "Papa will miss you, for one," she said.

"Anyone else?"

Tommie took a deep breath. "Yes, Edward," she said bravely. "I shall miss you very much."

"No more than I'll miss you," he told her. They looked at each other over the rims of their aperitifs, and he slowly put his glass down. She did the same.

"We agreed," he said stiffly, "to allow a little time to elapse before we marry—for your father's sake. That is why I propose to do some traveling during that time."

She sat back in her chair, smiled, and listened attentively.

"I have traveled all over the world, and I've lived in many places," he said. "Before I ever came to the United States, I had more or less fallen in love with this country, especially with the Western regions. Today, having lived and traveled through most of the West, I've confirmed my views. I've already made several investments, and I plan to make other major investments in the future.

"I hope eventually," he continued, "to make my home—our home—in the mountain country of Idaho or perhaps Montana, and I'm in hopes that I can become at least part owner of a fleet of riverboats because I believe that the future of the West depends on her commerce and the free movement of her goods from their points of origin to the great cities. The mere existence of New Orleans proves all that to me. I also find I'm eager to become an American citizen."

"Good for you!" she said enthusiastically.

All at once, he peered hard at her. "You've seemed, over a period of months, to be totally unaffected by the fact that I have considerable amounts of money. Does it really mean so little to you?"

"It means nothing," Tommie said.

"How so?"

"It's quite simple, really," she said. "As you know, as riverboat owners, Papa and I have been paupers one day, and we've been rolling in money the next. Well, we're the same people regardless of whether we have money or we haven't. It's all a matter of outlook. We wear the same clothes, we eat the same food, we have the same likes and dislikes, regardless of whether we're rolling in money or whether we're impoverished. I figure it's a person's character that counts, rather than whether he's rich or poor. It's a simple philosophy that most people don't seem to approve—"

"You're talking to the wrong person," Edward interrupted. "I happen to approve completely because that happens to be my philosophy, also. As I found myself falling in love with you, I also found that I didn't give a hang whether you had money or whether you were a pauper. I still don't care! What *does* matter to me is your common sense and steadfastness of purpose and other qualities that are quite rare. I must say I don't care particularly for your rather odd habit of dressing in men's clothes and emulating a ship's officer instead of behaving like the owner's daughter as you should, but you were brought up in a certain way, and I can't blame you for being yourself."

"That's very kind of you, thank you," she said a trifle sarcastically, and it was obvious that his words miffed her.

"If there's one thing I've learned about you Americans since I've been on this side of the Atlantic," Edward said, "it's the fact that you're all individuals. You must be accepted for what you are, not what you can be. I have no right to dictate alterations in your personality, any more than you have the right to dictate them to me. Each of us must accept others for what they are, not for what they might be or for what we wish they were."

Her father had been telling her for years that when she got married, her husband would insist that she give up her activities in male clothes on board ship. Therefore, she could hardly believe her ears. "Do you mean that you wouldn't object to the work I do on the *Big Muddy*?" she demanded.

Edward shrugged. "I might not like it," he said, "but I have no say in the matter. You must make such decisions yourself."

Tommie did a violent mental flip-flop. Perhaps her father—and her own better judgment—were right. Perhaps the time had come when she should give up the activities of a tomboy on board ship and should settle down into more decorous, feminine behavior.

Edward reached across the table and took her hand. "You needn't be so serious," he told her. "There's no need for you to reach any decision right now, on anything. We've left the ship to enjoy an evening's dinner, and I suggest that's what we do!"

Her smile was elfinlike.

They ordered large helpings of food, which they proceeded to eat with gusto. Both of them gnawed happily on barbecued spareribs, and with it they consumed a large plate of fried potatoes. Then, after they finished dinner, they wandered hand in hand down the waterfront back to the *Big Muddy*.

When they reached the Missouri River steamer, they received a shock that put their happiness out of their minds, at least for the moment, and gave them a frightful jolt.

A letter was tacked to the door of Edward's cabin. It said:

Dear Edward:

I will never be able to express my thanks to you for the great help you rendered me at a time when I needed it most. I was beside myself when you sprang to my rescue and saved me from Luis de Cordova.

All of that is in the past now, and I must face the future. I have chosen not to spend it alone, but with Karl Kellerman.

By the time you get this communication, I will

no longer be in St. Louis, but we will have taken ourselves elsewhere to begin a new, and we hope, a perfect life together.

> With my love,
> your cousin,
> Millicent

Edward was so shocked he was incapable of coherent thought. He handed the letter to Tommie, who shook her head as she read it. "My God, my God," she murmured. "I'm afraid the poor girl has gone crazy."

"What in the devil do we do now?" Edward demanded.

Tommie was silent for a moment, pressing her knuckles to her forehead. "Papa and I," she said, "are slightly acquainted with Commissioner Bowen of the St. Louis constabulary. I suggest that you and I go to see him early tomorrow morning and find out what additional information—if any—we can."

"Good," he said. "At the very least, it may be a start. One thing is certain, we can do absolutely nothing tonight because we have no idea where to even begin looking for her."

Dr. Anton Wizneuski, showing the effects of his sleepless night, walked down the hospital corridor to the visitors' room, where Chet Harris, Toby Holt, and Rob Martin awaited him.

"Our patient," he told them, "has successfully passed the crisis. In fact, it's quite safe now to predict that he's going to live."

"Thank the Lord for that!" Chet said.

"He's under sedation and will sleep for at least another hour or two," the doctor said. "When he wakens, you may question him briefly, provided he doesn't get excited. If you find that he's getting worked up, however, you'll have to stop questioning him immediately and wait until a more propitious time, after his recovery is further advanced. Do I make myself clear?"

"Very clear, Doctor," Toby said.

A few hours later, a nurse appeared and conducted the waiting trio into the sickroom. Once they entered, Toby and Rob lingered in the background, and only Chet Harris approached the bed.

Wong Ke's wife, the former Wing Mei-lo, sat beside her husband's bed, and although there were circles beneath her eyes, she was composed.

The patient was lying quietly in bed, his head and face and the upper portion of his body all heavily bandaged.

"Hello, Ke," Chet said casually.

The patient's fingers on the top of the bed sheets fluttered a greeting.

"Dr. Wisneuski," Chet went on, "says you've already passed the worst part and that you're going to recover completely. Not that I had any doubt that you would. You're too tough an old bird to let yourself be cooked for someone's meal. You're bound to give them indigestion first."

The expression in his partner's dark eyes indicated that Wong Ke appreciated his sense of humor.

"Do you want to talk about the—ah—incident?" Chet asked. "Do you know who did this?"

The fingers above the sheet fluttered a bit as Wong

Ke tried to speak. Mei-lo nodded encouragingly. At last the Chinese man was able to get the words out: "Tong—" he said slowly. "A tong was responsible."

A light began to dawn in Chet's mind. "I see," he said quietly. "I think I know," he said. "The attack was conducted by one or more thugs on the payroll of Kung Lee, am I right?"

Wong Ke's voice became stronger. "Yes," he said, "it was a hired hand of Kung Lee."

His partner dropped the subject instantly and talked of other matters. Chet said that he would attend to paying Toby and Rob the profits from their mine and also would attend to several other pending matters that had been on Wong Ke's agenda. Then he quietly took his leave, the two younger men following him without having spoken a single word.

"First," Chet said, "we'll stop at constabulary headquarters so I can pass this information to Captain Thoman—for whatever good it may do. Then if you don't mind, perhaps you two can escort me out to your ranch, Toby, and keep a sharp lookout for thugs who might be interested in attacking me. I'll explain the situation in full to you when we arrive at your place. In the meantime, I don't want to say anything because the very walls may have ears, and when Kung Lee is involved in a situation, believe me, it's impossible to exercise too much care."

A short time later they were on their way out to the Holt ranch. Chet Harris rode in the middle with Toby on his right and Rob on his left. Each of the younger men had one hand on the butt of a pistol and was prepared to use it at once if he saw anything suspicious or questionable.

When they arrived at the ranch, Clarissa Holt, filled with compassion for Chet, asked if she could get him some coffee or something harder to drink. He shook his head and thanked her, then went into the parlor with his host and Rob. They conferred behind the closed door.

"The person responsible for the outrage against Wong Ke," Chet said, "is the head of a powerful tong, one of the strongest and most notorious of Chinese gangs on this side of the Pacific Ocean. His name is Kung Lee, and he's diabolically clever and utterly unscrupulous. He may forget to reward friends occasionally, but he never forgets to inflict cruel punishment on those who are opposed to him. Unfortunately, my partner was, and is, totally opposed to Kung and all that he stands for."

Toby well knew that any involvement with a tong was certain to be dangerous. The way of these gangs was not the way of the Occident; they operated in a strange and often mysterious manner, with human life counting for little or nothing.

"Wherever Kung may go," Chet continued, "he's always accompanied by a bodyguard, Ho Tai. This man is a wild beast who exists for only one purpose—to protect his master. As I understand it, he's an excellent shot with both pistol and rifle, and I hear that he has no equal when it comes to knife throwing."

"Toby," Rob said loyally, "is no rank amateur himself when it comes to wielding a knife."

Chet shook his head. "Toby is a civilized man, not

an animal, and he can't possibly compare in ferocity with Ho Tai. Toby," Chet said curtly, "has a sense of fair play and a conscience. I can assure you that the tong strongman possesses neither."

"Since we know this fellow, Kung Lee, is responsible," Toby said, "suppose you or Mrs. Wong brings charges against him immediately."

"It's not all that simple," Chet said, shaking his head. "Unfortunately, my partner knows that Kung Lee was responsible for the attack, but there's no way it can be pinned on him. It's Lee's unsupported word against theirs, and you can be certain that Kung Lee will have many witnesses to testify that he had nothing whatsoever to do with the incident."

"Then what can be done?" Toby demanded.

"I don't really know," Chet replied. "We face the identical problem that everyone faces who tries to fight the tongs. People are afraid to give testimony against them, and in addition, the tong members always have alibis."

"It strikes me there's only one way to meet fire," Toby said. "With fire!"

"That," Chet replied gloomily, "is far easier said than done. First, the problem is to find someone who will volunteer to take on the tong as an enemy. We'll pay almost any amount of money for the right person or the right organization, but so far we haven't encountered anyone. And then, assuming we do find someone, how will he go about it? It seems to me that we face a hopeless quest."

Toby and Rob exchanged a long, significant look.

"Your search has ended, Chet," Toby said. "You and Wong Ke have not only been our business associates but our good friends as well. You're like family. The least Rob or I can do is help. Rob, I know, is pretty tied up with his work for the railroads, but I've got my affairs at the ranch in order and have some time available. I volunteer to take care of the tong, but I'll accept no pay for what I do. I'll get myself deputized by Chief Thoman, and then I'll immediately go to work. But don't ask what I'll do; I have no idea."

"All I can add to that," Rob said grimly, "is that with Toby on its trail, the tong of Kung Lee is in for the fight of its life."

Later that day, Mei-lo came out to the ranch to spend the night and to attend a dinner party hosted by Clarissa and Toby for their old friends. The Blakes from Fort Vancouver attended, accompanied by Cindy Holt; Kale and Rob Martin were there, as was, of course, Chet; and even Stalking Horse and his ward, White Elk, attended, for they were like family to the Holts.

While the women were busy in the kitchen, arranging platters of meats and vegetables and breads and bringing them out to the dining room table, the men went to the parlor. There Toby and his stepfather discussed recent events, including the death of Luis de Cordova. The rifles he had stolen had, of course, all been recovered, and the U.S. government had confiscated his warehouses and all his other properties from Portland all the way to St. Louis. Now it remained for Toby to put an end once and for all to the treacherous San Francisco tongs. Their nefarious influence had extended even as far as Portland, and it appeared that the lives of the Holts and the Blakes were also going to be affected.

Memphis, a city located in the southwestern tip of Tennessee, sat high on Chickasaw Bluff overlooking the broad Mississippi River. A rapidly growing community, it was expanding so fast that it liked to think of itself as "the New York of the South."

Memphis was genteel, with an overlay of antebellum society; at the same time it was a raw, progressive river city that was bursting at the seams. It had long ranked second only to New Orleans as a cotton port, and with the building of a railroad line that connected Memphis with Charleston, South Carolina, it had doubled in importance. It also ranked first in the shipping of various hardwoods, and in more recent years, Memphis was the site of a growing series of small but vital consumer industries.

Former Sergeant Karl Kellerman arrived in town with Millicent Randall on his arm, and they immediately took up quarters in one of the fancier suites in the staid old Memphis Hotel. Kellerman was almost blinded by his good fortune. He was happily accompanied by a woman far more attractive than he had ever imagined himself keeping company with, someone who made no secret of the fact that she looked up to him and was in love with him, too. Furthermore, she eagerly accepted his lovemaking. Millicent, unaware that her personality had been completely altered by the Gypsy potion, even though she was no longer being given doses of it, knew only that she found Kellerman sexually irresistible.

Karl had resigned from the police force and collected his retirement pay, spending it lavishly and arranging for them to engage a suite on board a paddle wheeler down the Mississippi that left Memphis at noon the following day. Meanwhile, Millicent, who had been left in the hotel suite while Karl made the travel arrangements, had nothing better to occupy her time, so she wandered in and out of the shops and looked at the store windows in the building adjacent to the hotel.

After making the arrangements, Kellerman found Millicent staring in the window of a jewelry shop, obviously in a highly excited state. Her eyes glistened as she concentrated on a huge, cat's-eye ring. "Look, Karl," she breathed. "Did you ever see anything so gorgeous?"

"That's a rather unusual yellow sapphire," he said.

She made no reply, but continued to look at the ring, clasping her hands in front of her.

"You want it, I suppose?" he said indulgently.

She sighed. "This is terribly wicked of me, and I've never in my life reacted this way to anything, but the answer, I'm afraid, is yes. I'd love to have that ring, more than anything in the world."

Kellerman was sufficiently enamored to take her request seriously. "We shall have to see," he said.

They strolled about the town arm in arm for a while and looked at the magnificent view of the mighty Mississippi from the heights above. Then, at Kellerman's suggestion, they returned to their hotel, and Millicent retired to take a nap for an hour or two before supper.

"What will you do?" she asked him sleepily.

"Oh, don't worry about me," he replied airily. "I'll probably drop in on a couple of fellows I know."

That is precisely what he did. He walked a short distance from the hotel to a nondescript building, and as he stepped inside the door, two hard-faced men came forward. "Kellerman," he said curtly, "here to see Jason."

In a few moments, he was admitted into the presence of a grossly overweight man who overflowed his office chair. Sitting in his shirt-sleeves, he looked the picture of cherubic innocence, except for his eyes, which were cold, glittering, and utterly merciless. "I hear tell you've left the St. Louis constabulary," the man called Jason said.

Kellerman nodded. "You have good sources of information," he replied. "Yes, I finally walked out. You were right, of course. Only suckers work for police pay, though it's also true that while I was on the force I made certain contacts—among them, yourself—who paid me well to look the other way when they were up to something."

"Where are you headed now, Karl?"

"On strictly private business," Kellerman replied curtly.

The fat man did not take offense but neither did he smile. His gaze remained expressionless. "Good for you," he said. "I wish you well."

"Thanks, I need your good wishes, and those of a lot of other bosses like you. Do you still control the Dixieland Jewelry Shop next door to the hotel?"

"Could be that I do," the fat man replied casually. "What of it?"

"The way I figure it," Kellerman said evenly, "you'd like to do me a favor as a token of good faith in my future and as a token of my accomplishments on your behalf in the past. Specifically, I'd very much like to have the cat's-eye sapphire ring that sits in your window."

"You've got good taste, real good taste," Jason said with emphasis. "That ring was just appraised for me a couple of days ago, and it's worth one thousand dollars if it's worth a penny. You want it, Kellerman? It's yours for a thousand, no questions asked, and you're on your way with it free and clear."

Karl Kellerman shook his head. "There seems to be a slight misunderstanding somewhere," he said. "As you undoubtedly know, it's only been a couple of days since I left the constabulary, and I haven't yet begun to build up a nest egg working on my own." He drew a sharp, double-edged knife from his belt and casually proceeded to clean his fingernails with the point. "Within a very short period of time, the sum of a thousand dollars will mean nothing to me. In fact, ten thousand will mean nothing, so I'm in hopes, for the sake of our past associations and our working together for so many years, that you'll be good enough to advance me the credit, so to speak, and allow me to have the ring now. In return, I give you my solemn promise that you shall have cash in full for it in one week. As a matter of fact, knowing how you operate, I'll even give you a ten-percent bonus."

Jason emitted a high-pitched giggle. "How I wish I could only do business with friends and on a basis of perfect trust. Unfortunately, in this wicked world, I'm able to do neither. When you're able to pay me one thousand dollars in cash for the ring, it's yours. In fact, I'll hold it at that same price for you for another week.

Next week, it'll go up to eleven hundred, the following week, twelve hundred, the week after that, thirteen hundred—and so on. Is that satisfactory?"

"No, it very definitely is anything but satisfactory," Kellerman said, rising to his full height. "In fact, I was hoping we could avoid unpleasantness, but if we've got to face it, then that's the way it must be. The lady in question wants the ring. She's expressed a desire for it, and that means she wants it now. That means I *want* it for her now. And I intend to have it for her now."

He pointed the knife at the fat man and slowly approached him. Then, leaping swiftly and with great agility, he landed behind Jason and put his hands on the fat man's shoulders just as Jason rang a hidden bell and three of his subordinates came into the room.

Karl Kellerman faced them, his knife in his right hand, a genial smile on his lips. "Your employer," Kellerman said calmly, "is one of the most friendly human beings in the world, and he wishes to prove his amity by making me a gift of the yellow cat's-eye ring that happens to be on display in the jewelry shop next to the hotel. Naturally, I can't accept a gift of such priceless value from him; therefore, I will use you three as witnesses to the effect that I will pay him the sum of one thousand dollars within the period of seven days. Are we all agreed?"

One of the hard-eyed men reached for his pistol. Before his hand touched the holster, however, the blade in Kellerman's hand pricked the fat neck of Jason. "I'd be very careful, if I were you," he said. "You don't want to see your dear employer hurt in any way, do you?"

The man's hand relaxed and dropped again to his side.

"That's more like it," Kellerman announced. "Now, then, all we need is Jason to verify what I've said about the cat's-eye ring. Will you tell the boys to procure it for me immediately, please?"

The Memphis gangster was tough. He had no idea what penalty he might be required to pay for his silence, but he clamped his thick jaw shut and refused to utter a word.

Karl Kellerman reacted instantly. The knife blade whipped out and, neatly and instantly, lopped off one earlobe of the fat man's head.

Jason winced in pain, uttered a muffled scream, and brought both hands up to his ear. Discovering he was bleeding profusely, he took a handkerchief from his pocket and held it to his ear in an attempt to stem the flow of blood.

Kellerman remained impassive. "I reckon," he said, "your hearing isn't what it once was, Jason. Should I repeat the question, or do you think you can give the boys proper directions now?" He shifted the knife significantly from one hand to the other.

This time, Jason spoke with alacrity. "He's a rough, tough, fighting fool, boys," Jason told his subordinates. "Do exactly what he says. Go get him the ring, and mark down an IOU for a thousand dollars to be repaid in precisely one week." He continued to hold the handkerchief to his injured ear in a vain attempt to stem the flow of blood.

One of the henchmen bolted out the door and returned in a short time with the ring, which he breathed on, rubbed on his trousers, and then handed reluctantly to Kellerman.

The former sergeant took it, examined it carefully, and then dropped it casually into his waistcoat pocket, making certain it was secure there. "If you've got a paper for me to sign, I'll be glad to oblige you, boys," he said.

Someone produced a document, which he scanned hurriedly and then scribbled his signature below. "You can go now, lads," he said. "I have some other business to attend to with Jason, and I'd rather we talk about it in private."

The three looked at their superior, who nodded, and they filed out reluctantly, closing the door behind them.

"I suppose you know this is it," Kellerman said flatly.

"I know," Jason answered. "Once a leader loses face with his gang, he's had it. All right, what shall it be? You going to put the knife in my heart, or what?"

Kellerman shook his head. "I'm not that stupid or that inexperienced," he said. "If I get rid of you, I'm a marked man for the rest of my days. Your whole crowd will be after me, and sooner or later, believe me, they'll get me."

"I got to give you credit," Jason said. "You were around when brains were being passed out."

"Give me your six-shooter, handle forward," Kellerman ordered perfunctorily.

The fat man blanched. "Geez! You're not going to shoot me down in cold blood, are you?"

The former sergeant made no reply. He opened

the chamber of the other's pistol and emptied all bullets save one from it, and those that remained he left littering the desk. "I think," he said, "you'll put this one shot into your own brain. It's much neater that way, and it saves us a lot of complications afterward."

"Hold on now, not so fast," Jason said, speaking rapidly, a note of alarm entering his voice. "There's got to be some other way out of this mess."

"You tell me what it is," Kellerman said, "and I'll be glad to listen to you. You'll be known from now on as the man with one earlobe, and everybody in the business will realize that I'm the man who lopped it off for you. All the young braves in your organization are going to want to prove themselves by taking potshots at me, and the one who succeeds in killing me will be a great hero and will stand to succeed you. I want to remove all temptation from the path of your followers, thanks very much. As a matter of fact, I crave a financially comfortable old age, and I have every intention of living long enough and living well enough to get my wish. I'm sorry it was so difficult to persuade you to accommodate me on the temporary loan of a small piece of jewelry, but we all make mistakes, and I'm afraid that you made a rather major one there. If there were some way you could avoid payment for it, I'd be the first to find it for you, but what's at stake is your future or mine, your safety or mine, your life or mine, and naturally, I choose mine. So here's your gun." He slapped the gun into the fat man's flabby hand. "I'll go and join your boys in the outer room, and I'll wish you well in hell. I'll see you there some year in the future. Good-bye, Jason, and good luck." He turned on his heel, and even though he might have been shot in the back, he slowly left the office, closing the door gently behind him.

Jason, alone behind the desk, was trembling. As Kellerman had said, he had lost face. He could not imagine going on any longer, a man disgraced. He breathed in deeply, tremulously, and slowly raised the pistol, which he pressed to one temple.

The four hard-faced young men lounging in the outer office looked up as Karl Kellerman joined them. He gently removed his own pistol from its holster, moving slowly and gently in order not to alarm them. "I think, gents," he said, "that I've reached a meeting of minds with your boss. There are certain rules that have to be obeyed in this game, and he knows it as well as I do. He's ready to do what's needed."

He had scarcely spoken the words when a loud, single pistol shot sounded from the inner office. The quartet were on their feet instantly.

Kellerman made no move. He nodded faintly and smiled. "That's what I meant," he said.

One of the men raced into the inner room, returning a moment later, ashen-faced. "He's dead," he cried. "Jason has shot himself!"

Kellerman observed quietly, "He died the way he lived, according to the laws of our own peculiar brand of jungle."

All four turned toward him, their faces carved in granite. "You did this," one of them said.

Kellerman leaned against the edge of a desk and looked for a moment into the muzzle of his own six-shooter. "I think not," he said. "I was in this room with you when the trigger was pulled. I didn't hypnotize Jason, and I didn't blackmail him or otherwise threaten him into killing himself. He did what he did because he was a coward, and that's the end of the matter."

"Like hell it is!" a member of the Memphis gang said viciously. "There was nothing in the world wrong with Jason until you came along with your lousy demand for that ring, and the next thing you know, he shoots himself. I'm damned if you're going to get away with it."

Kellerman surveyed him coolly. "Just what do you think you're going to do about it?" he demanded, not raising his voice.

The Memphis gang member made the mistake of reaching for his own pistol. Before he could draw it from his holster, however, Kellerman fired and struck him in the heart. The man crumpled and slid to the ground without making a sound.

"Does anyone else care to enter into a little discu sion of the right and wrong of the things that have been happening today?" Kellerman demanded.

There was a surly, shocked silence.

"As a matter of fact," he said, "I believe I'll take that little IOU that I gave you earlier." He looked at each of the three in turn. One of them reluctantly withdrew the paper from his pocket.

Kellerman took it, lighted a sulfur match on his thumbnail, and set fire to the sheet of paper. "There," he said, "that should pretty much even the score and take care of all the trouble I had to go to today." He rose slowly to his feet. "I think our business is concluded, gentlemen," he said, "so I'll bid you good evening. Let me just issue one word of warning. Your leader is dead, and one of his associates has now died. If the rest of you value your lives, you'll keep your distance from me at all times, and you'll point firearms of any kind at me at your peril." Nodding and smiling pleasantly, he left the building.

It was dusk, and the heat had been drawn out of the day with the setting of the sun. A cool breeze blew off the Mississippi, and Kellerman enjoyed the balmy fresh air enormously as he strolled back to his hotel and went up to the suite that he shared with Millicent. She was just awakening from her nap when he entered their bedroom.

Kellerman turned on a small gas lamp on the far side of the room, then went to the bed. Sitting on the edge, he put his hand behind her back and lifted her to a sitting position. He kissed her at length, tenderly, and then he said, "Don't open your eyes."

"Why ever in the world not?" she asked in child-like wonder.

He made no reply, but fishing in his waistcoat pocket, he withdrew the cat's-eye ring and slid it onto her finger. "All right," he said, "you can open them now."

Millicent's eyes widened in wonder. She shrieked aloud and, throwing her arms around Kellerman's neck, kissed him ecstatically. "You did it!" she cried. "You really did it! You got me the ring!"

He chuckled indulgently.

"I didn't mean that I wanted it literally," she cried, hugging him fiercely. "I was just playing a sort of little girl's game and wishing out loud, but you took me seriously, and you got it for me. How wonderful!"

They embraced and kissed passionately.

"You spoil me terribly, darling," Millicent whispered.

"After all," he murmured, "you wanted it, and that was good enough for me."

"I can see," she purred, "where I'm going to have to be careful expressing what I want and what I like."

"Not at all," he replied, stroking her gleaming, thick, dark brown hair. "All you have to do is tell me what you want, and I'll move heaven and earth to get it for you."

Millicent looked at the ring, and wave after wave of happiness engulfed her. Had she known how the ring had been acquired, she would have been horrified.

Seeing her expression, Karl Kellerman was not only pleased for her but also proud and delighted with his own ability to provide for her slightest whim. It in no way bothered him that the ring had cost two members of the Memphis criminal gang their lives. After all, results were all that counted.

The headquarters of the St. Louis constabulary was a large, solidly built compound that faced the Mississippi River. The core of it was a four-story headquarters building of red brick, behind which stood a three-story dormitory and training center for officers. Adjacent to that was a two-story lockup for prisoners on their way to sentencing and subsequent incarceration in state and local penitentiaries. The night shift was just going off duty when Tommie Harding and Edward Blackstone appeared to see Commissioner Bowen. Cleaning women scrubbed the floors, filling the air with the scent of a strong yellow soap, and assistant commissioners and their aides bustled in and out, all of them glancing with undisguised curiosity at the handsome, well-dressed young couple awaiting the commissioner, both of whom seemed so thoroughly out of place in their surroundings.

At last, Commissioner Bowen appeared, carrying a greasy bag filled with jelly donuts. A pot-bellied, gray-haired man who had grown old in the service, he resembled a mild-mannered civil servant at first glance, but his eyes were hard and unyielding, his expression was formed into a perpetual frown, and his voice resembled a Mississippi River foghorn.

"Well," he said, "I don't often have fancy visitors, 'specially at this time of day. Come in and tell me what I can do for you." He motioned them into his office and then insisted on pouring them cups of coffee that his secretary had prepared. Not until they had also tasted the donuts he served them was he satisfied to hear their story.

Edward launched into the curious tale of his cousin, Millicent Randall, and of her strange association with the crooked Luis de Cordova. Holding that tale to a minimum, he related how Sergeant Karl Kellerman had joined their ship in Lexington, Missouri, and had stayed with them until they had arrived in St. Louis, at which time Edward had received a peculiar communication from Millicent.

He handed the letter to the commissioner and then sat back in his chair, sipping his bitter black coffee as he waited for a reaction.

"Karl Kellerman," Commissioner Bowen said, "gave me a big jolt when he resigned from the force just recently. He was a tough policeman, and I was sorry to see him leave. But then I guess I really wasn't surprised."

"How so?" Tommie asked curiously.

"I guess I always knew a service career wasn't what interested him," the commissioner replied. "Not enough money in it. You see, he developed a liking for the finer things of life. He appreciated fine clothes, fine horses, fine food and liquor, and if you'll pardon the expression, ma'am, he also appreciated the beauty of attractive ladies. I'm quite certain he's not married to this Miss Randall, with whom he's gone off now."

Tommie flushed slightly.

"No," Edward replied curtly, "I'm afraid that he has not married her."

"Knowing him, I strongly suspect he has some money-making scheme in mind, something that's going to make him, if not wealthy, at least comparatively well-off. I'm not necessarily suggesting that this scheme is illegal, although I wouldn't deny that possibility, either."

"We're none too concerned," Edward said, "with the ways that Sergeant Kellerman has devised to earn a living for himself now that he's no longer a member of the constabulary. What concerns my fiancée, Miss Harding, and me is where we can find him and where we can locate my cousin, Millicent, whom we're very anxious to return to the family fold."

"I appreciate your anxiety," the commissioner said. "Unfortunately, the West is a huge area in which to search for someone who has no known peculiarities, who makes a habit of attending to his own business, and who creates no waves."

"It occurred to us," Tommie said, "that perhaps his personnel file might contain some hint as to his present whereabouts."

The commissioner nodded. "We'll soon find out," he said, and sent a secretary for the file. When the thick document came, he glanced through page after page in silence. Apparently the material it contained was confidential because he neither commented on it nor offered to share the information. Offering his guests additional donuts, he continued to study the file at great length. Finally he put it aside.

"In a manner of speaking," he said, "the entire Mississippi River has been Karl Kellerman's beat, from the upper regions in Minnesota near Minneapolis and St. Paul, down through the connection with the Ohio River at Cairo, Illinois, and on down through our own St. Louis, through Memphis, Vicksburg, and other communities in Mississippi, all the way to New Orleans and the river's delta. However . . ." He paused for breath.

Edward and Tommie waited anxiously.

"It appears to me that in the past year or so, Kellerman had more business in New Orleans than anywhere else. I can't identify his interests for you. All I can say is that apparently he seems to have formed some sort of connection with another man in a business enterprise. I'd be inclined to suspect that now that he's left the constabulary, he's gone off to join his companion in a full-scale business venture."

"I see," Edward said.

"I can't guarantee that you'll find him, much less locate your cousin," Commissioner Bowen said, "but it seems to me your chances of locating both of them are somewhat better in New Orleans than anywhere else."

They thanked him effusively and soon were walking back along the waterfront toward the *Big Muddy*.

"It appears," Edward said, "that I won't have to change my travel plans after all. I'll still sail on the *Mississippi Lady* to New Orleans as I had planned. On my way, I intend to locate Cousin Millicent and Sergeant Kellerman."

"I'm going with you," Tommie said suddenly.

He didn't think she should be subjected to the risks and uncertainties of such travel, but he kept his opinion to himself. Knowing her, it would be better to wait, save his ammunition, and then present her with a flat ultimatum that she could not accompany him. But even then, Edward well realized, he might lose. Tommie would do what she believed was right—despite what Edward might say, even despite what her father might say.

In truth, however, Edward was not displeased at the prospect of Tommie's traveling with him. She had become such an important part of his life that the thought of going to New Orleans without her was suddenly inconceivable to him. With Tommie by his side, life for Edward was filled with more joy, more happiness than he had ever imagined possible, no matter what dangers might lie ahead.

Coming this summer . . .

WAGONS WEST★ VOLUME XV

MISSISSIPPI!

by Dana Fuller Ross

Searching for his missing cousin Millicent Randall, the dashing Englishman Edward Blackstone and his pert, attractive fiancee Tommie Harding travel down the Mississippi to the glamorous, exciting Queen City of New Orleans. Meanwhile, Millicent suddenly finds herself in dire straits when her lover, the ex-policeman turned criminal Karl Kellerman, tires of her and includes her among those he and an unscrupulous Greek ship's captain are shanghaiing to the Orient.

Toby Holt is called upon by the U.S. government to put a stop to Kellerman's operation. Joining forces with the most unlikely of people—the New Orleans crime boss Domino—Toby encounters great danger in the Mississippi bayous, and later, great temptation in the form of Domino's sultry, beautiful associate Martha.

Buy MISSISSIPPI!, on sale May 15, 1985 wherever Bantam paperbacks are sold.

★ WAGONS WEST ★

A series of unforgettable books that trace the lives of a dauntless band of pioneering men, women, and children as they brave the hazards of an untamed land in their trek across America. This legendary caravan of people forge a new link in the wilderness. They are Americans from the North and the South, alongside immigrants, Blacks, and Indians, who wage fierce daily battles for survival on this uncompromising journey—each to their private destinies as they fulfill their greatest dreams.

☐	24408	INDEPENDENCE!	$3.95
☐	24651	NEBRASKA!	$3.95
☐	24229	WYOMING!	$3.95
☐	24088	OREGON!	$3.95
☐	24848	TEXAS!	$3.95
☐	24655	CALIFORNIA!	$3.95
☐	24694	COLORADO!	$3.95
☐	20174	NEVADA!	$3.50
☐	25010	WASHINGTON!	$3.95
☐	22925	MONTANA!	$3.95
☐	23572	DAKOTA!	$3.95
☐	23921	UTAH!	$3.95
☐	24256	IDAHO!	$3.95

Prices and availability subject to change without notice.

TALES OF BOLD ADVENTURE AND PASSIONATE ROMANCE FROM THE PRODUCER OF WAGONS WEST

A SAGA OF THE SOUTHWEST
by Leigh Franklin James

The American Southwest in the early 19th century, a turbulent land ravaged by fortune seekers and marked by the legacy of European aristocracy, is the setting for this series of thrilling and memorable novels. You will meet a group of bold, headstrong people who come to carve a lasting place in the untamed wilderness.

- ☐ 23170 Hawk and the Dove #1 $3.50
- ☐ 23171 Wings of the Hawk #2 $3.50
- ☐ 20096 Revenge of the Hawk #3 $3.25
- ☐ 22578 Flight of The Hawk #4 $3.50
- ☐ 23482 Night of The Hawk #5 $3.50
- ☐ 24361 Cry of The Hawk #6 $3.50

<u>Prices and availability subject to change without notice.</u>